Blood Fable

Blood Fable

Oisín Curran

BookThug
Department of Narrative Studies
Toronto, 2017

The production of this book was made possible through the generous assistance of the Canada Council for the Arts and the Ontario Arts Council. BookThug also acknowledges the support of the Government of Canada through the Canada Book Fund and the Government of Ontario through the Ontario Book Publishing Tax Credit and the Ontario Book Fund.

 Canada Council **Conseil des Arts** Funded by the Government of Canada   Financé par le gouvernement du Canada | **Canadä**
for the Arts **du Canada**

 ONTARIO ARTS COUNCIL
CONSEIL DES ARTS DE L'ONTARIO
an Ontario government agency
un organisme du gouvernement de l'Ontario   **Arts** NOVA SCOTIA

BookThug acknowledges the land on which it operates. For thousands of years it has been the traditional land of the Huron-Wendat, the Seneca, and most recently, the Mississaugas of the Credit River. Today, this meeting place is still the home to many Indigenous people from across Turtle Island and we are grateful to have the opportunity to work on this land.

LIBRARY AND ARCHIVES CANADA CATALOGUING IN PUBLICATION

Curran, Oisin, author   Blood fable / Oisín Curran. —First edition.

(Department of narrative studies) Issued in print and electronic formats.
softcover: ISBN 978-1-77166-294-9
html: ISBN 978-1-77166-295-6
pdf: ISBN 978-1-77166-296-3
kindle: ISBN 978-1-77166-297-0

   I. Title. II. Series: Department of narrative studies

PS8629.U7678B56 2017   C813'.6   C2017-900744-0
C2017-900745-9

PRINTED IN CANADA

For my parents, who spread their dreams under my feet;
for Fianan and Neva, my fire and my water, and for
Sarah, who made them and remade me.

'It is curious that I can't say who I am. That is to say, I know it all too well, but I can't say it. More than anything, I'm afraid to say it, because the moment I try to speak not only do I fail to express what I feel but what I feel slowly becomes what I say.'

—Clarice Lispector, *Near to the Wild Heart*

DEATH FALLS! my father cried, and whirled his axe, Death falls on your neck! Axe flashed through the sky and fell—birch log snapped in two; Myles rested, glasses crooked, head bound in a white rag, black hair on end—demented samurai. I caught up the log halves, stacked them, and placed a whole one upright for division.

He was half answering a question half-heard.

The night before, a drunken hunter had mistaken my cat Shadow for a raccoon and shot her. Or so we guessed—we never met the man, but armed drinkers were known to stagger through the woods, and Shadow did look a bit like a raccoon, especially at night, which is when they're hunted in these parts. In any case, she was dead. We found her in the morning under her favourite tree.

Though she was my first love and though the blood from her bullet wound covered me, I didn't cry. My mother wrapped her in an old bedsheet while my father dug her grave. As she disappeared under handfuls of dirt, it occurred to me that she'd been likewise invisible before I watched her slip from her mother's body four years earlier. For that invisibility I had no name; perhaps it too was death. The rest of the morning I considered the matter with desperate attention to quell the sob welling in my chest because I thought it would kill me if I let it. For added distraction, I spoke to Myles.

Do we go back to death because we're born from it?

(Half-heard, half-understood.)

Death is simple, he declaimed, Unlike birth, which is a feat of unparalleled difficulty. A feat of rage—explosive. We each of us seek our incarnation.

Axe fell again and wedged in the log. Face locked in a vicious grin, Myles raised axe with log and hammered both against the stump. Sweat flew from him and from the rag on his head and the rag at his neck and his dripping shirt, until the log sundered and he leaned against a tree, breathless and purple.

You chose us, he gasped, straightening his glasses. You picked us out and now we're in for it.

From her position nearby, where she was planting a spindly pear sapling over Shadow's grave, Iris called out that although I was, without question, the cause of their union, I couldn't be blamed. Myles replied that I certainly could be—it was only logical.

I blame him, he said proudly, but I admire him—the effort it must have taken to force the two of us together. To beget is simple—to be gotten is a trial of cunning and tenacity.

Iris raised her dirt-streaked, tear-stained face at this and retorted, For a man to beget is to pleasurably pollinate. For a woman—nine months of possession ending in painful dispossession.

An event you bungled, Myles grunted as he smote the next

log. I slapped blackflies and gaped at a smeared rainbow of spilt chainsaw fuel. I daydreamed, or tried to, but it was no use...their voices rose inch by inch.

Like Caesar's mother, Myles went on, You required a blade.

Iris paled.

Inform your son where you were then! she exclaimed. Bidding adieu to your other lovers while your child was cut from my body.

Myles sighed.

It was a joke! he said, I don't fault you that our son refused to come out the way he went in.

The way he went in? said Iris, I see Catholic school left you with medieval fantasies about human reproduction!

Myles ignored this, saying that as for severing ties with lovers, he'd done that long before, *months* before, and, as she well knew, on the day of my birth he walked with trepidation in the hospital gardens as though in some anti-Gethsemane, awaiting the arrival of his son, his heir, his fate.

Yes, of course, now Iris remembered (how could she forget?) that he had strolled among the lilacs while she bled.

This, said Myles, Is rank exaggeration, as usual, but how, in any case, could she be expected to remember anything from that glorious day when she was doped to the gills for the knife, while he, *he* was in a state of ecstatic transport as he beheld and held me in his arms for the first time.

As they disputed, I felt a strange interior tug, as though a different source of gravity were pulling me at an oblique upward angle. The combined force of the twinned gravities, one internal, one terrestrial, produced a lateral floating sensation.

I remember, I said quietly but abruptly, and fell to the ground.

HERE IN the woods on the coast of Maine in 1980, a hundred years had passed since a shovel had delved this soil, or axe split the local wood; the stones of an old farmhouse foundation had become the outline of a frog pond, and trees swarmed over the swampy ground, shrouding all signs of human toil. Then Myles and Iris joined a nearby Buddhist community, bought these few acres, and began to reclaim them with chainsaws and fire. For my part, I advanced with a pint-sized saw through the close alders, whispering apologies to the saplings I gingerly severed from their roots and watching salamanders start slowly from beneath overturned stones. And later, after the wreckage and the bonfires, the crack of hammer blows bounced back from the receded forest as my father and his fellow disciples raised beam over post and a house stood once again on the land.

In the middle of that land, on a clump of grass I now lay, feet to the trees, head to the house. Loose corners of black tarpaper were flapping, and the plastic over the window openings bellied and smacked in a wind that blew over the forest from the ocean. And how do I recall these details? I don't. Nor do I remember my parents kneeling above my damp body, waving away the blackflies, panic-stricken as I spoke. They tell me my eyeballs were rolling in their sockets and my joints were rigid. I was muttering something about an old building full of new music, an accident.

Myles picked me up from the grass and carried me to the car. Iris rushed ahead to prepare a battery of flower remedies and herbal tinctures. Settled on the back seat of our station wagon, staring blindly upward, I continued, something about sad hallways, illness, death waiting, threatening.

My poor little pumpkin seed, Iris cried, climbing in next to me, squirting liquids in my mouth, massaging ointments into my temples. Hurry! she said to Myles, who threw the car into reverse, tore out into the dirt road, and bounced off over the potholes at top speed.

Slow down! said Iris.

Make up your mind! shouted Myles, compromising between her two commands by easing off the gas pedal for a few seconds before flooring it again while saying, Write it all down.

I went on, speaking of a fugitive on the run, but the images were scattered, no story jelled.

My little beetle, said Iris, by now typing dictation at warp speed on her manual Olivetti, which was rarely far from her side. In the months that followed, those images became a story. As I told it, Myles also took notes, scrawling in his nearly illegible (but aesthetically intriguing) penmanship. When I retrieved those notes years later, he told me he still intended to devise from them a vast mythopoetic hermeneutic, just as William Butler Yeats had done with his wife's automatic writing.

For her part, Iris had undertaken structural adjustments and revisions of my muddled, run-on sentences. The onionskin sheaves of her typing would, over time, come to contain great quantities of cross-outs and notes in the margins, alongside the sketches she planned to turn into illustrations. It is from my parents' combined records that I have reconstructed that narration, so it comes filtered through the syntax and vocabulary of three adults.

In the back seat of the car I apparently babbled of a bridge spanning the interior of a glowing world.

Dimly I heard my father exclaiming from the driver's seat that I was experiencing some kind of visionary state.

Or a seizure! said Iris, unhappily.

Or a mystic trance! Like Edgar Cayce, said Myles, He may have access to another plane of consciousness.

Just hurry, said Iris, But not too fast.

A seizure? No. I knew about Edgar Cayce, the Sleeping Prophet, the mystic clairvoyant. Back then it was hard to avoid him. My parents and their friends spoke often of his various predictions—especially, and with secret hope, the imminent disappearance of California under the waves. But for my part, no. No seizure, no vision. I'd grown sick of the heat and of my parents' argument and felt dizzy enough to lie down. Well, maybe I fainted a bit, I won't deny the possibility. And if I did, that would explain the little bits of dream I spoke as I came around. The combination of collapse and surreal utterance electrified Myles and Iris. They stopped bickering and bent their attention on me. I couldn't disappoint them. And anyway, I wanted to find out what happened next. So I went on, as best I could. It's not as easy as it sounds, making things up and pretending you're not, especially when there's so little material, just a small, strange jumble of images. Among them: a traveller in need, in peril, sheltered, smuggled to safety; a headless bird, feathers and blood everywhere, shining guts; a gleaming treasure trove; a sinking boat—there were more, but in my fainting spell they'd spat themselves at me too fast to hold. Then they slowed until, at last, they settled on a scene of quiet waves sieving through a pebble beach.

WRAPPED IN an old coat, I sleep on a beach. Stones squeak. Lonely sound—hollow shoes on hollow planet. City shoes, expensive once, strange for a sailor, which is what he is—the one wearing them. At least, I think he is. He could be lots of things. Hard to tell how old he is too. Thirty? Not yet, but on the verge. He walks up to me where I'm lying in the cloudy light, and says all is ready, the ship prepared, crew assembled, and I should come at midnight because he'll be on watch then and can smuggle me aboard.

Rook (that's his name) makes a strange face that bends his broken nose (but that's the shape of his smile) and then walks away. His hair looks like black springs that bounce when he walks.

I don't follow him, won't press my luck—following was how I got to him in the first place. Last week I saw him smoking on the beach and realized he was from the *Lizzy Madge*. I took my chance and asked him to get me on board. That was the first time I saw his snarl-smile, his big black hair, short thick braid in the back, wide black eyes, brown skin, long, thin, twisted nose. He wanted to know if I had any money. I had a little. He nodded, scratched his chin, said he'd think about it.

So, this day, three later, full of hope and fear, I go to my sea cave, the driest of the holes in the headland on the border of the beach. It's where I've lived for the past weeks, subsisting on raw bivalves and leftovers from the back-alley trash cans of Night Harbour.

Where I come from I don't remember. One afternoon I woke up on the beach not far from the mouth of the sea cave. No past, no old life to recall, no idea who I was or where I came from. Just some images, or pieces of them, which I hold tight since they're all I have of who I once was. Every hour of every day I tend my collection, gathering it in my mind's eye—my little trove of visions. I lay them out one by one in the darkness of my thoughts, to contemplate and polish.

an old house in the night, music leaking out
a car accident on a long road
a green waiting room, death in the shadows
the belly of a glittering planet
a man from a faraway country seeking refuge
an axe on a bloody stump, head of a bird on a bed of
feathers and shining guts
a treasure of silver coins
two people up to their ankles in water on a sinking boat
a spectre on a desolate road at night
a ghost with a gun, a shot, a wound
a rainbow of light flashing on a wall in a room full of
children
firewood dragged on a sled from a broken forest
through blue snow, cold blue air
a round loaf of bread hot from the oven, end cut and
buttered, steam rising from it
a woman (my mother?) in bed, pale, in pain
an explosion of light in the middle of a dark night
a brown-haired girl betrayed, face once vivid, now
ashen
an old book with my own life printed inside it
two men fighting in thick snow, moon behind sky-
spanning clouds, dark trees pointing up to it.

I march those images onto an interior stage and let them
play and replay while I survive. And there they form their
own kind of gravity, which pulls me toward a final sight, a
city. It's a place I've never known, but I can see it clearly: tall
buildings with a big river flowing between them in waterfall
after waterfall, and somewhere nearby there's a park full of
lilacs. So many lilacs the scent is strong, sweet, almost sickish.

The city isn't just a city, it's City. I feel it in my muscles, my sweat, my nose and tongue. It pulls my bones like the earth pulls a stone, but the direction it pulls me is out to sea.

I heard from town gossip that the *Lizzy Madge* is chartered to take a strange crew of people on an expedition to find an island in the Southern Seas. The island is supposed to have some secret, or treasure, maybe a fountain of youth. The rumours are airborne. I don't care about the island—all I know is that to find City I have to get on a boat.

After dark I say goodbye to my cave, bundle up the few clothes I've stolen from Night Harbour clotheslines, and head for the port.

The moon is out, a half moon, in its light I look back at the beach. Goodbye, beach.

Something near my cave, something in it. A person? Animal? Hot animal smell on the wind, but it moves too quickly to tell what it is. The moon's not bright enough. Whatever it is, the back of my head heats up instantly. To cool it, I turn away and walk fast.

Night Harbour is a backwater, barely quaint, stinking of diesel and brine. But at the end of its rotting dock the *Lizzy Madge* floats in its own private atmosphere of scruffy glamour, promising other waters, other shores.

I walk up the gangplank, feel the fresh coat of tacky paint on the bumpy railing and the engine throbbing in it.

A hand grabs me and pulls me through a door. I hear Rook's voice say, Quiet! and the door closes and locks and I'm in the dark.

MY VOICE fell silent at last, and in the quiet that followed, I heard somebody gently urging me to lie back and relax. I was in the hospital. Wires were attached to my chest with round stickers and a nurse patiently chatted with my nervous parents as she watched a screen. She made a printout and a doctor came in and looked at it and said, No, there's no problem with his heart. Let's get an EEG.

Then somebody wheeled me into a windowless room and stuck wires on my head with some kind of goo and flashed lights in my eyes over and over in different patterns for a long time. Eventually they printed something out and a doctor looked at it. He shook his head. No, there was no problem with my brain.

So then another doctor sat with us and said it was probably just a fainting spell from the heat. Iris noted that my cat had just been killed and the doctor said, Yes, a sudden shock plus hot sun could cause you to faint, so I wouldn't worry about that. Try wearing a hat from now on. And speaking of sun, what about this?

He pointed to Iris's leg where her shorts rode up and showed a black mole just above her knee. It was blotchy and big, and Iris said yes, she knew, she should get it checked.

No time like the present, said the doctor, and with her permission, he scraped a little bit of it onto a glass slide and took it away.

RUST SMELL cuts mould. Rivets ping, steel creaks. The sun shines through cracks around a trap door in the ceiling. It forms a square outline that slides across the walls and floor. My only clock. I think I might lose my mind in the dark so I unpack the shards of my memory and burnish them to stay alive. It's an unpredictable exercise—sometimes the images grow and extend, become thicker and more detailed; other times they shrink in time, in colour, texture, until they're nothing more than passing glimpses, or the notes for a memory, shorthand variation on a thought. This time they grow...

an old building at night muffling strange music that trickles out through the dark trees outside and the bright lanterns strung between them
  car skidding out of control on a broad highway lined by a leafless forest
  a grey-green waiting room full of people quietly waiting to find out when they are going to die
  a room shaped like a giant beach ball lit from the outside—the interior of a hollow, glass planet
  a man with frightened eyes in need of refuge
  a stump, an axe, a dead bird, feather, guts, blood
  piles of silver coins glimmering in a small wooden box
  a boat sinking under two people rowing to shore through cold water...

Once a day the trap door blows light and Rook's hand comes down with a plate of bread and butter or boiled potatoes or beets. Once sausages. I ask him to let me out—it's too dark and the little metal room burns me. He says to be patient and tells me that in his hobo days he was locked for a week in a boxcar maintenance cabinet the size of a coffin. No food and only leaking rainwater to drink. So he almost died before another tramp heard and freed him. Coming out, he stretched in the raw air and saw through the boxcar's open door that the train rode the back of a snowy mountain range. He looked down on wild goats and flying eagles and ate the hard, green crust of bread that he was given.

Your circumstances are infinitely more luxurious, he says.

The door closes again and later my room cools and I sleep.

I wake shivering and put my clothes back on. The steel walls and floor freeze me fast. We're going in the wrong direction.

The trap door opens, and from the crash of light I hear Rook's voice warning me of frostbite—he says he lost three toes to a snowbank when a plough accidentally buried him while he was sleeping off a bender. He was frozen there for months before a thaw freed him. Accustom yourself to this, he says. This is the life of a drifter—wretched and free.

Blankets fall on me, and hats, all moth-eaten. We're plying the Northern Seas, he says.

Let me out! I yell. We're going the wrong way.

He's sorry but it's impossible—the people on this boat are lunatics. They belong to a society, he says. The Silver Apple, or maybe it's the Gilded Branch... The Order of the Knotty Pine? Anyway, they're nuts about this island. But we have to go north before we can go south. A matter of geography.

He reaches down a cigarette, places it in my mouth, and lights it, but I choke. I've never smoked. He lies down on the floor above me, props his head on his hand, and lights a cigarette for himself.

By the time I was your age, he says, I was hacking twenty butts a day.

CIGARETTES?! My mother groaned in a confusion of longing and disapproval, which brought me from my story. She opined that this Rook was a terrible influence to be pressing tobacco on a child—she didn't like him. Reproving her for interrupting me, my father said that Rook was but a young man after all, raised rough and following the hobo's code of honour to help a fellow drifter in need and share what little he had. Myles liked him, cigarettes or no. After all, had not Iris chain-smoked menthols from the age of sixteen until she met him?

It was night. I lay on my bed, Iris perched on a chair with her Olivetti on her knees, and Myles sat on a brown mat on the floor, legs crossed in the half-lotus position, a blanket draped over his head and shoulders for warmth. His red plastic fountain pen was poised over a yellow legal pad. My head throbbed from what was evidently a hangover, for I remembered that earlier that night I had surreptitiously downed a bottle of homebrew.

We had been to dinner at the Krimgold-Gragnolatis' after a long Sunday of salvaging lumber from a condemned nunnery. We needed the salvage to finish our house. The K-Gs needed it to build one. At the beginning of the day, the grown-ups set me and the younger Krimgold-Gragnolati siblings, Artemis and Apollo, to work pulling nails from old boards while Myles and Bill Krimgold eased windows from their frames and floorboards from their joists. Iris and Bernadette Gragnolati toiled over the plumbing, with Bernadette's eldest daughter, Athena, releasing two bathtubs and three sinks from the mineralized shackles of century-old pipe fittings. Later, the roof of the station wagon weighted down with timber and porcelain, we drove to their tiny cabin to recuperate.

Bill and Myles considered the virtues of hops and malt as they sampled each other's homebrew, while Iris and Bernadette parsed the weather and the weeds and their gardens and the farcical campaign for president of Ronald Reagan. Artemis and Apollo and I played Parcheesi. Artemis was a year older than me—jutting chin, long black hair in braids, bell-bottomed overalls. Apollo was a year younger, a year softer too, with a sweet-natured moon face under a page-boy head of straight red hair. Their sister, Athena, sat in a corner reading *Anna Karenina*. She was in Grade 12. A serene, flash-eyed girl of terrible beauty. When she walked it was as though she floated, a demi-goddess from another world. She was seven years older than me, and if she smiled at my gaping face, the brilliance of her teeth between plum-coloured lips made me shiver.

Myles dilated on the subject of etymology and the surprising, yet inexorable path that led to the root of all language and culture, which turned out to be Old Gaelic, or rather Gaeilge, as he corrected himself, the word *Gaelic* being no more than another anglicization inflicted on the mother tongue of poets by perfidious Albion, and he paused momentarily to swallow the buildup of phlegm in the back of his throat, for one can't talk for so long without needing to spit unless otherwise trained, and in that pause he smiled uncomfortably for an instant, as though aware of his own loquacity, and, mildly embarrassed yet incapable of stopping himself, or at least unwilling, he launched awkwardly but swiftly out of the pause by swallowing fast and picking up where he'd left off while the swallowing action was still descending, because if he paused for an instant longer...

But it was too late, Bill had already seized the opening to say, only half-jokingly, Do you know what you are, Myles? You're a Celt-supremacist! But hey! he went on before Myles could protest, It's OK, I like those Celts. Crazy bastards. You ever read Caesar's *Gallic Wars*? Vercingetorix and his crew? Anybody who runs screaming into battle wearing nothing but some paint deserves respect. Speaking of French Celts, speaking of Gaul, guess what kind of car de Gaulle was in when the OAS tried to assassinate him? A '55 Citroën DS! Just like the one I've got out back. They say it was the superior suspension system that saved him. Even though the tires were shot out, the driver was able to accelerate out of a skid and get away. Funny, because my suspension is in trouble— cracked strut, but I've got a line on a good welder. Hard to believe I got the Goddess for three and a half bucks back in grad school. Mind you, her engine was shot at the time...

All this while I was quietly working away at a bottle of stout that I'd purloined from the table and soon I passed out on the ox hide that covered the piano bench. Sometime later I dimly heard exclamations at the empty bottle discovered in my clutches. And later still I came to in my bedroom at home.

Above and around me, planks of unfinished spruce were attached to the walls with infrequent brackets, and they swayed under the weight of books. In my line of sight, the red spine of *The Rise and Fall of the Third Reich* was compressed between *Adrift* and *The Jataka Tales*. I turned my head on my pillow and saw, as usual, *Journey to the Interior of the Earth, The Demigods, Building the Energy-Efficient Home, The Three Pillars of Zen, The Viking Portable Jung, The Voyage of Maeldun, The Tibetan Book of the Dead*, and *Finnegans Wake*. The long sagging lines of volumes had the upright disorder of teeth. They comforted me; they oppressed me. They were backed by pink fibreglass insulation caught in a Jupiter storm behind stapled sheets of cloudy plastic. My eye fell on the bench next to my bed and, taking in the luminous pair of new tube socks and the freshly patched corduroy jeans and the carefully folded velour sweater, I recalled the source of the misery that had driven me to drink: school.

Claude O. Cote Elementary School squatted on a concrete pad in a hollow just north of the town's two rival general stores and just south of the gravel pit. It was a box sided with grey asphalt shingles, the lower rows of which had been gnawed away by generations of bored, malnourished children. In its dark interior hallway, a portrait of Mr. Cote gravely surveyed his beneficiaries as they shot from the classrooms at the close of the day and slunk back to them at 8:00 a.m. Each morning, we endured hour-long captivities in stinking yellow buses wherein the young, the small, and the weak sought front seats within the radius of the driver, while the violent and the pubescent sprawled across its back rows, and a crescendo of insults, threats, and seductions was snuffed out by the driver's roar, only to bubble up again in a repeating cycle.

The bedlam of the bus, ejected into the parking lot, was reconstituted in subtler, age-segregated hierarchies within the carpeted, high-ceilinged classrooms. There, the dispirited teachers sought vainly or sternly or ingratiatingly to quell the flames with which we burned, for we were alight and knew it and saw these creaky humanoids as messengers from an empty future. Their classes were nothing more than preparation for the purgatory of adulthood. Or something like that. Really what I remember are the buckets placed under leaking ceilings and the bad kids zigzagging to catch the droplets on their tongues. In the meantime, we must suffer the shrilling of bells, pedagogical droning, and ritualized pledges while the hours in their thousands ground by as we progressed glacially, imperceptibly toward that clear, impossible light of late June.

I waited for September with predictable dread. Ripening tomatoes, lowering sun, lengthening shadows, first crimson leaf hidden in green—all auguries portending the Bus, on board which I endured the Top 40 radio babbling at low volume, the nausea induced by the endless stop and start and the diesel exhaust farting through the windows with each rattling hammer blow when the back wheels hit another prodigious frost heave. Outside, the tracts of blueberry barrens scanning by were nothing more than external manifestations of the Bus's psychic landscape. Inside was the filthy banter of children recently overwhelmed by the idea of copulation. Further inside, in my interior, was the now familiar sideways pull of alien gravity, which brought me floating into a dark metal box within which I sat, listening for the sound of hawsers, hoarse shouts of sailors, the swallowing sea.

In my metal box I wait. Rook comes and goes with food and my toilet, a dented tin pot with an old plate to cover it. No light but the sudden rush of sun with Rook's visits. In the dark with nothing to see, nothing to do but shit and eat and read with the flashlight that Rook lowers to me, a copy of *You Can't Win*. He says it's the only book he owns.

I sit wrapped in layers of blankets, only my face and hands touch the bitter air. I need my hands free—one to hold the flashlight and the other for the book. My breath steams in the thin tunnel of electric light, which bounces off the page and lights up my little box.

The room is ten books long, six high, and five wide. Big for a coffin. Darkness and fear give me bat ears. Or I am crazy because I start hearing hollow, faraway talk from around the ship. Voices thinking about navigation, a chorus practising opera, piano tuning, some yelling, happy or sad? And also the hammering engine. Radio signals come and go, plumbed fathoms ping under us. If the ship goes down, I go with it.

Potatoes! somebody shouts. Have you seen them? The voice is close.

Then Rook yells, Not there, NOT THERE!

But it's too late, the trap door is hauled off and a whole sun thuds down on top of me.

Dark eyes stare down at me. The woman with the eyes pulls me into blinking sun. She's young, smooth hair and skin, not much older than Rook, but the steep wing pattern of her eyes makes her seem more grown-up. She thinks I'm a prisoner, she's worried about my health. Her name, she says, is Quill. She's the cook and she was looking for potatoes. I tell her I'm not a prisoner, I stowed away and nobody knew.

I knew, Rook says.

Rook, it turns out, can't lie, even if he gets in trouble. This is either a virtue or a weakness, depending on circumstance. Right now the former, in my opinion.

Quill calls over Severn, the captain. Captain Severn is tall, sinewy, yellow hair a flag in the breeze. I figure he's in his forties although his face is lined from facing down gales, or maybe from smoking, which he does non-stop. Quill puts her hand on his arm as she explains what happened and he doesn't move away. He turns his hard hawk nose toward her and his hard blue eyes focus and soften when they meet her dark gaze. I see an angry man who hates his own anger and wants to shake it. Maybe Quill has something to do with that. In any case, he's kind, but it's hard for him. And he punishes Rook with extra work anyway.

Somebody shouts, Squall!

In the west a dark wall with lightning. Severn orders me below deck and then turns and shouts commands.

I curl on an empty bunk to avoid the crew. Footsteps above me, hatches hammer down, the ship shakes. Through a porthole, I watch the sky go black.

The storm is coming for me, hot, thick, wild animal smell just like when I saw the creature entering my old cave—it's following me. The back of my scalp burns again.

I turn from the view, close my eyes, and unshelve my pictures.

car accident
green waiting room
planet-room
refugee
axe, bird, feathers, guts
silver coins
sinking boat

That's not a good image to think of. And worse, as I run through them, there's one missing. Which one? Desperately, I claw through my brain for it. What was it, what was it?

The sea blows open.

We dive with lightning and the whole screeching sky to the bottom. But the screeching might be me. Hard to hear anything over thunder pounding all around.

LURCH OF the bus rounding a sharp bend returned me to the end of my ride.

Then I was walking down the steep dirt road, kicking stones and trying to catch falling yellow poplar leaves for luck, but no luck—and then the little bridge over the mouth of the bay where I stopped and stared out across the water for some time and burned my eyes on the brilliant wave tops, then turned in the other direction toward the marsh whose creek ran through the giant culvert under me to the bay and on to the open ocean. In the marsh, fat rosehips formed and a great blue heron unfolded its wings and drifted into the sky.

Now I hurried past the empty farmhouse where blank windows mirrored the sun and trembled in the wind, adding to an atmosphere of muted horror that trailed me up the long narrow corridor of road hemmed by snarling woods. Deep in the trees someone tried to start an engine, which, though it thudded bravely, failed to cough into life, so the sound diminished and died away. Into adolescence I would remain convinced of the mechanical origin of this noise, admiring, pitying, resenting the persistence of the mysteriously inept owner of the engine that could never start. Then one day, while peeing in the woods I saw a bird, a grouse beating the ground with its wings, and the sound it made was the noise of that reluctant motor.

I was distracted by a dark shape in the bushes and, for an instant, I thought it was my cat, Shadow. But just as quickly I remembered she was dead and tamped down the pang that followed.

I turned in the driveway and heard yelling from the house. My mother's voice, raging. Walking as quietly as possible to the open kitchen window, I stayed out of sight and listened.

I'm not going to die! she shouted.

I didn't say you were, said Myles quietly.

I have a son! An eleven-year-old son—I can't die!

The doctor didn't say you were dying. He said it was serious—very serious—and we need to think about all the possibilities.

I have a child to raise, said Iris, and her voice was murderous. I'm not dying.

She stomped out of the house, slammed the door behind her, and headed for the garden.

I snuck off to the outhouse even though I didn't have to use it. A tiny, shed-roofed collection of old boards and posts, it stood about fifty feet from our house with a doorless opening facing the woods. I sat on the closed seat and contemplated the bushes and trees. Where forests are newly cut, the borders look gapped and raw, wrongly exposed like a layer of ripped skin. Still, the chickadees and finches and red squirrels seemed to enjoy it—hopping from root to branch in their war over pine cones. Artemis told me she once saw a squirrel eat the head off a living baby chickadee while its mother attacked from above in vain. There was no such carnage on view now, just chirping and hopping, scrambling. A few mosquitoes made desultory, whining passes through the chilling air, in search of a last blood meal before they frosted to oblivion.

A deep grunt and sudden crashing to my right startled me upright to see the antlers and rump of a white-tailed buck vanishing into the bushes. What was I thinking? I didn't know what to think. I was trying not to. Would Iris vanish like Shadow? And if so, what would I do then? Now, there was an empty grey hole in my stomach and all my thoughts were sliding into it along with the rest of my life. I felt pressure in my chest—the old sob for Shadow swelling. I was either going to blow apart or collapse into the grey hole. Maybe explode first, then implode. To dodge either disaster, I jumped up, hoisted my backpack onto one shoulder, and made my way to the garden.

Iris knelt among her tomato plants, weeding furiously, weeping silently, and so I sat down beside her.

I know you're sick, I said matter-of-factly, I heard you before.

She looked at me intently and then leaned forward and pulled me to her.

I'm not leaving you, she said in my ear, and her voice sounded so ferocious I believed her.

She wanted me to tell her about school but instead I told her of my latest vision. She wiped her dirt-encrusted hands on the grass, unpacked the Olivetti that she now carried with her at all times for just this reason, and began to type.

As I spoke I watched her fingers strike the keys with rapid power. That rhythmic, assured percussion is among the most vivid of my childhood memories. The clatter of the steel alphabet transferring words to crackling paper in an authoritative blur of movement thrilled me more than any music, I think, other than peepers crying in the swamp next to us. And also I suppose the call of the hermit thrush, not to mention, while I'm at it, crickets. But those noises were seasonal, whereas Iris typed all year long. She typed stories that she wrote first in longhand. She typed short pieces for the newspaper. She typed poems and essays and papers for Myles.

In the garden, for those twenty minutes, all other sound was muted by my own unbroken voice in my ear and the hammering of the Olivetti. My mother's sun-browned cheekbones, her broken nose, her bow-shaped mouth pursed in concentration, her eyes slate-blue and her blond strands falling from their pins, all were focussed on my story as it tumbled out of the darkness into the dry autumn light. Or so I would like to be able to say—it wasn't until many years later that I was able to see my mother as somebody else, not me. And it would be many years as well before I could see the shape of that story I told her, or rather the shape of how I told it to her and Myles, how it started as a lark but, beginning that day, grew steadily more burdensome the more deeply attached to my lie we three became. It was, to be honest, still a pleasure to gloat over my mother's attention, even as the tears dried on her face, because in those early days I chose to believe her declaration that she would not die. No, it was impossible that she could die.

When I had finished, we rose, typewriter and pages in hand, and made our way slowly back to the house, pausing in our progress to remark the late new blooms of calendula and the cucumbers under siege by slugs. Iris bent to pick several yellow bodies from a tattered leaf and flung them bitterly into the woods, wiping their slime from her hands on a pile of uprooted weeds. But she mastered her humour quickly and agreed with me that the blue of the Chinese forget-me-nots closely resembled the lapis lazuli earrings that Myles had given her some years before my birth, but which she never wore due to the absence of piercings in her ears.

These earrings were kept in a box of yellow leather embossed with curlicues. To open this box gave me a pleasure nearly comparable to that of opening a book. When the lock sprang open, it hit the box with a small thud and the box itself acted as resonator, augmenting the sound. Attached to the underside of the lid, a mirror reflected a mass of coloured stones and wrought metals. A ruby-coloured glass necklace tangled with Bodhisattva pendants built of silver set with amethyst. Myles's gold wedding ring resided there, for it was too uncomfortable, he said, to wear all day. Sitting quietly in the darkness of the treasure chest, his gold band had gathered a dull patina, its edges sharp, its two decorative slashes distinctly visible. By contrast Iris's ring gleamed yellow, soft and round with use. When she washed her hands or picked up a bottle of beer, the gold knocked against porcelain or glass with a reassuring clank, the satisfactory quality of which I remarked only many years later, when my own wedding ring collided with dishes and stones. I think, in fact, that it was only upon the recognition of this familiar sound that I understood myself to be finally an adult. I had become a ring wearer, bound by covenants once obscure, to sentiments that had mystified. But even then, as a child, rummaging in my mother's jewelry box, I knew those two rings carried more symbolic weight than they could bear: one tarnished and hard in the dark, the other glittering softly in sunlight—the marital equation was too exact to be tolerable. Too exact, yes, and therefore not accurate, because their marriage, like most, was an indecipherable stew of ambiguities, inscrutable, I later discovered, even to them.

Myles was spattered with house paint as usual—even his glasses sparkled with white droplets. He first scraped the lenses, then his beard with a razor, and we all changed into clean clothes and walked out onto the dirt road and followed it west, back the way I'd come from the schoolbus, between the swampy trees, past the ominous farmhouse, across the giant culvert now feeding the marshland from the ocean's surging tide. The sun collapsed over the bay, a colossal jellyfish trailing raw purple. And from there the road sloped upward gently past the home of the Silvers, also under construction but having reached a more advanced stage of completion than our own. And here the slope abruptly reared up into a hill. We walked up, conversation lapsing with the effort. Half-way we passed the Bojanowskis' miniature house. Herman Bojanowski was always building new rooms, but inexplicably the house appeared to grow smaller and smaller with each addition.

As we approached the top of the hill, we could hear the screams of peacocks mingling with the tuning of strings and a purring crowd, all punctuated by giant laughter and vocal scales. Strung lanterns fought the dusk through a screen of trees. A male peacock with fan unleashed staggered, iridescent and absurd, along the shoulder of the road like an eighteenth-century debutante straying from a ball.

Then we were in the crowd, some freshly dressed, others stinking vehemently of manure and sawdust. Mallards and chickens were underfoot, squawking from time to time when someone, already pickled in vodka, stumbled over them.

In the forest of adults, I found Artemis and Apollo, who were morosely plotting to blow up the concert barn. Nobody we liked would die, they assured me, but this horde of assholes must learn. I asked what the horde must learn, but the plotters were already heading for their target.

The barn was still empty as we crawled under the stage to lay the charge. Artemis dumped a pile of gunpowder that she'd collected from stolen bullets. She punched Apollo, her protege, who was gaping up through the cracks in the floorboards. The daydreamer shook himself and produced a fuse that he uncoiled. I fretted that the powder was directly under Willard's piano bench. But that was the point, Artemis explained with satisfaction, Willard would blow sky-high in the middle of the "Bemsha Swing." They had told me nobody would die and here they intended to kill off the Teacher, who was indubitably somebody.

That's where I was wrong, Artemis insisted, Willard wasn't somebody, he was a monster.

How? I asked. Something horrible had happened, but they wouldn't say what. Nor would they ever, in fact, ever, ever say what.

They were already backing out from under the stage, uncoiling the fuse as they went.

Then we wandered in the crowd, establishing an alibi. The disciples had been joined by well-heeled locals who had come to gawk as though at exotic fauna. They adored the Teacher and called him Maestro and he did not correct them. They filed reverently into the barn, admiring the authenticity of its rough-hewn timbers and their reflections in the gleaming black flank of the grand piano. And gingerly, genially, they lowered themselves onto the motley stools and benches, rocking chairs and sofas that populated the dirt floor. In the glow of the kerosene lamps that served as footlights, Willard hopped lightly onto the stage. His thick, grey-black hair spiralling straight up from his head in an explosion of short, tight curls radiated a glow of pleasure as applause rose around him.

Nobody knew exactly where Willard came from. Some said he was a Black Indian, the descendant of Louisiana slaves who escaped their masters and found refuge with local Choctaw. Others said his mother was a Brahmin from Jaipur who scandalized her family by marrying a Chinese fisherman. Still others insisted his father was a Sephardic Jew from Ethiopia. A man claiming to have gone to high school with him said Willard was just a Schmidt from New Jersey who tanned easily. Willard himself neither confirmed nor denied any of these rumours. Where we come from is irrelevant, he would say. We must erase our past, our selves. We must become the wind.

That's what he always said. That's what he was saying now, more or less as he stood on the stage of the barn.

Thelonious Monk, he said, grand poo-bah of the bebop ivories, prince of the percussive attack, emperor of improvisational jazz. And what is improvisation? It's making do with what you've got, what's right in front of you, right now, right here. That also happens to be an A1 description of zen practice. Monk's compositions are musical zen. In a given moment they use no more nor less than the precise note required. To play Monk, to listen to Monk, to really play, to really listen, is to be immersed in *samadhi*. Let's do that, cats. But before we do, a moment to reflect on the moment, which contains a reality that is neither welcome nor unwelcome; it simply is and must be faced.

One amongst us, he said, Has a life-threatening illness. Our dear friend Iris, he went on gesturing toward her, Has cancer. She is in our thoughts, but not just in our thoughts, in our actions too. The proceeds from this concert will go toward paying her medical bills.

And with that he bowed and turned to his piano. Nobody looked at Iris, but it was as though the peripheral stares of the audience bore down on her, and she shrank, mortified, in her chair. Later she would accuse Myles of revealing private information to Willard and god knew who else to humiliate her in public. To which Myles would say he had no idea that Willard was going to announce it at the concert, but in any case it was a very kind gesture and they certainly would need the money and why must she be so bloody private all the time and from there the argument travelled a well-worn path along one of the major fault lines between them—in this case the division between a Reticent New Englander and a Garrulous Irishman.

The lights flickered with Willard's brisk movement. In the silence the manure-encrusted hems of his overalls knocked gently against the legs of his piano bench as he sat and splayed his giant, work-swollen, splinter-ridden hands over the ivory teeth of his grand, its belly wide open to the barn. Beside Willard sat his page-turner, his aide-de-camp, Ms. Ohm, my piano teacher, a woman who, in every other context, could hardly restrain herself from grinning, but here, in the shadows of the barn, sat concentrating still and grim through the "Bemsha Swing."

No sooner did the music begin than I started to squirm. These concerts were torturous endurance tests during which I attempted the rapt stillness or quiet swaying and head-bopping of the adults around me. I even tried closing my eyes like them. After an eternity, I had to accommodate myself—my bones were growing as I breathed. While notes roared by, or tinkled pitifully along the ground, my sinews stretched and twisted new strands, my teeth pressed themselves out of my jaw, and it became imperative that I shift in my seat to release all this inner movement. So, at last, as silently as possible, I twisted my torso in the wicker armchair that imprisoned me and was met by the disapproving glare of Jack Blatsky, the violin maker. Swiftly I reverted to my original position and just as swiftly my body was agonized by interior crowding. I slammed my eyes shut. My skull was expanding at such a rate that I could feel the ligaments stretching, my throat distending, knees bursting their caps off, and I knew myself to be rolling in salt air.

THE STORM passes, not finding me. The ship still floats. The porthole window dries fast but I can't see much through it except for horizon, sun, sea.

Rook finds me, gives me a hat, an apple, a biscuit, and points me up to the crow's nest, on Captain Severn's orders. We've been blown off course and now must hunt for land.

From the top of the mast, the world is a giant disc under me and I rock above it. Sheets of colour everywhere. Above me the dome of the sky is an upended purple bowl that slowly becomes a mercury-red curtain in the west, where the sun sets into a horizon made of blood. And that blood flows over the waves to me, turning pink as it reaches the boat, and then quickly fades to galvanized steel and finally whelms into black in the east on the far side of the world.

I turn my eye inward and hunt for the missing picture. I have so few I can't afford to lose any of them. But it's gone, completely. Yet I can still feel the gap. It would almost be better if it disappeared without a trace, but some residue remains, like the glue left in an album where a picture was removed, and that residue feels nearly as vivid as the image itself, and so all the more painful. What was it, what was it? I sort through my collection one by one to safeguard those I have left. There can be no more losses.

accident
waiting room
planet
refugee
bird
treasure
boat
spectre

gun
rainbow
firewood
bread...

The *Lizzy Madge* is a tiny shell beneath me.

Rook and a skinny, bearded man wheel a piano out from a large cabin on the foredeck. A little while later, the bearded man brings out a bench, opens the piano, and tunes it. When he's done, a tall woman in a big straw hat sits down. A small, brown animal moves like water to the bench and flows up onto it to sit next to her. It's an otter. Why do I know that? The woman's fingers move up and down the keys a few times and play a strange, sad song that tires me.

To stay awake, I scan the deck. Toward the back, Rook juggles oranges. He stares straight up at his flying fruit and walks around like it's nothing. He juggles to the music. Maybe the woman at the piano notices, because she plays faster. Rook speeds up. So does she. They keep going until the juggling and the music are both going so fast they'll brew another storm. I look up and don't see storms but land. I ring the bell.

The sea is still, and in the middle of it is a small island made of bare yellow rock. It's little but tall, at least as tall as my nest and with cliffs as straight as the mast. All in all, it looks like the top of a drowned castle and even has doorways cut in the stone along the inside walls of the rock. Nothing grows on it, and the whole place is as mournful-looking as a cemetery. But if I could, I'd climb out of the crow's nest and fly straight to it because the gravity of City pulls me there.

This feeling slams into me from behind. One moment I'm coolly sizing up the place and the next I *must* get onto it. Why? There's no city there, no waterfalls, no lilacs, no room

38

for car accidents or waiting rooms or rooms that look like planets. But still I must, still it's here I have to go.

The place is inhabited. There's a small dock cut from the rock. On the dock a few people with nets and ropes. They don't look happy to see us, but maybe they can tell me the way to City. Maybe that's why I must go ashore. But for now I wait.

The *Lizzy Madge* lowers her anchor, and Captain Severn jumps into a small motor boat with Rook. When they reach the dock, Severn cuts the engine and from the ship we hear voices back and forth. Rook seems to be trying to speak with the people in different languages. Apparently his wanderings have turned him into a linguist.

When the launch comes back, Rook says they don't speak any of the twelve languages he knows. It sounds like our tongue, he says, But it actually isn't at all. He seems happy about this. He pulls out a small mechanism and plays back a recording of a man saying:

Hostage sounds or rather silence held hostage by incessant sound, darkness imprisoned inside street lights, clock light, brake lights, moonlight, Sound and light, immobility kidnapped by earthquakes and engines.

Then a woman's voice:

Towns floating on rivers of blood, on torrents released into the innocent air, but was there ever anywhere an innocent ceremony to drown? The sighs, the shouts, the ecstatic flood, the rush, the din.

A child's voice says:

Nothing there nothing there, now hear this here. In recent days the course of blood, the inward wind that wails down my spine all the time but only now and then heard and then too loud to reach so then propitiated with coinage and chants.

Finally, the man again:

We dwelt and slew the hours one by one, inch by inch, till the whole thing was through, black spider sun, competing moons, the approaching orbit of the joyous bug, wings thrown, jaws wide, furred antennae of a demigod. Indifference to the eternal, if eternal there is. What is to love is what flees, what is—

Severn turns the tape deck off impatiently.

Tell the whole story, Rook, he says. We were still able to communicate. Hand gestures may not be as refined as language, but we got through to them. I drew a picture of our destination in the sand and they pointed east.

The deck of the *Lizzy Madge* is crowded. Everybody looks east. Nothing but horizon.

All right, says the woman who played the piano, Let's go.

She's quiet, but everyone listens to her. She sounds rich. Maybe that's why. Why everybody listens, I mean. She's regal somehow, tall, her long, grey-black hair in a thick braid over her shoulder, her grey eyes are shaped like hawk wings, her mouth a thin, proud line.

Yes, they all say, Let's go.

They move fast to make it happen.

Rook asks Captain Severn if we can stay a little longer to record more of the strange language, but the anchor is already raised.

Severn turns to Rook and says, It seems the consensus is against you.

You mean Chisolm is against me, Rook says, and looks at the rich-sounding woman who is playing the piano again.

She's the one who chartered my boat, says Severn, and heads for the bridge.

No!

I hear my voice before I know it's mine.

You can't leave. This is the place you're looking for!

Severn stops and stares at me. Everybody does. Stowaway vagabond shouting at captain. But what else can I do? The boat is turning and City is yanking me back toward the island with such force I feel like I'm going to throw up.

And how would you know what we're looking for? asks Severn.

It doesn't matter how, I say. This is it.

Silence from Severn—nose hard and sharp as a knife. He turns and walks away, the others go back to work, the boat pulls away. We're not going back. It's too late for me to swim for the island. I'd never make it. I'll come back, I think. I'll turn this boat around. Somehow. It's like having two poles of gravity pulling me in two different directions. There's the usual force pulling me down and then the island yanking me sideways. I feel sick; I lean against the gunnel and grab at the pictures in my mind to steady myself.

Accident
Waiting room
Planet
Refugee
Bird, axe, feathers...

The images soothe me. They're like polished stones, all surfaces, no pain or dizziness, only dim heartache. The ache of the missing whole. They are pieces of some larger picture, some other story. What story do they belong to? My story. What is my story? It's still out of reach, but the ache of missing it restores me, drives away nausea.

Chisolm plays the piano and looks at me. So does her otter. Friendly? Unfriendly? Can't tell. I look away when they look.

THE POUNDING of claps jumbling in every direction woke me to the concert barn.

The show was over and Willard was taking his bow. He had failed to blow up.

The gunpowder was a dud, said Apollo with disgust when I came upon the siblings in the crowd. Willard has survived, but not for long, Artemis vowed. Not for long.

Iris found me and hustled me from the barn, desperate to clear out in advance of solicitous querying from all the concerned citizens who had been alerted to her condition by Willard's pre-concert announcement.

How dare he, she muttered as I struggled to keep up with her down the hill. How dare he, I would never ask for charity.

I couldn't tell if she was speaking of Willard or of Myles for disclosing her diagnosis. Maybe both. In any case, we'd left Myles behind—a familiar scenario in that Myles moved always according to his own timetable. If he found himself in convivial conversation with plenty of chatting to be had, he was not about to cut such parlance short simply because Iris wanted to go home, as she typically did. Nor was Iris prepared to wait for him to bring his discourse to a close, since she'd heard it all before and, in any case, on this particular evening she had reason to be pissed at him. And as per usual, I was enlisted to accompany her home, which was fine with me as there were books to be ingested. This evening I was re-reading *Treasure Island*. But the day must have gotten the better of me, for I had barely tucked myself into bed and cracked the volume before my eyes began to close and I found myself rocking in bright water.

I HELP Quill in the kitchen. Because she found me, Quill thinks she needs to take care of me. Rook is her assistant. Before letting me work in the kitchen, Rook trims and washes my hair, washes my face, clips my nails.

Where are you from? he asks.

I don't know, I say. He looks at me and smiles. Not really a snarl, I realize, more of a sad smile and also somehow bright. He has crooked teeth and a crooked nose and all in all it's a nice face. Quill thinks so. I see her looking sideways at him, surprised, as if she forgot why she wants to look.

And everybody knows Rook loves Quill. He hides it, but can't. They fight about everything—how to chop vegetables, how to cook rice, if the sky is clear or cloudy. Sometimes the fights get bigger. Quill walks away with dark eyes darker. Rook follows, saying he's sorry, even though he's not sorry.

I ask Rook why they fight.

You know, he says.

Maybe, but not really, I say.

It's because, he says bitterly, Quill is engaged to Severn and she won't break it off.

Why not?

But he stalks away without answering.

In the following days, they fight on, but when somebody else fights them, the gap between them seals shut.

One morning a small, jittery man comes to the galley door. He wants to talk to Quill about onions.

You're using them too quickly, he says. The ship will be entirely onionless in a matter of weeks. Do you propose to provoke ship-wide scurvy?

Quill's small, round brown face turns red.

You can call yourself third mate if you want, she says, But you're a fool!

Rook steps between them.

Nolan, this was your mistake, he says. If you had paid any attention to the supply list we gave you, this wouldn't be a problem.

Nolan talks about statistics and budgets and then stops because he sees me. His eyes widen and he smiles. His teeth are white and straight. He shakes my hand slowly. His hand is thin and strong.

So pleased to meet you, he says, staring at me.

I hate him.

I don't like onions, I say. Does that help?

He smiles again. He laughs. It's a big laugh. He backs out of the galley.

Land! somebody shouts from the crow's nest, and rings the bell.

Another island. Engines cut, anchor down, and Severn and Rook board the launch.

Hot wind chops the waves white. White clouds in the blue, blue sky. The island is also white—short white houses on top of white cliffs that fall down into a green valley. Quill looks through a telescope. She says the valley is full of vineyards and the streets of the clifftop village have cafés where people drink wine.

I hope this is the place, she says.

But it isn't. Severn and Rook come back frustrated. The

people on the island laughed at them when they said what we're looking for.

It doesn't exist, they say.

And when Rook told them about the island where we'd just been, they laughed again.

That doesn't exist either, they said, and went back to drinking their wine.

Now everybody on board the *Lizzy Madge* looks at each other.

If the island that we saw does not exist, says Nolan, Then that is the island we seek.

Obviously, says Chisolm. She says it quietly, but everybody hears her. And I see she's looking at me again. Everybody is.

Captain Severn orders the boat about on a return course. The crew runs.

Chisolm walks to me. Her otter follows.

How did you know? she asks. Her otter climbs onto her shoulders. Its long whiskers twitch.

There's something in her voice, some kind of sound she's trying to keep out of it. She's close to me, staring. I can't tell what's going on behind those grey hawk eyes and I don't care. At least, I don't think I do, although I probably should.

I'm not sure, I say.

She doesn't move, her eyes don't move. Her face doesn't move.

Then she turns suddenly and walks away. She touches Severn's arm as she passes him. The otter slides down and circles his feet. Severn stops what he's doing and follows Chisolm. It looks like he doesn't have a choice, like he's miserable. As he goes, his blue eyes turn to Quill, who stands in the stern of the boat with her back to him, watching the island get smaller. For a moment I can see her as he might see her, a young woman with long hair so smooth it looks like tea coming out of a spout. Come to think of it, her skin is smooth and tea-coloured too.

Quill is Chisolm's daughter, says Rook, who's suddenly next to me. His voice sounds like acid, and when I turn I see that his face is twisted more than usual. He must have seen the way Severn watched Quill.

They don't look like each other, I say.

No, says Rook. Very different types too. Quill is Quill, of course, as you know. But Chisolm—well, you saw. She was measuring your soul for drapes.

Does Quill know about that? I ask, pointing my chin after Chisolm and Severn, who have now disappeared from view.

Rook shakes his head silently.

Why don't you tell her?

He smiles at me sadly and shakes his head again. Then he rolls a cigarette, lights it, and strolls over to lean against the gunnel next to Quill.

That island might not have been the one we were looking for, Rook says, But its geology seems to have been influenced by the lost civilization in question, for, according to the ancients, that original language had both a hieratic and demotic form—the demotic was spoken by the human tongue but the hieratic was written on the landscape in shadows and light, in waterfalls and birdsong or the crashing of waves. The outcropping and cliffs of the island have been subtly altered in ways characteristic of this language, to speak more clearly to the stars. And this might have been neither capricious poetic whimsy nor metaphysical gesture, but rather mercantile semaphore, or better yet, all three.

Does Rook even know what he's saying? I think he doesn't.

I think he's saying anything besides what he feels. Or maybe he's saying what he feels but in a very strange way. Or maybe he's saying that he can't say what he feels or that the only way to say it is this.

And surely, he goes on, It was the very capaciousness of such signifiers that allowed the local maritime demotic tongue to grow into a polyglot composed of borrowings from every other language in the world.

But no, says Quill, It is precisely not a patchwork language, but rather a direct descendant of the original demotic from which all others were born. It bears all the signs of that mercurial first language whose grammar shifts like a tide, whose relationship between word and the object it names is barely symbolic, can alter at any moment, and is, more often than not, invented on the spot. This language could be called Greek or English, Chinese or Hebrew, for one could read a text or listen to speech in any of those languages. Even, for instance, the most banal advertisement can be reread in the original demotic as something else entirely—a prayer, a love song, a lament, or a shopping list. Its rules are elastic, intuitive, yet rigid in as much as, from moment to moment, there are accurate and inaccurate means of expression.

Quill is pretending she doesn't understand what he's trying to say, or maybe she's not pretending. Maybe she has no idea what's going on.

Rook turns away from the island and throws four knives in the air. The knives are long and sharp. They flash as they turn before he catches and tosses them back up one by one in a wheel of blades. Rook says he understands this language to be synthetic, declined with the classic cases of nominative, accusative, genitive, and so forth.

Blablabla! I wait, hoping to hear him break through his own word shield, hoping he'll say what he needs to say.

Indeed, Quill says, It is, and yet its categories are more numerous than one expects and very different, for there are no genders nor are there quantities. And the declensions are composed musically—a word spoken in the lowest register is, as one might expect, Subterranean; in the highest register it is Extraterrestrial; soft utterance is Angelic; mouthed speechlessly it is Divine; spoken glottally with mouth hanging open it is Organic; and the Synthetic is indicated by a nasal tone.

My head hurts, heart falls.

And in written form? Rook asks as a knife falls and stabs the deck.

The categories are indicated by colour and letter shape, Quill says, still looking back at the island.

But, Rook says, Can any of this be counted on? For surely there were no primary documents in existence and only the commentaries of learned antiquarians relying on hearsay and legend.

Rook winks at me as he says this and I realize he's not going to say anything. All this has been a way of not saying it. Not because he fears revealing himself, but because he fears hurting her.

But when Quill turns and lowers her binoculars, she says, Rook, I know very well that you already know all this.

Does she know, then? Does she understand?

You were drawing me out, she goes on, To flatter me, but I went along with your game because it was not for your sake that I was speaking, it was for the girl.

And she looks at me and smiles.

GIRL?

From his position wedged under the station wagon, my father's astonished voice shot up through the tangle of pipes, wires, and engine block. I explained impatiently that before I was born I was a girl. I couldn't blame him for being surprised. My girlness in the story was an element that arrived as an unlooked-for twist even to me, its author. But once revealed, it seemed inevitable, even logical. Yes, inescapably logical when it comes right down to it. There was no response from Myles as he wrestled with the bolt on the oil pan, cursing gently and exhorting the object to capitulate. I watched his feet, which were all that were visible of him. They jerked and twitched with effort. At length he noticed my silence, remembered where we were, repeated the word *Girl* in a bemused tone, and then urged me to carry on. But the spell had been broken. I switched off the tape recorder he had placed on the engine block under the open hood. The bleary sun had set, and a thin, cold drizzle began to fall out of the darkness. Myles declared his need for a flashlight and a larger wrench.

I covered my head with my coat and hurried to the shack where Myles kept his tools. He called out to my retreating back that the wrench could be found just inside the door, to the left, above my head, the flashlight should be on the table saw. My spirits, already low, fell to the level of the mud I splashed through, for even in daylight I found my father's instructions rarely helpful and the navigation of his tool shed a fruitless exercise. I entered the door, bumping into an old window that had been enthusiastically purchased at a recent garage sale. Having broken a pane, I carefully collected the pieces, my fingers bitter in the damp cold, and stacked the glass in a corner, catching now the roar of my father's voice impatiently demanding to know what was taking me so long. I called back that I was looking, but all the while I pondered whether he had said to my left and up or up and to my left, and was that left as I entered or as I exited. These subtle variations should not have made a difference in a space equivalent to the interior of a car and yet the truth was that no level of descriptive precision could have helped me in that bedlam.

The spotty light cast by the fading flashlight (which I had found not on the table saw but on the vice) shone on jumbled stacks of old jam jars full of unsorted rusting nails, bolts, and screws removed from salvaged wood by me over the course of tedious, sweaty afternoons. Suspended from the rafters were squares, levels, cords, and chains in such profusion that proceeding in any direction was hazardous to the skull. An array of circular saws were strewn in varying degrees of disrepair, and on the narrow rocking surface of the table saw sat Myles's antique power sander, a device with which he accomplished tasks that ordinarily entailed the use of five or six other tools. The distant thunder of his voice reached me again and I slumped, sensing defeat, but I could not return empty-handed. My forehead cracked against a dangling pipe wrench, but as wrenches went, this one was out of the question since I knew it to be useless from previous attempts to proffer it as a substitute (why then it persisted in that shed, I don't know). No, this time the best I could do was a hammer—known to my Grandfather, Padraig, as a Chicago screwdriver. It had been Padraig who replaced its cracked handle with a stick of whittled wood only a few months earlier during one of his month-long stays.

Though billed as vacations, these were, I would later learn, rest cures or, more precisely, dry spells. Once a year he was packed off to our remote spot far from bars or stores or drinking friends, and though from time to time he would press some money into my hand and propose that I ride my bike to the nearest vendor for a fifth of rye or gin or whatever was on offer—a scheme whose unfeasibility due to my minority age I was forced to explain repeatedly—for the most part he puttered away with apparent contentment, repairing tools and building benches and coming into the house at regular intervals to sit down and await the preparation of his breakfast, his lunch, his tea, his supper, all of which was resentfully served to him by my mother, who found his patriarchal expectations of her only slightly less irritating than my father's assumption that she would fulfill them.

And after he had finished his boiled egg, his toast, and his tea, he would launch into his repertoire of stories, buttonholing whomever was in range—usually me—with tales of hierophantic saints capable of covering whole islands with their miraculous cloaks, or tossing their walking sticks thirty miles without breaking a sweat, or he told of cannonballs bouncing into an ancestor's backyard, gone astray from a furious naval battle between a Spanish galleon and a British man-of-war, or of famous revolutionary martyrs hunted, hung, shot, or beheaded. And best of all, and most repeated, were accounts of tricksters he himself had known—men who used their wits to outmanoeuvre the overlords—buying property they could not buy through proxies, hunting animals they could not hunt by wearing disguises, finding hidden glens to make the whisky they were forbidden to make. In those years I still listened with great curiosity, and it was not until much later, when I had heard them all many times repeated, that I began to humour the teller, or to quiz him for further details, or to simply switch channels to my own interior monologue. But on one occasion he startled me with a story never before told and never repeated.

I remember that it was a summer night and that a thunderstorm was grumbling in the distance. Iris and Myles were at the kitchen table with someone—maybe Bill and Bernadette. Padraig sat in the rocking chair near the screen of an open window, and I perched nearby on a stool. We sat there together watching the lightning, and in the silences between thunderclaps we could hear mosquitoes clamouring at the screen. And Padraig abruptly began to say that he'd gone on a pilgrimage in Ireland three times, fasting for three days each time while marking the Stations of the Cross on his knees and muttering the rosary through the night in the Basilica. And all the while asking: should he go to America? But God gave him no answer. He asked his parish priest, who was not encouraging. He asked a Monsignor, who was similarly dissuasive. He had a wife and six children; he had a job at a time when jobs were scarce in the republic. Not only that, it was a government job—he was a member of the gardai, a cop. That was secure employment. But the pay was poor and he kept failing the advancement exams. Above all, he loathed policing—handing out fines to teenage girls for cycling after dark without a bike lamp, ensuring farmers were keeping the bracken weeds out of their fields, ferreting out illegal poitin stills, shutting down pubs for operating after hours—it was petty stuff when he was longing for adventure. He'd grown up hearing of neighbours who had made a fortune in the Yukon and come back loaded with gold. His own uncle had been a Forty-Niner before heading north and now they said he owned most of British Columbia. Most of British Columbia and a good deal of Alberta to boot. Padraig wanted to give it a go. So he climbed Mount Errigal, the tallest peak in Donegal. At the top he said a rosary in each of the four directions, according to the pilgrimage instructions. He took in the view flung down before him—green fields and stone walls shooting out to the brutal North Atlantic. Then he descended. Halfway down he bent to pick up a jacket he'd left on his way up. As he did, he felt God speak to him. The answer, at last.

How? I asked. How did God speak to you?

It was a shudder. He felt a shudder come over him.

A shudder. The contingencies that depended on that shudder overwhelmed me. Upon that shudder my existence depended. But for that shudder I wouldn't be standing in the dark of the tool shed gaping down at the hammer, mind adrift, hearing again Myles's voice hovering now on the edge of desperation. I shook myself free of mental drift and made my way back to the car. Myles was not pleased with the hammer—why could I never find anything in that shed? he wondered. Had I looked where he instructed? Were my thoughts circling the ionosphere? His voice was muffled by the engine block past which it travelled, and then it spiked suddenly into a fluent stream of curses because he'd whacked the troublesome bolt with the hammer and managed to flatten his thumb in the process. The filthy engine oil began to gush onto him, and as he cursed he scrambled to slide Padraig's chamber pot under the flow. He emerged at last—glasses, face, and shirt black with viscous fluid, eyes hooded with rage. He did not look at me but stomped away, lamenting the necessity of cars, the inadequacy of their design, the tyranny of matter.

An hour later the three of us huddled around the woodstove waiting for dinner to bake. Among the burning logs inside the stove, Myles had placed three potatoes wrapped in foil, along with two cans of B&M brown bread, even though, according to New England regulations, you were only supposed to have canned bread with beans and hotdogs.

Money was the problem, as always. How to get it, how to keep it. Myles wanted to travel—Iris wanted running water. In summer we bathed behind the garden in a tub filled with sun-warmed water—and that was luxury next to winter's few gallons of ice melted on the stovetop and splashed under the arms. The dollars my father earned painting houses spent little time in the bank next to Iris's newsroom wages before the chequing account was bled dry by the banalities of power and light. The savings for water pump and copper piping had just been emptied into the car's new transmission. And meanwhile Willard demanded his tithe of labour on his farm for the privilege of inhabiting the radius of his wisdom.

And beneath the oil changes, penury, and meditation was a substrate rarely exposed to open air, but if it were it might sound like this:

Myles: I can't go on painting houses forever. I'm a poet-mystic forced to petty labour by the exigencies of family, a family I never intended but the responsibility for which I honourably shouldered.

Iris: I'm too young—for you, for marriage, for a child. Biology shackled me to family before I had a chance to become the artist I dreamed myself to be.

Me: Since this is all my fault, I will make it worth your while. Let me tell you a story, a tale of derring-do, of cunning, tenacity, and ruthless ambition to become your child. It will be grand and miraculous and carved in stone, and when it is

54

done you will understand why I had to make you bring me into this world.

But for all my efforts, the waters that coursed above that bedrock were rougher than ever, thanks to the looming non-subject of cancer. Iris still refused to discuss her diagnosis, but the oil change had been made to prepare for a trip. We were going to Massachusetts General Hospital in Boston, where Iris had made contact with an oncologist through a friend of a friend of a friend of a friend. Iris was worrying about the trip and Myles was worrying about Iris, but neither of them was willing to talk about these fears, so instead they fought about money.

But then they stopped and I saw them turn to look at me, for I had begun to speak.

THREE DAYS after leaving the island of white houses, we come to the waters where we saw the first one. But it's not there.

A disappearing island is romantic to contemplate but aggravating to look for, says Rook.

But it is here, I say. I can feel it.

Captain Severn is going through his logbooks on the bridge and barely looks up when I enter.

The island, I say.

Yes?

Is below us.

Now he looks up and his face closes like a folding book. Even his eyes somehow shut while remaining open. He looks like he's strangling himself from the inside.

I point down.

55

He gets up. Is he going to throw me out? He turns some knobs on his sonar equipment.

There's something there, nine fathoms down.

Severn climbs into the two-person submarine that's stored on the deck. Nolan, small and wiry, climbs in after him with a big camera. Apparently he's not just the third mate, but also the expedition's documentarian.

The crane lowers the two of them into the water and they submerge. Here, up above, it's suddenly very quiet. Flat, flat water. Some people lean over the railings and look down. Others smoke and gaze at the horizon or the birds that have found us, even here in the middle of the ocean. Maybe the sunken island confuses them as much as us. Mood as gloomy as the clouds.

Chisolm and her otter appear next to me.

I hear, Chisolm says, That it was you who knew the island was below us.

I nod. I notice her eyes seem to have changed, grown larger, softer, soft enough to cushion my gaze, even absorb it.

Who are you? she asks, and her voice has changed too, no longer remote but now warm and curious, almost motherly. Her otter, which she calls Lutra, curls around her shoulders like a big, fluffy scarf, its black nose settled near her earlobe. My fingers itch, wanting to stroke its fur. Maybe Rook is wrong about her. And maybe her hold over Severn is a spell of gentleness and understanding, not cold scheming.

I don't know who I am, I say. I only know I have to get on that island.

Chisolm is about to say something but, just then the submarine resurfaces. Severn and Nolan climb aboard and report that the island is there all right—in the headlights of the submarine, they saw yellow fish schooling above the dock and sharks nosing the stone doorways. No sign of the inhabitants.

Now what? says somebody. There's a long silence.

There is a line in the prophetic tradition, says Chisolm, Which states that the Isle of the Dead rises to a fire in the sky.

There's a murmur of assent from the crew, but Severn seems unmoved.

What does that refer to? he asks. The sun? Obviously not. What other fire could it mean?

Comets, says Rook.

Very well, says Severn acidly, Let's leave and come back when a giant space rock is scheduled for an appearance in a hundred years or so. Or more. It might be a thousand years before that island comes back up for air.

Then everybody talks at once and I feel myself unspooling, losing myself, what little there is to lose. My pictures flash by me.

waiting room
bread
rainbow
firewood
bird
treasure
gun
ghost
invalid
duel
book
girl

Another one is missing. I scramble after it in my mind, but

the babble of the crew makes it impossible to think. I slip away. There's no time to waste trying to reach a consensus. I have to find City before I disintegrate.

I have to do something now.

Near the stern of the boat, the expedition's single-engine pontoon plane sits on its runners. I find the stays and release them and then open the cockpit canopy and climb in. How do I know what I'm doing? My fingers move of their own accord, guided by some obscure force or by muscle memory alone. But memory of what? When have I been in a plane before? No time for doubt or reflection. I strap myself in, start the engine, and watch the propeller blur in front of me. Then I taxi along the rails and into the air.

I can feel the air pressing up under the plane's wings, my lungs, lifting us up, up, up. My heart lifts too. I'm flying!

Banking, I see the dimly lit crew of the *Lizzy Madge* milling chaotically on the deck in uproar. I can't hear their shouts, but I know they must be shouting. I turn away from them to concentrate on the flight path. I know what I must do. Pulling back on the joystick, I force the plane into a steep ascent. Higher into the constellations I climb, higher into darkness. The night is black and silver and still except for the roar of the engine, which I'm pushing to its limits. The heat gauge nails itself in the red zone of danger, but still I climb into the thin, cold air. I find a strap and tie the joystick in position, then unbuckle myself, locate the parachute, and put it on. Under my seat I feel for the flare-gun kit. I load one flare and pocket the rest, tucking the gun into my waistband. Then I open the canopy.

As soon as it's unlatched, the wind rips it off and I'm nearly blown out of the cockpit by the force of the bitter, hard air. My face and fingers go numb almost instantly, but somehow

I pull myself out of the cockpit and, clinging to whatever handholds I can find, I crawl down to the left pontoon and stand on it. The wind is screaming in my ears, my eyes. I should be terrified, but instead I'm filled with wild joy. This is the way, the only way, forward and I have nothing at all to lose.

Hanging on with one hand, I pull out the flare gun, take aim at the fuel tank, and fire. For a moment I can't tell if I hit it or not, but then the flare lights up a hundred feet away. I lower myself to sit on the pontoon and grip it with my legs as I reload the gun, fighting the wind and the numbness in my fingers. Now the flare is loaded, but a sudden gust flips me over upside down. I don't have the strength to right myself in the terrible wind. Hanging from the bottom of the pontoon, barely gripping it with my legs, I use both hands to aim at the fuel tank and fire. I think I see a tiny hole in the metal, but before I can make sure, another jolt shakes me loose, the wind rips me away, and I'm falling.

In freefall on my back, the night suddenly opens up to me and all the stars rush in as though I'm falling upward, as though I'm flying, pushed by the wind into space. Something brushes my face—feathers? Far above me the plane still climbs, climbs, explodes.

I'm far enough below to see the fireball billow outward in purple-and-yellow waves of flame several seconds before I hear the roar of the explosion. The plane carves a burning arc down the sky, cutting open the blackness. Will it work? It has to work.

I spin around and face the whip of freezing air and the giant void of the dark ocean looming up at me from below. I pull the cord and feel a great jerk as the wind drops and I dangle at the bottom of a drifting parachute.

Far down below me, the plane hits the water without a sound. Flames spread across the waves, then slowly disappear with the burning wreckage, and the ocean is black again except for the deck and mast lights of the *Lizzy Madge*, pinpricks in the darkness. I load another flare and fire. How angry they must be. They'll declare me crazy, dangerous. They'll want to leave me here and let me drown. But Chisolm won't let them. She understands now that I will lead them where they want to go because I am desperate enough to do what none of them dare to do. As the cold waves rise to hit me, I close my eyes and collect my pictures.

a treasure of silver coins
a rainbow of light flashing on a wall
a ghost with a gun, a shot, a wound
a loaf of bread still steaming from the oven, butter melting
a pale woman in pain, in bed

You sank my plane, says Captain Severn in a choked, choking voice after he fishes me out of the freezing water. Even Rook looks furious. I'm too cold to answer, too bruised from landing to care. When he and Rook bundle me on-board the rest of the crew is shouting at me. I think they might push me back overboard. But before they can, the *Lizzy Madge* heels over and we fall.

We're going down! somebody shouts.

But we aren't. We stay where we are on a crazy slant. Captain Severn lights the ship's spotlight and swings it around. The *Lizzy Madge* has run aground.

How? shouts Quill. We were anchored.

But as the light uncovers the ground beneath us, everybody recognizes it. We're on top of the Isle of the Dead.

No, no, F sharp! yelled Ms. Ohm. She was in the shower. I could hear the splashing behind her muffled voice. Two rooms away I was trying to pick my way painfully through the prelude to "The Well-Tempered Clavier" at her white Yamaha piano. Because I had, as usual, failed to practice, the going was slow and full of errors. I corrected the note and continued. The shower stopped splashing, I heard her humming, lighting a cigarette, and then heading into her kitchen. A short time later the toaster popped and there was the unmistakable sound of a knife scraping butter onto scorched bread. The delicious odour of raisin-bread toast accompanied Ms. Ohm as she came wandering into the room clad in her bathrobe and munching her snack. She was tall, slender, round-faced, cheerful, energetic to a restless degree. The only time she was still was at the piano.

Are you hungry? she asked, absently. Then before I could answer, she sat next to me and began to play the right-hand part.

You see? It should flow together, like a brook flowing over stones. Each note is a stone, but the water keeps moving.

A car horn outside signalled the arrival of my parents and the end of the lesson. I jumped to my feet, thanked her, and ran out the door.

Tell your mother I said good luck! called Ms. Ohm.

Our station wagon was a monumental vessel in the back area of which I was able to lie down full length and read. From that vantage I looked up from time to time to catch a glimpse of my mother's head—her posture anxiously upright, her blond hair wound loosely up into a spiral while my father slouched cavalierly behind the steering wheel, occasionally handing her his glasses to be cleaned as he discussed the highway system, which led him to the subject of the military-industrial complex, which led to Eisenhower and thence to Truman, and from there to Hiroshima and onward, to his days in Kyoto—the cigar-chomping zen master, the boiling baths, the flight to New Delhi, and so on—all punctuated by Iris's semi-regular gasps, strangled warnings, Myles's irritated responses that while she had been in two car accidents, he had been in none—her riposte that he might consequently be more sensitive to her consequent fears... I lowered my eyes to my book.

It was a beautiful volume discovered at a yard sale for ten cents. Crumbling, cloth-bound, title embossed in gold. The paper, browned at the edges and faded subtly to the pale middle of the page with the delicate shift in hue of a clear sky, gave off the faint smell of dried mushrooms. The font was slender, serif, elegant—little could take my eyes from it, even the knowledge that Iris was suffering nearly unbearable anxiety as the car slowly approached Mass General, where her fate would be determined. Or, of course, the book was my distraction from her pain, just as Myles's extemporized soliloquy was his, and perhaps from his point of view it was an attempt to distract her too. Their lives were organized around a meditation practice that eschewed distraction as delusion and exhorted engagement with immanence as the only path to illumination. Yet what power distraction had. Diversion, your qualities have not yet been adequately sung! And when it comes to distraction, little could beat what happened next.

A profound thud shook the car, everything tilted toward the rear left corner, followed by a catastrophic scraping. Iris shouted, Myles fought with the steering wheel, and I sat up abruptly. Through the mud-spattered, dust-caked back window I saw a car tire—no, a car *wheel*—bound enthusiastically back down the stretch of highway we had just driven, veer into the opposite lane, hop a ditch, sail off an overpass, bounce off the road below, and come to rest at last in a stand of firs. Miraculously it narrowly missed half a dozen cars and, beyond our dislocated nerves, there were no injuries. Myles brought the Fairlane to a grinding halt on the shoulder of the road and three cars stopped to help. Later it would be determined that the wheel had sheared off at the axle, and Myles recalled that to economize at some point he had taken the car to an unlicensed mechanic for a brake repair job only to discover him on his back under the car hard at work with a hacksaw sometime later. When Myles pressed him, the mechanic's explanation was so incoherent that it was clear he was pie-eyed. Myles took the car elsewhere, not realizing that a third of the axle had been shorn through.

Grandmother saved us. That's what I called her, I punctiliously insisted on pronouncing the full three syllables like I was Little Red Riding Hood, while my cousins invented a happy array of pet names for her, as normal children do.

Grandmother was Iris's mother. Small, laconic, kindhearted, she arrived in her powder-blue Buick, peering over the steering wheel at us, a lit cigarette dangling between her immaculately painted fingernails. Not until her final years of decline did I ever see her without makeup, coiffed hair, a skirt showing off her calves, and permanently arched feet in high heels. Widow of a war hero she had adored and who, by all accounts adored her, she quietly, dutifully, sardonically fulfilled her allotted span of years, taking pleasure in her grandchildren, Red Sox radio play-by-plays, cigarettes, and highballs.

She seemed unsurprised by the Fairlane's missing wheel. I suppose by that time she was accustomed to the disasters that pursued my parents—product no doubt of their indifference to money until such time as they had need of hers. And now was such a time. I don't remember my mother's mortification, but I have no doubt that she was mortified to ask and receive Grandmother's financial help. What I remember is the cupboard and refrigerator stocked with sugared cereal, store-bought bread, pre-sliced cheese, and iceberg lettuce. Iris's will to police my diet was currently sapped by a preoccupation with her mortality, and so I gorged on giant, multitiered sandwiches, followed by heaped bowls of fluorescent cereal and containers of ice cream topped with Cool Whip. All this consumed in front of the TV, a device that had never crossed the threshold of my parents' house.

Grandmother lowered herself into her chair, crossed her elegant legs, lit up a cigarette, sipped her highball, and absorbed Iris's murmured worries. The enumerated concerns: lost income, the irreparable car, the unknown prognosis —all was a background hum to the magnificent exploits of the Dukes of Hazzard, the Hardy Boys, the California Highway Patrol, Starsky and Hutch, Evil Knievel and the Boston Celtics. Extolling the virtues of Celtics point guard Tiny Archibald, Myles rattled off his vital statistics before launching into the story of his (Myles's) bid for the Canadian Olympic basketball team, an ambition crushed by a weightlifting injury to his lower back.

When at last I went to bed in my aunt's old room, I raided her bookshelves searching through the fat volumes about spies and racetracks for all the tawdry scenes of gunplay and sex before drifting to sleep, empty, grey, unsated.

The next morning before we left for the city, I walked into the trees behind Grandmother's house. Unlike the fir and maple forests around our own house, Grandmother's woods were made of towering white pines that had evenly distributed a soft, melancholy, faded brown floor of long needles. It was nearly silent in there save for the wind hissing through the living needles far above. The softened contours of a long-abandoned road were still distinguishable between the tree trunks, and I followed them deeper into the gloom. The atmosphere of those woods extended the air of mourning permeating Grandmother's house. The yellowing black-and-white photographs of my grandfather, handsome and sturdy in his uniform on a battlefield in France, the paintings of Prague that he'd sent back, the *Croix de guerre* framed above her desk, all bathed in the same nicotine-coloured light, the same forlorn palette as that forest strewn with dead pine needles. There was an embankment on one side of the old road, and I stopped and looked over it to the slope below, where rested the rusting carcass of a beautiful old car. The tree into which it had crashed had incorporated the front fender in its girth. All the windows were broken and I could reach in to grip the wooden steering wheel. Standing on the running board I wielded an imaginary Tommy-gun. Surely that was how it had happened—the car careening wildly as it tried to shake the Heat, guns blazing through some 1920s night with a trunk full of rum. Then the crash, the sirens closing in as the dazed mobsters and their molls crawled from the wreckage and disappeared into the soft, concealing woods, a pack of bloodhounds on their trail.

I heard my name bellowed in my father's voice and patted the car's hood before departing. And then Grandmother was waving goodbye in the rear-view mirror of her car, which we'd borrowed to drive to Boston. There was nothing romantic about the Buick, but at least its axles were intact.

Even though Myles and Iris had both lived in cities, they

had already managed to forget how to enter and exit one. And there are few things more distressing for rural drivers than approaching the tangled maze of metropolitan entranceways. As the high-rises climb the sky, the bridges and tunnels and on-ramps and off-ramps, the sudden splits, the lane changes, the inconsistent signs all contrive to give the impression of a secret code, a lock with a forgotten combination, if it was ever really known, that opens onto some battle zone of an urban class war, where you risk being dragged from your borrowed bourgeois vehicle and torn asunder by a grim and ruthless proletariat who remain deaf to any cries of solidarity.

That, at least, was the tenor of my mother's rising panic as we wandered grimy neighbourhoods, having taken a series of wrong turns. But in fact the local proletariat, if such they were, appeared to take no interest in us until, at last, reassured by their indifference, Iris worked up the courage to roll down her window and ask directions. Naturally we were on the wrong side of the city, but with two simple turns we were set on a straight course for the hospital. And now Iris's strung nerves began to vibrate in a discordant twanging of recriminations and regrets—those ten years of chain-smoking, those burnt summers in the midday sun.

Myles's hearty agreement with these assessments was only gas on the flame. Was he incapable of sympathy? Iris wondered. Did she want him to lie? Myles asked. But here they clammed up, for my voice was suddenly speaking.

I had inched up from the back seat and stuck my head between their battling voices, and my own was saying that the *Lizzy Madge* was wrecked on top of the Isle of the Dead.

THE NIGHT is black, the moon sharp. Captain Severn and Rook lower a ladder and check the hull with a flashlight. They climb back on board looking upset. When it came up under us, the island's stones ripped the boat open so badly that it's beyond repair.

Send a mayday, says Captain Severn to Rook, Lower the boats, and abandon ship. This island could sink under us at any moment.

We cannot radio for help, says Chisolm. No one can know the location of this island.

Captain Severn doesn't look at her. This expedition is finished, he says. My plane is gone, my boat useless.

Chisolm doesn't care.

This place has been secret for millennia. It must remain so to all but the most dedicated seekers. No radio message until we've explored the island. In the meantime, yes, prepare the lifeboats.

You do not give the orders, says Captain Severn angrily.

As they argue, I slip away. Still shivering uncontrollably, I run to Rook's cabin, shuck my wet clothes, and pull on some of his. They're far too big, but I belt the pants in and roll up sleeves and cuffs, then run down to the engine room. It takes a few minutes to collect what I need, but when I get back up on deck with a can of diesel and some matches, the crew are still arguing about what to do. These people are decent, as people go, but they lack decisiveness. The key is to keep the momentum going or they'll stall, and I can't afford to let that happen. I need them—I can't take off on my own. I'm resourceful, but it's important to have a clear understanding of one's weaknesses. Mine is that I'm being chased by something too frightening to think about, and there's safety in numbers. At least, I hope so. I have to convince them that there can be no retreat. There's only one way to go and I will force us there if I must.

With the help of the gasoline, the lifeboats catch fire more easily than I expected. Before the crew notices the flames, the deck of the *Lizzy Madge* suddenly tips violently and everybody crashes into the gunnels.

I can hear Rook shouting, The moon! The moon!

Looking at the horizon I see that the moon's coming up fast. Too fast. The island is sinking again. Good. Just in time.

To the lifeboats! shouts Captain Severn, too late. As the crew run toward me they see boats engulfed in fire.

We've come too far to leave! I yell from the gunnel, then turn and jump.

Because the boat has tilted so far over, the ground is just a few feet away. I land on smooth stone and, without looking back, head east toward the rising moon.

I hear the crew behind me, cursing, shouting, jumping down. Everybody follows. They have no choice.

I feel the island under me. My feet know every stone. Did I walk it before? Did I live here?

I don't look back. Waves hit rocks as the island sinks. I can't hear the crew over the surf, but I know they're behind me. My legs walk on, remembering what I can't.

Hidden stairway down to a grotto. Water already up to my waist. I splash across it to a tall doorway cut in the rock. Pitch-black inside, but Severn has a flashlight—we're in a big cave with a high stone ceiling. It doesn't look man-made. At the far end of the cave is an opening to a descending stairway. There's a strange glow coming from those stairs, pale, from another world.

We'll drown in here! somebody says.

The water pours in behind us.

Wait, I say.

The water runs into a channel. The channel takes the water through a small gap in the rock wall. The opening is blood-red. A second later we hear a hiss. Then scraping behind us. Slowly, a huge slab of rock rolls out from a pocket in the wall. It's twice as thick as I am tall. It slides across the doorway, sealing it tight. No water after that.

Lava, says Severn. A steam-powered door.

We're trapped, says Rook.

We're saved, says Chisolm. The girl has saved us.

For what? asks Captain Severn. We'll be buried alive under the ocean.

Turning to me, he shouts that I'm a lunatic who's destroyed our only chance of escape.

I feel like the stone around us. His anger has no effect on me. Why not? I don't care that he's angry, I don't care that he's scared. And he is scared. The fear is leaking out of him. And when I feel his fear, a sudden rush of pity nearly topples me. I try to calm him by telling him I will lead them where they need to go.

Where?! he shouts. The island is above us, a drowned pile of stones, nothing more.

He rounds on the crew yelling, It's insanity to follow this child! She's a maniac, she's unhinged! You say she rescued us, but it was her madness with the plane that raised the island and shipwrecked us. And the burning lifeboats? Her handiwork again, no doubt.

Chisolm looks at me too. She says, Where are we going?

I see the look Severn gives her. It's a look of raw hatred.

I point to the stairway. To City.

And that's where I go. I walk down the steps. The strange glow lights my way. The stairs aren't really stairs. They're big chunks of rock slabbing down through a winding tunnel. I hear the crew behind me as they follow. What else can they do? They mutter to each other, What city?

The original city! says Chisolm. The girl speaks of the lost birthplace of civilization! We thought the Island held a secret and now we know what that secret is. It is the gateway to the past. To our origins.

There's more muttering. How can they trust me?

She has led us this far, says Chisolm. She was sent to guide us. She knows where she's going.

Sent? By whom? I remember no instructions. And do I know where I'm going? I walk, but feel blind. Each step is the right one, but I can't see the path in my mind. I follow my feet where they lead. I have that and my pictures and City, its waterfalls and lilacs and tall buildings forming an invisible magnet pulling a lodestone in my belly. And why? Why do I know where to go? Why do I need to get there? To find out where I come from.

The cold of the ocean finally begins to seep out of me as we descend, because the temperature goes up the farther down we go. The pale light strengthens. It lights the grey-pink stone of the tunnel walls and the bands of minerals that run through. Behind me I hear talk.

Perhaps, says Severn, The light comes from some kind of powerful mirror, relaying the sunlight down here.

Yes, says Rook. From some rock near the island. The sun should be rising now up there.

Quiet for a while. Thinking about the island makes us all think about the *Lizzy Madge*. That's what I think of. How it's probably rising with the rising water at first. And maybe even floating as the island disappears under it. Floating alone, abandoned. And then the sea will come in through its torn hull until it sinks on top of the island. And I suppose that it will go on rising and sinking as that island rises and sinks until it crumbles to dust.

I wonder if Captain Severn is thinking about his boat.

The light may come from phosphorescence, he says grimly, Or from the fires of hell, for all we know.

And then the stairs end and the passageway levels off.

Stop, says Chisolm. We must rest for a bit.

I stop. They stand around and some sit on the ground. I move away from them and squat against a wall. They leave me alone.

I hear something. Or think I do. Back up the stairs—a quiet sound, maybe claws? Burning head, stink of wild animal. Just like the cave, just like the storm. The back of my skull is boiling. It's after me. How did it find me? How did it get past the door?

We keep going! I say. And without waiting, I run.

I THINK this hallway resembles your underground tunnel, said Myles. We were lost in the Massachussetts General Hospital, trying to find the room where Iris had been taken to recover from surgery.

The light, Myles continued, Is similarly dim, the vague threat lurking. Don't touch anything! Every surface is crawling with mutant bacteria that could devour your lungs or skin. Yes, we too are marching through the subterranean passageways of your mother's illness in hopes of returning to the relative peace of our precancerous past.

Was that it? I wondered. Was my story just an elaborate metaphor for our current circumstances? Or was Myles displaying his talent for finding meaning where he needed it?

And what did he mean by our pre-cancerous past? Wasn't the cancer Iris's?

A steel triangle hung above Iris's hospital bed, and she gripped it to pull herself upright when she saw Myles and me coming through the doorway. Myles said she looked pale and drawn and she thanked him sarcastically, trying to let the remark slide off her but being so drained from surgery she couldn't muster her armour and sank against the pillows as though in response to a slow-motion blow. And it was only upon seeing this that Myles realized the brutality of his observation and tried to soften it by alleging that actually she looked quite good, all things considered, quite healthy given that she'd just been under anesthesia for several hours.

Not to mention, Iris muttered, that a chunk of her leg had been cut out. They took the lymph nodes, the butchers, because they wanted to be sure, and they're students so it looks like they did with a hatchet.

She was certain of this although she had not yet seen the wound since it was hidden under gauze. And, she went on, lifting herself up to see me better, I won't know for months whether they got it all. What, she wanted to know as she ruffled my hair, Had I done that day?

In fact, it had been one of the best so far of our week in Boston. On Iris's instructions, while she was poked, prodded, scrubbed, tested, X-rayed and cut, Myles had taken me on a tour of high-rises and children's museums, playgrounds and swan boats. That day we had visited the least likely of locations, the Christian Science headquarters, within which was the best room I'd ever seen. It was round, completely round. In fact, it resembled my globe lamp at home, only on a giant scale. A giant spherical room, then, with doors at opposite ends of the equator and those doors were linked by a catwalk that spanned the room. As we stood in the centre of the cat-walk, Myles said it was as though we were floating in a secular cathedral, because the sphere was made entirely of stained glass that was backlit and glowing. The stained glass was multi-coloured and each colour represented a different country. I imagined that we had been miniaturized and gained entry to my globe lamp at home and that the names of the countries had been reversed so we could read them and that instead of being lit from within, it was lit from without. But the names of many of the countries were unlike those on my globe, as were the shapes of the countries, and this was due, Myles explained, to the fact that this room had been constructed in the 1930s. All things, he intoned, Are in flux, they wax and wane, there is no stasis, no certainty in this world. Thus the British Empire that you see there has crumbled, and India, for instance, is ruled by Delhi rather than London. Likewise, the French no longer hold sway over West Africa—empires crumble and others are born: Latvia, Lithuania, Estonia, all subsumed into the Union of Soviet Socialists. And thus also, your mother is with us now, but in the space of a month or a year she may be gone, and our lives too tremble on a slender catwalk above doom.

His Sermon on the Maps was typical of his general out-look that day, which had been manifested earlier at the science museum, where we had paused before a small display featuring a massive number. Words next to it identified the number as the world's human population—the final digit ticked upward quickly, relentlessly, representing the rate of births worldwide, and Myles said gloomily, The human race, of course, is damned—soon we will overrun the continents and be wiped from the surface of the earth by famine and disease, if not by nuclear apocalypse or by some alien race who will introduce an invasive predator species to control our demographics as we have introduced foxes to fix rabbits, or snakes to snooker rats.

It was his prevailing mood and it continued even in the hospital, where Iris, who had listened with enthusiasm to the story of my day, at last succumbed to her pain and pressed a button for a nurse. And as we waited, Myles tried to be helpful, saying, The pain arises from difference, which arises from judgment—erase judgment, breathe into the pain, become the pain.

Go away, Iris cried, You dime-store Roshi! And then, having said this, she lay back and breathed deeply. She relaxed, and by the time the nurse came she noted that the pain had subsided a bit. Nevertheless, she accepted the nurse's pills and as she lay back on her pillows I told her that the night before I had dreamed that far below the Island of the Dead everybody was running.

THEY'RE CHASING me. Rook catches up. He calms me. I can't hear the Follower anymore. Can't feel it either. We have to go, I tell him. We have to get to City.

Yes, he says, Yes. We're going. But we can't run the whole way.

Everybody else is with us now. They breathe hard, they look at me hard, they're not happy. I don't tell anybody about why I ran. I start walking and everybody follows. We go on until we can't and stop.

Where is my Follower? Does it even exist?

The dim, strange light begins to fade and soon disappears, leaving us in darkness. A darkness so complete I can't see my own hands waving an inch from my face. Severn and Nolan have pocket flashlights, which they use to help everybody find a more or less comfortable spot to lie down. The mineral floor is hard and wavy, but smooth at least, and we are tired. The lights snap off and soon I can hear the breaths of individual crew members make the shift to sleep. Deeper, louder. Somebody snores lightly. I can't sleep. I'm suspended between terror and happiness. Happiness because we're on the path to City and whatever secrets it holds. And I am terrified that I won't reach it in time, that my Follower will catch me first and fold me into its stinking feathers where I will suffocate and vanish. Feathers? What feathers? I know it has them—dusty, mouldering, hot stench of wild animal. I lie awake waiting to hear its scrabbling claws and feel the heating of my scalp. But no sound comes.

I do, eventually, fall asleep and the next thing I see is Quill and Rook moving about in the thin light of what must be dawn. Apparently, before jumping off the *Lizzy Madge*, they threw some provisions into a pair of backpacks. They hand out a few crackers and sardines, a sip of water.

Quill wants to know how far it is to City. Will the provisions last?

I don't know.

All I know is the direction we must take and so I take it. Behind me, I hear the crew fall into step.

Soon we come to a long, thin tunnel. It thins and thins until I'm the only one who can walk forward easily. The others bend over and move slowly. The light fades as we walk until we're in the dark just as the tunnel comes to an end and we can stand. Flashlights come on and, in the beams of light, we see bodies on the ground.

Does somebody scream? Do I? Not sure because there's a crashing in my ears—must be the blood leaving my head because suddenly I'm dropping inside my skin and need to crouch down to keep from falling over.

Quill has a candle lamp in her pack. She lights it.

It's a huge cave. Gold shines on the ceiling between green stalactites. Purple stone rivers, pink waterfalls, and crystal fountains all frozen in time as though we stepped inside a photograph. None of that matters. There are bodies everywhere. Severn crouches down and pointlessly feels for a pulse. We all know these are corpses—there's something subtly, but horribly wrong about their postures.

Dead, he says quietly. Then he gently turns the corpse onto its back to see its face. And then he shouts and leaps backward. I've never seen anybody look so scared. No wonder. The corpse's face is his own.

Somebody turns over another body—it's Rook. And another is Quill. And Chisolm. We're surrounded by our own dead bodies. Is mine here? I hunt around but can't see it, but maybe it's hidden somewhere. It doesn't matter—this is a waking nightmare, devised by some unknown force (my Follower?) to stop us in our tracks. And it's worked. The crew is paralyzed. I look around and see them frozen in place as they gaze down at their own deaths. And when they come to, they'll want to retreat—understandably. I'd like to leave too. Flight is the natural reaction. But there can be no retreat. And no delays. Something must be done quickly.

Behind me, above the tunnel opening, I see several stones precariously wedged into the ceiling. Slipping out of sight of the others, I find a good rock, slightly larger than my fist, grip it tightly, and aim it where it needs to go. My aim isn't good. I barely nick one of the stones, but it's enough. Moments later several rocks come tumbling. And then more.

And then the roof of the cavern crashes down on us and we run.

Red glow on the walls of a tunnel opening. We race in and head down and feel heat. But we can't turn back—the cave-in crashes stones down the tunnel after us and plugs it.

We come out on a cliff edge. We're high on a shelf overlooking a giant cavern. The ceiling of the cavern is so high it's hidden by huge, rolling orange clouds. They're orange because they're lit from below by a river of fire. Lava pours across the floor of the cavern a hundred feet below.

To our left a thin stone bridge bends over the lava to a shelf on the other side. And there's an opening in the cliff face across from us—another tunnel.

Our clothes drip sweat.

The others stand and stare down, scared to stone. I walk to the bridge and step on.

Wait! somebody yells, maybe Severn.

Wait? That's all they ever want to do. It's that kind of thinking that gets you into real trouble. Never wait. Why would I? There's only one way to go on and I have to go on. There's no return, no retreat, no time to stop and think.

The bridge isn't man-made. Water made it maybe, and lava. Not constructed, in other words, for human feet, or any feet at all, for that matter, so the crossing is hard. Very hard. Because it's thin and lumpy, I crawl on my hands and knees. Soon I can hear the others behind me, swearing quietly, breathing loudly. Single file, inch by inch, we shimmy forward. My knees tear open on the rock, hands grow slippery with sweat, heat from the river of lava below bends the air, distorts my sight.

Halfway over, a scream behind me. I try to look back but

nearly tip over, so lie down to get a better grip and turn my head back.

It's Nolan. He's slipped and hangs by his fingertips, legs dangling in space. Rook reaches for him, but it's too late.

Horrible silence as he falls.

Instead of melting, he lands with a sickening crack on a chunk of rock riding the lava like an iceberg. Lucky, or maybe not. He lies still on the gliding rock in a limp pile.

We yell to him as he sails away, but he doesn't move. There's nothing we can do but helplessly watch his body slide out of sight around a bend. I don't know Nolan well enough to be sorry for him, but I'm still sorry for him. Sorrier for myself. Now I've seen somebody fall, it seems more likely that I'll follow suit. I stay down and inch like a worm on a stick. That's what I am. A burning worm. And the heat makes me dizzy. I begin to slip sideways and don't mind it. Falling is a relief.

Stop fucking around and go! Rook is right behind me. His voice is sharp and scared. I keep going.

Fear and a need so far away it's an old dream—the need to go on, the gravity of my pictures, of City.

sinking boat
rainbow on a wall
ghost with a gun
butter on hot bread
axe, bird, stump, blood
firewood
lilacs
waterfalls

What have I lost? Which ones gone? My mind has a hole in it and my treasures are leaking out. I'm going as fast as I can, but I have to go faster. I won't make it, but I go on, on, on. If the last shift forward worked, there's a chance the next one will. And it does, and it does, and again. Until finally I'm on the other side, helping others off the bridge. First Rook, who kneels on the ground, breathing hard. Then the others, one by one, Chisolm behind Lutra. Quill is the last. Unlike the others, she's upright. She steps off the bridge lightly, as if she's been walking above lava all her life. Maybe she has.

I hear the sound of gulls.

GULLS, IRIS said dreamily. That's a welcome change. There's so much darkness in your fable. Poor Nolan.

We were standing on the road looking out at the bay. Iris was on crutches. The day before she had been released from the hospital and had insisted Myles drive us home immediately. We had arrived at midnight to cold but familiar air, drying herbs, acrid scent of the incense Myles burned while meditating, ashes of a fire lit in the woodstove by a neighbour earlier in the day.

Myles was still in bed the next morning, but Iris had woken me to accompany her to the bay and she gamely hobbled on her crutches while I, still half-asleep, recalled my dreams to her.

My trance narrations had elided quietly into dreams without comment from my parents. A trance, a dream, what did it matter where the story came from? And it's true that I sometimes dreamed of underground landscapes and journeys, but more often I woke with jumbled pictures (strewn corpses, blue seagulls, lava) and glued them together into something semi-coherent, and tried to suppress my guilt for masquerading a yarn as truth.

It's wonderful, Iris said, To dream in sequence and with such clarity. I will write it all down when we return to the house.

Below us stretched the slick grey mud flats. She stared at the slender current that wound its way out to sea in the distance. Low tide, she said. I'm at low tide too.

The gulls squawked above the bay, hunting mussels. We turned away from the slaughter and made our way home before we had to watch the poor shellfish dropped from great heights to smash open on the barnacled rocks below, their exposed, snotty guts fought over by a tribe of dagger-eyed birds.

At home I made breakfast and Myles was roused and he and Iris poured the thin, smoky syrup he had made of swampy maple sap over the heavy patties of fried dough that I called pancakes and Myles noted their consistency and the weakness of the coffee and Iris told him not to be an ingrate.

There was a knock at the door—Charlotte and Jane, two of my parents' fellow disciples, had walked a half-mile from their adjacent houses carrying baskets laden with pies and quiches to ameliorate Iris's convalescence. There was no turning them away, even if Iris had wanted to—and she did. Nevertheless, she took pleasure in the *fact* of company if the company were previously known. I wonder why this is. I am largely the same. In my case it is a matter of working up the reserves necessary to dial down the noise of my interior world sufficiently to hear the sounds coming from outside — not the demandless noises of the world—the rattle of a passing truck, or a calling bird to which I listen with pleasure, but the sound of human language to which I feel obliged to listen closely and to respond in kind, matching not merely the subject of the speech, but, more dauntingly, the feeling with which the words are spoken. This kind of thing requires a switch in modes of attention that is not pleasant to contemplate when I'm happily ensconced in the feelings of my own thoughts. I think this might have been (and might be) similar to my mother's temper, and thus explains her polite, but reluctant greeting of Charlotte and Jane and the inevitable chorus of You shouldn't haves and But yes we should haves that followed.

As for Myles, his sensibility allowed of a very different reaction—contrary to Iris, he thrived on new acquaintance, in fact the novelty of new personalities and new backstories was one of the few things capable of breaking through to still his internal flood of cerebration for a short time while he harvested a person's name, upbringing, and tribal history before some detail would send him off in a torrent of uttered thoughts, an outgoing tide of free association. When it came to Jane and Charlotte, for instance, familiarity had bred, if not contempt, at least indifference. They could offer him nothing new, and as far as he was concerned, small talk lacked flavour. However, they had one important piece of information—he was late for a work session at the zendo garden. This he had entirely forgotten, and the news suddenly transformed him from slothful tea drinker to hurricane.

He vanished upstairs to change into his work clothes, exhorting me to follow, for I was conscripted to join him in the morning's labour. Our house was tiny and nearly doorless and so from upstairs, as I belted on my jeans, I heard the voices of Charlotte, Jane, and Iris sunken to a murmur, and as I came (very quietly) down the stairs I caught Jane's voice saying, We cannot expect to understand Willard's motives and methods. Common morality does not apply.

Iris didn't agree, but Jane was firm, saying it was not a question of agreeing or disagreeing—in fact there was no question to be asked, as Willard himself would say, only a reality to be experienced. In any case, she went on, It isn't as though he raped anybody. I was there, I saw the whole thing. It was at the last Gathering. Of course, Robert and I have experienced Willard before. Bill and Bernadette should consider themselves lucky—

But here Iris coughed loudly because she'd spotted me trying to slip unobtrusively closer to better hear the women's conversation. Myles descended, dug out a hunk of Charlotte's rhubarb pie, shoved it in his mouth, beckoned me, muttered goodbye, and flew out the door. So I never found out exactly what Jane meant by Experienced, which was probably just as well.

Myles and I ripped out of the driveway, narrowly missing a passing truck, and went jouncing over the washboards of the dirt road at top speed. Climbing the hill, Myles waved at Willard, who stood in the doorway of his ancient farmhouse playing his piccolo.

A few hundred yards later we swung into the little parking lot, which was full of rusting Dodge Darts and other assorted beaters, and nearly sprinted the sumac-lined wooden platform steps that led down the hill next to, and sometimes over, a narrow but very active brook. We heard, before we saw, the hammer blows and rattling machinery. The steps ended, the woods gave way, and in the sunlight we saw the rolling acreage upon which the cascading rooftops of the meditation hall sat in Japanese style, surrounded by a rectangular moat of whitened beach pebbles, overlooking a pond overlooking a wooded valley.

To our left, next to the pond, men laboured to erect a fence while others carted soil. The sound of machinery came from a tractor that towed a tilling device. This tractor was a denuded Volkswagen Beetle welded to the chassis of a truck. It was driven by its maker, a tall thin, blond man who bounced away earnestly on the tractor. On weekend evenings he took to the stage of the concert barn and released his tenor to the rafters —he was a powerful singer who worshipped Puccini and Gershwin in equal measure. I could hear him crooning over the sound of the engine, practicing a solo from *Boris Godunov*, I think. Meanwhile a bald, muscular man was pounding a post deep into the ground as another, slight, bespectacled, and bearded, clad in a ragged army jacket and hat, held the post in question. The military garb was the only material trace that remained of his tour in Vietnam. Other evidence could be found, according to Myles, in his sorrowing eyes. Nearby, a small, mustachioed, handsome man, nattily attired in carefully patched overalls, toted a wheelbarrow full of manure. This was Robert, Jane's husband, who had also, apparently, Experienced Willard. He greeted Myles sardonically, asking if he was late because he'd been hitting the books.

This was a reference to Myles's recent decision to undertake a graduate degree in English literature. As though, Willard had sneered when he learned of this, The academy has anything to teach. There is nothing there but desiccated thoughts chasing themselves in an ever-tightening circle of irrelevance. There is nothing to learn there because learning is a delusion. There is nothing to learn, nothing to unlearn, there is only emptiness, only the eternal flux to be encountered in every moment, every breath as you saw wood, hammer nails, muck stables, sit on a cushion—it is *these* activities,

and not the wasted hours of abstract thought in dusty librar-
ies, bent over the dead words of dead fools, that will bring
illumination.

But Myles had persisted, feeling the need to quench a
mental thirst and pursue some advancement in the material
world, delusory or not. And so, Willard, finding intolerable
the notion that he must share his authority over Myles with
bespectacled deans and musty professors, began a campaign
of belittlement—singling Myles out at work sessions and
meetings, asking if he had any new wisdom to share, proposing that Myles teach instead of Willard, seeing as he was
becoming a Master of Fuck All, calling him egghead, calling
him Professor of Farts, calling him Piles. How are your piles,
Myles? And, of course, all the other men laughed uproarious-
ly and joined in, chuckling and shaking their heads whenever
they saw Myles and asking him questions about Milton and
snickering when he launched enthusiastically into descrip-
tions of *Paradise Lost.*

And still Myles persisted, his stubborn streak hardening
rather than weakening in the face of disapproval. Encour-
aged by Iris, he took out loans and drove the hour to the
university twice weekly.

For instance, the Monday following that zendo work session, Myles picked me up after school and I went with him as
I often did to roam the hallways of the English department
at the University of Maine, while he sat in class or taught
composition. Those bleak corridors are strangely vivid in my
memory—the beige linoleum tiles beneath an atmosphere of
suppressed dread that lingered in the lounge with its crumbling bookshelves and stench of ancient coffee boiling to tar
on its slow-drip machine above the stained and mildewed
carpet, bug-splattered windows, glare of fluorescent lights,

walls of concrete block painted mustard yellow in some vain effort to cheer the ambience.

A basket next to the coffee machine held a collection of candies, small rolls of toffee individually wrapped in shiny, crackling foil. I transferred the bulk of these to my pockets and then wandered to the elevators, which I rode up and down for what seems in my memory to be hours but was, very likely, no more than a few minutes. But in that time I observed the vacant or anxious or keen faces of students, the fatigued, thousand-yard stare of the graduate candidates, the self-congratulatory decrepitude of the professors, even the younger ones, and I swore to myself that I would never surrender to the academy. No, once I was done with high school, it was the open road for me. There were seas to be sailed, tombs to be explored, perils to be survived.

I abandoned the elevators for the lounge, where I sprawled in a chair idly flicking through *Paideuma*, the department's literary journal devoted to the works of Ezra Pound. Barely reading, my eye snagged on a quote from an Italian philosopher named Giambattista Vico. The threefold labour of great poetry is (1) to invent sublime fables suited to the popular understanding, (2) to perturb to excess with a view to the end proposed: (3) to teach the vulgar to act virtuously.

I muddled over this for a while and decided I liked it. But could a poem teach Willard to be more virtuous? I felt certain he was in the habit of vulgarity. Paging further I landed on a poem...

BE in me as the eternal moods
   of the bleak wind, and not
As transient things are—
   gaiety of flowers.

Have me in the strong loneliness
　　of sunless cliffs
And of gray waters.
　　Let the gods speak softly of us
In days hereafter,
　　the shadowy flowers of Orcus
Remember thee.

As though the words of the poem worked a spell, they
canted me sideways until I slipped down, down through the
linoleum tiles, through concrete and rebar, through ducts
and fluorescent lights and ceiling tiles into the open air of the
mathematics department, and on down, down in a free fall
two more storeys and into the basement past the furnace and
hot water heaters through the floor and into the soil beneath,
tunnelling through layers of gravel and granite schist, down,
down far below where gulls coasted the face of those sunless
cliffs, which rose over grey waters.

ON THIS side of the bridge there's an opening in the rock
face. I get up and head in, not waiting for the others. They
come behind me anyway.

This new tunnel is very short. I'm barely in before I see pale
light ahead. Then I'm on the other side. Gulls everywhere.
They flap, they call, they shoot the air and land on a beach. A
beach! We're on the shore of an underground ocean.

There are waves all the way to a flat horizon. Even though
stone walls on either side of us go up hundreds of feet before they bend into a ceiling high above, standing in that
much open space after the oppressive tunnels feels miraculous. The strange light is brighter here because it bounces

off water. At the bottom of the cliffs, the shore goes on and on out of sight.

None of us move. We stand or sit and stare and breathe. The air is wet and rusty. Yes, that's the problem. We can't stop for long or we'll rust, the air will freeze us up like old bolts. I can see it happening. Everybody's stalled—the sight of our own corpses, Nolan's fall—it's all coming on. We have to leave the caves behind.

We keep moving, I say to Chisolm.

Where? she asks.

I point to the far end of the sea. And then to the boats, because there are boats. Five of them. They're in bad shape, but we have to fix them and set sail.

No, she says, No, we stop. We need to stop. You've led us into hell.

Obviously, the bodies in the caves have shaken her will. That's bad—I've lost Chisolm and she was my fulcrum for prying everybody else loose. I fight with her. I shout, but she doesn't answer. Nobody answers. They sit and stare at waves, which are full of jumping fish. Lutra looks hard at them, but Chisolm holds her tight to keep her from jumping in after them.

If I can't use Chisolm, I must find another point to pivot on.

Quill and Rook give everybody cans of sardines. I eat half of mine and save the rest. The light fades and the crew lies down on sand and sleeps. Severn takes first watch. I pretend to sleep until I see his eyes close and yellow hair fall forward.

My Follower is close. I can feel it—feel the wind from its ragged feathers, feel my pictures slipping away, the little shreds of my forgotten past fading one by one. We have to go on. I walk to the boats and look them over. Rotten gunnels, cracked planks, dried caulking falling out. Where did the wood come from? Who built them? Why did they leave them here? Too heavy for me to drag to the water. And I don't know how to sail. And even the best one would sink under me.

Lutra curls tight to sleeping Chisolm, but the otter wakes up as soon as I crouch in front of her. She growls, but I hang a sardine in front of her nose and she snaps it down. I hold another one out and she comes for it. I get her to the water's edge and give it to her. Then I take the last one, show it to her, and throw it as far out in the water as I can. Lutra jumps into the water and swims out after it. Small silver fish jump in her path and she dives. It's nearly pitch-dark when I think I see her head surface again far out. Then she dives again and disappears. She's gone. I rake away my footprints on the sand but leave Lutra's. I lie down and now all the light is gone so try to sleep.

I wake up to screams. Chisolm is at the water's edge in thin dawn light, on her knees, crying, then screaming for Lutra, then crying again. Others stand and call to the otter. No sign.

You did this, says Rook in my ear. He looks at me, not smiling, and says he knows it was me, he should never have brought me aboard, I've led them into a nightmare.

I have to go on, I say.

Fix the boats! yells Chisolm. We must find her.

Some of the crew are carpenters and they brought a few tools, mostly hatchets and penknives. They get to work, pulling good wood off bad boats and fixing the two best ones. They work hard all day. Chisolm stands on the beach staring out at the water. Rook won't talk to me. Everybody else seems to think Lutra left on her own.

Light's nearly gone when we climb into the two repaired

dories. At first we bail non-stop, but then the wood swells and the gaps slowly close. Somebody sewed old shirts and coats into sails, which now hang from oars that have become masts. A little tuft of breezes comes along and bellies them enough to blow us slowly out to sea.

The dark grey air electrifies and I turn just in time to see, or think I see, a flicker near the tunnel. My Follower. I'm barely ahead of it.

I sit in my seat at the prow of the lead boat and eat the can of sardines Quill hands out.

Captain Severn sits behind me. He looks as pale and drawn as his own corpse from the caves. That nightmare seems to have broken him. He doesn't argue about where we should go but pulls out his compass and looks at me. I point over the waves and he sets a course.

We sail for three days. A light wind sends us over green water so clear we can see the mineral sea floor below us—crystal and iron, fool's gold glinting, pink granite. Here and there islands of smoothly rounded pink rock pile up on top of each other like whipped egg whites. The ornate rock ceiling is so far above us that from time to time fluorescent orange clouds drift beneath it. In places elegantly long, solidified drips of purple stone hang from it like gargantuan icicles.

But the nights are so dark we stop. There are rusty anchors in the boats. Severn and Rook tie together old ropes and throw the anchors overboard. Nobody talks about what we saw in the caves. We don't talk about much at all.

We're scared at night. In daylight we see glowing animals slide under the water too fast to tell how big they are. They're big enough. Fish too, schools of them. But at night every noise is huge. Waves slip and sigh, something boils the water nearby—fins? One night we hear a fight. Splashing water, roaring—two monsters? But the next day there's nothing, except strange sky-blue gulls flying around us.

Chisolm sits in the bow of the other boat staring at the waves for Lutra. No Lutra. I stay where I am, looking at the horizon. My eyes are like Severn's compass, they can bounce away but they always swing back. That's why I'm the one who sees the island first...

...HURRY, SAID Myles, jostling my elbow, I'm late.

We were down the hall, out the door, in the car, and leaving campus before I'd fully relocated. Then pushing the speed limit on Route 1A to Frothingham, which was the big town this side of Cove. There, at the corner of Main and Water, was the homeless shelter where Myles worked four overnights a week. Inside, the spotless halls smelled of floor soap and boiled potatoes. I trailed Myles, who rushed in, apologizing for his tardiness to Sister Mary Catherine, whose place he took at the office desk.

I would fire you, she said not unpleasantly, If I could find a replacement. As you well know.

Myles began to concoct an explanation, but she waved a hand to silence him. There's an intake to do. I'm going home. Good night.

The intake was a young man from Nigeria who was waiting patiently in the hall.

For Myles, doing an intake was a natural extension of his propensity for story-harvesting. This was the best part of his job there. He arranged himself comfortably on top of several pillows on the office chair and listened carefully as Bayo told his tale. So did I.

They killed my father, he said, And said they would kill me next.

An internecine struggle, clan rivals, he had to flee the country. Then, he said, I was in Ghana for a while, selling jeans and T-shirts on the street.

I had money I'd brought from Nigeria, he said. I used it to pay a sailor on a merchant boat. He shut me in a metal box under his cabin. He was too afraid to let me out in Spain, so I froze when we went north and then I nearly died of heatstroke when we went south. I was in the box for three months. In New Orleans I walked off the boat because I'm black. Nobody noticed me. They thought I was a dockworker. I went to a shelter there and they said I should go to Canada. They put me on a bus here.

That makes sense, said Myles. We're the closest shelter to the border. But that means you're an illegal. I'm afraid you can't stay here.

Myles called Father Malenfant, who agreed to give Bayo sanctuary in St. Mike's until arrangements could be made to smuggle him north. The evening had begun well, with a good story and some law-bending, and Myles was flush with energy when Iris arrived to pick me up. Her day of proof-reading the newspaper had ended and she was ready for home.

Iris was quiet all the way back and over our dinner of left-over egg rolls.

You should go and visit Apollo and Artemis tomorrow, she said when she'd finished eating.

I guessed that she was worrying about Bill and Bernadette but didn't feel she could go see them herself yet for fear of offending them with her sympathy. So she would send me as an emissary, or proxy. My friendship with the Krimgold-Gragnolati kids would, by association, refer to her friendship with their parents.

Bill's blackjack and pistol lay quiescent on a bed of loose .45 calibre bullets. The bullets lined the bottom of a wicker basket on a side table in the Krimgold-Gragnolati kitchen. I stared at the blackjack, which I knew about from Tintin, who was always getting knocked out by one. It was made of polished black leather, seams stitched in red, and I wanted very much to hold it but didn't dare.

Bill had the weaponry because he'd been an officer in the military police in Vietnam. Now he worked as a paramedic and volunteered with the police and fire departments, which explained the scanner that sat behind the basket of bullets, broadcasting anxiety at low volume.

Six foot five, flaming orange hair now balding, enormous blue eyes, lean and handsome, he loomed around by turns jittery and brooding, full of sudden erratic laughter, unexpected questions, and mid-conversation lapses.

Bernadette was slim and tall, dark-haired, quick-witted. Despite having defected to the counterculture with Bill, post-Vietnam, she retained a military decisiveness from her role as army wife stationed by turns in various outposts of Middle America. Normally, she was exuberant and tough. Today she was neither. She and Bill had gone practically mute. They were avoiding each other, smiling with painful awkwardness at me and the kids and focussing intently on household endeavours. Bill was installing baseboards and Bernadette was repairing Apollo's three-speed. Athena serenely canned pickled beets, either unaware of her parents' disquiet, or unwilling to care about it.

I couldn't tell if Artemis and Apollo knew about the Gathering, but they knew something. Artemis was surlier and Apollo further out in his personal ether. He might also have been in shock. A bandage on his calf covered the hole made there by their rooster's spur earlier that day. The rooster had long been troublesome and vicious, and as far as Bernadette was concerned, this attack on her son put things in a mortal light. Artemis, Apollo, and I were sent to the chicken yard with a hatchet and thick leather work gloves to dispense justice.

I helped the siblings corner the doomed bird, but nothing prepared me for the raw shock of the chopping block. I gripped the legs while Apollo did his best to hold the bird in a position horizontal to the stump. His hands were invisible among the feathers of the wings, which kept flapping free, but moments before Artemis raised the hatchet the rooster stilled, as though resigned to or stunned by the imminence of its death.

Then feathers and wings flew everywhere as the headless body thrashed among the wood chips, blood welling from its open neck. The head and an inch or two of the neck remained on the stump, unmoving, eyes open. Nauseated, I squatted to avoid fainting while Artemis and Apollo pranced gleefully around the twitching body of the rooster.

You look a little green around the gills, said Artemis, ruffling my hair. Don't worry, it didn't feel any pain. The body moves automatically after you cut off the head.

Where do you think food comes from? said Apollo scornfully.

I'm a vegetarian, I muttered.

Not us! declared Artemis, rubbing her hands together in anticipation. Time to dress this bird. No need for you to stay if you don't want to.

Leave if you're a candy-ass, added Apollo quietly. I knew

very well that Apollo was soft, like me, but the rest of his family was hard and so this was how he callused his softness to belong.

I stayed anyway, to spite Apollo. I watched as he and Artemis plunged the carcass into hot water, plucked the feathers, cut open the anus, and removed the liver and heart and stomach all shining and slippery. Artemis showed me the gravel in the gizzard and the contents of the oil sac.

The wind was cold in my hair as I rode my bike home. That night, as I tried to read myself to sleep, the faces of the Krimgold-Gragnolatis went by me, grim, distracted, mortified, oblivious. And I thought of the rooster whose coincidental violence had doomed it. But had the butchery lanced the pent misery in that household? It was hard to know yet. These thoughts conspired to keep me awake, and against my will my blood-soaked vision veered underground.

THE ISLAND is lumpy, strange, but we're happy to see it. Scared too. We need supplies, we fear a fight. But the closer we get, the quieter it looks. The little wind dies and the stronger crew members use old rotting oars to row us in.

Now we see it up close, small, flat, rocky. And the lump is astonishing—an enormous ship tilted halfway across the island. Blue gulls fly in and out of big holes in the steel hull and perch on the handrails of the deck, high above the rocky beach.

Big ships come from big cities. Which means I'm right. There is one down here.

We drag our dories up on the shale. Gulls the only sign of life.

Hello! shouts Captain Severn. But there's no reply, nothing but a metallic echo.

Then there's a faint noise in the ship, and a head with neat brown hair pokes out a window. Two bright, bright eyes look at us. We're so surprised to see somebody, we don't recognize him at first.

Nolan! says Quill.

It is. He disappears and we wait, stunned. Soon he hops down from a hole in the freighter and comes toward us slowly, limping, sideways. He's dressed well and looks good for somebody we last saw on a rock floating on lava.

I have no memory of any of that, he says. I remember falling and that's all until I woke up on board this ship here.

We're happy to see him and he pretends to be happy to see us. But I can tell he's not. He's angry. Why? Can't ask him that. Anyway, he's telling us what happened.

The river of lava brought him to the sea, where the crew of a passing ship rescued him. The ship's doctor tended his leg, which fractured when he fell. The crew took good care of him, and after a while he realized he could understand them, but they had a very strange accent. The ship went on, stopping at small ports along the coast to load and unload goods. As his leg got better, he began to help, taking inventory, swabbing the deck, cleaning berths.

But it's been just a few days since we saw you last, says Rook. How could your leg have healed in that time?

A few days? says Nolan. I've been here for months and I was months aboard that ship before that.

Is he telling the truth? He doesn't see how confused we are, or doesn't care. He keeps talking.

There was a storm like I'd never seen before.

He was ordered to his cabin, where he stayed until he felt

95

the boat drive aground and fall sideways. He left his cabin and he was alone. The crew abandoned ship in their lifeboats and forgot about their passenger in the rush.

Luckily, the boat was well stocked with supplies, he says. I've managed to survive.

He brings us on board and shows us how clean all the cabins are, all the halls, the walls. He's very proud of it. We climb ladders until we come out on the top deck and look out to sea.

Did the crew talk about a city? I ask.

Yes, says Nolan. He waves at the flat horizon.

I look at Chisolm. I was right and she was right to trust me. But she doesn't seem to care. She wants to know if Nolan has seen Lutra.

He hasn't.

We have to go on to City, I say. I can practically hear the rustle of my Follower's wings as it makes its way toward us.

But Nolan isn't ready to leave. He wants time to pack. He says he'll cook a hot meal for everybody if we stay the night. The crew is hungry and tired of bailing and rowing and floating. They vote to stay. I argue, but nobody listens and I can think of no new trick to get them going.

So we pull our boats up higher and follow Captain Severn's instructions. The carpenters check the hulls and clean them. Others patch the tattered sails. Nolan won't let anybody help him make his stew. He cooks in a giant pot from the ship's galley over a driftwood fire.

He works so quietly it looks like he's barely moving, but he must have because we can see and taste the stew. We sit around on rocks and eat, and everybody likes the food, except me, but that's just because I don't like stews. I pour it into the sand when nobody's looking and eat some of the nuts I've been hoarding in my pockets. Maybe it's my empty stomach that keeps me awake when everybody lies down on the beach to sleep in the warm night.

It feels like hours go by before I finally begin to doze a bit and see a lightning bug crawling across my mind, blinking as it goes, until it turns into a moving lamp. I blink and wake and see the lamp is Nolan's. He's walking from body to body and picking up an arm or a leg and letting it drop. I don't move. Too scared. He comes closer and I can hear him *sniffing* the sleeping bodies. That sound creeps all over me with freezing little feet. He checks six of us and then starts tying hands and feet with rope.

I see a knife shine in the lamplight. Nolan puts it under the piano tuner's beard. Then he pulls it across. The piano tuner's eyes bang open. He gapes his mouth but he can't talk. Dark blood pumps out of his neck. He wriggles for a second, then stops. He lies back. His eyes are still open, but he doesn't blink. He doesn't move. He doesn't breathe.

Nolan stands and walks to the next person.

I see all our bodies in the light from his lamp. I've seen them like this before. Everybody's lying the same way our dead bodies were lying in that cave. The cave was the future. It was now. He's going to kill us all.

I shake Quill, then Rook, but can't wake them. They must be drugged. Nolan's sniffing Severn's body. I've got seconds before he puts knife to throat again. I find a smooth rock that fits my hand and run behind him fast and quiet, trip, fall.

Nolan's light turns toward me. I lie still. Lamp turns back and he bends over Severn.

I get up and run at him and jump. He hears, turns, and slashes. Cold on my arm and I drop the rock. But Nolan falls under me. My arm's cut. He gets up, stumbles, curses, trips, falls and I'm on him. Grab another rock to brain him, but he's got my wrist. Arm's bleeding so I wipe my free hand across it and smear the blood in his eyes. When he tries to wipe it off, he lets go of my wrist and I grab sand and grind it into his eyeballs with the blood. He screams and rubs at the grit while I grab a rock and hit his head as hard as I can. He tips over and lies still.

I've got to keep moving, because I'm afraid if I sit down I won't get back up. Severn is still sleeping, still alive, head on his rucksack. I search it because sailors have rope. The lamp shows a long piece of thick cord. I tie Nolan's hands and feet. I don't know good knots so I tie a lot of little ones as tight as I can and then knot the loose end around a boulder just in case.

Finally, I take the time to clean my cut and look at it. It's a long, shallow slash across the bony side of my forearm. The bleeding's nearly stopped. I wade ankle-deep in the water and clean it again before wrapping it with a rag from one of the boats. Suddenly I realize that I'm starving. A can of sardines from Rook's backpack goes down fast. I sit down near Nolan, rock in one hand and his knife in the other.

I don't mean to pass out but I must because I wake to find Nolan's teeth nearly on the knife. Behind him the rope stretches so tightly it digs into his wrists and ankles. I give him a light whack with the rock because I don't want to kill him. Not just yet. He groans and lies down again. The morning light begins to spread and my crewmates start to wake.

When they do, Nolan shouts that I've gone insane. He woke to discover me slitting the piano tuner's throat and jumped me, etc.

He's lying, I say when he's finished talking. He was going to kill us all.

But why? Captain Severn says. He still doesn't trust me. I'm a stowaway from nowhere who could very well be insane, as far as he's concerned. I can't really blame him—I've certainly done enough bizarre things by now to warrant his suspicion.

The piano tuner's wife holds her husband's limp head in her lap and rocks back and forth, his cold dark neck blood on her dress. I can't look at her.

Follow me, I say. And they do, as they always do. I think I'm beginning to understand why. Rook and Quill follow me because they care for me, they worry about me, Chisolm follows because she believes in me, Severn because he's in love with Quill and in thrall to Chisolm. And the rest, as far as I can tell, are sheep.

Severn brings Nolan, holding a knife to his back, and I lead the way to the wreck. Inside we walk the hallways. Nolan yells. He wants us to untie him. He shouts that I'm the murderer, he's the victim. I open a door, then another, another. Empty rooms, boiler rooms, storage rooms. Not what I'm looking for. I hear crewmates muttering. Nolan is louder, nervous. I'm getting close.

Another door. Here it is, yes, this must be it. A room full of neatly folded clothes and neatly stacked human bones. We walk through it, everybody quiet. There's a second door at the far end. We go through it and find them all. All their parts. Hearts pickled in sea brine; ears, eyes, and arms and legs smoked and salted, hung from the ceiling by fishing lines.

Did Nolan's fall break something other than his leg? We leave the room full of human meat and go back outside. Nolan won't answer any questions at first, but then he does.

I had no choice, he says.

When the ship wrecked on the island it was far from the shipping lanes, and all communication instruments were destroyed. A month later the crew ran out of provisions. They started fishing and gull-hunting—but the fish in this part of the sea are few and bony and the gulls are smart.

One day a young sailor named Oliver got sick and died. The crew was starving and the captain ordered them to gut the body and prepare it. Most said no. They couldn't, wouldn't. But in the end, their hunger got the better of them and then they ate Oliver.

Everybody listening shakes and twitches. Nolan notices and gets mad.

For your sakes, I hope you never learn what it's like to really starve to death, he says. Your body starts to eat itself and you can feel it. You cannibalize yourself. You're a cannibal whether you want to be or not.

He stops talking, but Rook gets him to go on and he does.

Oliver didn't last long between them all and after a while they were hungry again and once you start down this path it's hard to stop.

The custom of the sea, says Captain Severn, nodding.

Meat is meat, Nolan says. He shrugs when he says this and I don't like the shrug. I don't think anybody else does either.

The captain said they would draw straws. But the captain was the one who drew the short one, so he found his gun and shot himself in the head.

A man of great character, says Nolan, Although it's too bad he wasted his brain. It's too nutritious to spray across a beach.

They went on following the dead captain's orders until the only one left was Nolan.

For a long time after he stops talking, nobody says anything. I think we're thinking about our provisions. We're wondering how long they'll last. Who will make the best meal if it comes to that?

I look down and see a dark stain on the rock under my feet. Old blood maybe.

Suddenly I see Nolan in my mind stepping over his dead crewmates. Slippery guts spill out with blood.

I'm not the only one thinking this. Severn doesn't believe Nolan. He's asking him questions. Why is the storeroom so well stocked? If the story is true, the crew would've gotten smaller one by one, each body eaten before the next game of straws began. In the end, there shouldn't be any provisions, just Nolan slowly starving to death.

If it wasn't for the girl, you'd be butchering us now, Severn says.

Nolan doesn't answer.

Poor Grimm didn't escape, says Chisolm.

We look at the dead piano tuner and his wife, who still holds his head.

It's time to go, I say.

We pile up the smoked and pickled remains of the ship's crew and burn them. What else can we do? Nolan goes crazy. He screams, foam comes out of his mouth. He tries to escape. Severn ties him up even more and gets some help to throw him in one of our boats.

We do what Grimm's wife asks and build a raft of driftwood. We lay him on it, pour diesel from the wrecked ship on the wood, tow it out to sea, and light it. Behind the raft flames, we can see the fire on the island. So can Nolan. He looks like he's given up.

Suddenly he stands up and jumps overboard. He disappears for several long minutes, then comes back up. He got himself free of the rope somehow. He swims back toward the island. Nobody tries to stop him. They all turn away and look at the horizon. But I can't look away. It takes a long time for Nolan to get back. When he does, we're so far away I can barely see him. He's trying to put out the fire. There's something else. What is it? A flicker. Behind the fire. The back of my scalp burns—my follower is there on the island with Nolan.

I turn away, sweating. Rook bends down in front of me and picks up a small mussel shell from Nolan's seat. It must be what he used to cut himself free. Rook looks at the shell, then throws it overboard.

GOOD LORD! said Myles. Why so macabre?

He was looking at Bernadette's latest canvas—blood-coloured paint spattered over a drawing of a woman holding a man's severed head by the hair.

It's Judith beheading Holofernes, said Bernadette. It's macabre by nature. Nothing I can do about that.

It seems to me, said Myles, massaging his belly, That there's no need for such excessive grotesqueries.

We had just finished brunch at the K-Gs'. Iris's scheme had apparently worked because after my visit we were invited for waffles.

I disagree, said Bernadette sharply. We can't turn away from the grotesque, we must face it. Suffering, pain, and death—it was only when Siddhartha realized those were the bedrocks of experience that he was able to step onto the path to enlightenment.

Myles was preparing a rejoinder, but Iris interjected suddenly to ask whether Athena was the model for Judith. Athena smiled enigmatically from the window seat where she sat with a book.

Just then Bill came in with Artemis and Apollo and showed me a strange piece of paper he had recently discovered in the attic. It looked ancient to me, yellowed, torn, and partly burnt.

It seems to be a map, he said.

And it was. Examining it closely, I saw that not only was it a map, it corresponded to the K-Gs' property.

It's a map of this place, I said.

Do you think so? said Bill with surprise.

On the map was a large X drawn above a boat in the northwest quadrant. The sketch of the boat matched the old dory sinking into the grass of the sloping lawn. I ran to it with Bill, Artemis, and Apollo close behind me.

The boat, filled halfway with soil, was overflowing with dead flowers, a portion of which had been wrenched from the ground and left to compost on its surface. Rifling through the weeds, I came upon an old glass bottle, and inside it was a note on paper that resembled, in its state of decay, the map. It read: My Prow Knows the Way.

What could it mean? asked Bill as Artemis, Apollo, and I dug around in the bow of the boat but found nothing. Hunting beneath, I found nothing again and circled to the stern, staring pensively at the yard. I was too caught up in the hunt to note that Artemis and Apollo were not really helping but rather lurking and nudging each other in the background. In the near distance was a chickadee bustling its wings in the grotty old birdbath. The prow pointed straight at it. Away flew the chickadee as I sprinted forward and, after peering quickly into the depths of the bath, reached in. Trying to avoid contact with the fresh white and pea-soup bird excrement, I pulled out a metal container. It was an old travel case for soap—I had one at home that I'd acquired at a yard sale and in which I kept a tuft of Shadow's hair cut before burial. Opening the lid, I found a small brass compass. I dried it off and noticed a deep nick in its frame. When the compass's arrow lined up with the north setting, the nick indicated west and so I went that way, Artemis and Apollo in tow.

Dead birch and maple leaves crisped under our sneakers, dampening in the chilled grass. A lone snowflake wafted from the clear sky. Clue by clue, we made our way from one end of the yard to the other, coming finally to a miniature ceramic castle, and as we climbed up to it I noticed suddenly that the evening was coming on fast. The castle, known to me from childhood playdates with the siblings, had a drawbridge, and when I lowered it I found a cigar box. Artemis and Apollo crowded around me. Bill had disappeared in the gathering dusk. Iris and Myles were loafing near the house, talking with Bernadette. On the heels of the dark came the cold. I pulled up the collar of my coat and, with fingers red and trembling from the chill and anticipation, I lifted the lid of the box.

Explosion to our left. A shot of fiery purple arced high into the sky and blew up in a rain of pink sparks. Then a red one followed. Then blue. It went on.

Happy birthday! shouted Bill as he came striding from the fireworks, What did you find?

I looked down and saw by the exploding lights that the cigar box was crammed to the brim with silver dollars.

It was three days before my birthday, but Iris had brought a cake and arranged for the surprise with the K-Gs because it was the weekend. Although the cake was delicious and the ice cream sweet, I felt strangely let down by the party. I didn't like attention, didn't like surprises, and the atmosphere of gloom in the Krimgold-Gragnolati household was so deep that not even balloons and streamers could brighten it. Above all, the party made it impossible to ignore the fact that the entire treasure hunt had been staged—I'd suspected as much, of course, but hoped I was wrong.

It was treasure, nevertheless, and while Artemis and Apollo noisily ate seconds, I brought my hoard to a low table in the living room and stacked the coins in neat heaps. Iris helped Athena clean up in the kitchen and Bill plunked down his chess set on the dining room table in front of Myles and began to set it up. A match between Myles and Bill was a ritual event and could last hours. Myles was good but impatient. Bill usually won because his method was virtually fail-safe. He played defensively, taking no risks, waiting, waiting until Myles impetuously made an error out of boredom.

Bernadette rose abruptly and paced for a bit before settling on me. Well? she asked.

One hundred dollars exactly, I said.

It's too much, said Iris, emerging from the kitchen. Much too much.

Not at all, said Bernadette, rounding on her. Finders keepers.

They settled on a couch to talk. In the tiny kitchen Athena dried dishes, a world away as she stared out the window and sang along quietly with the radio on the windowsill, *Is there life on Ma-ars?*

Artemis and Apollo had also grown quieter now as they began working on their third helpings of cake and ice-cream, while next to them a dense silence radiated from the chess game between Bill and Myles, and I, for my part, refurnished my cigar box with its coins, perfectly stacked. It wasn't hard to see, even at the age of eleven, that my treasure trove was directly linked to Iris's diagnosis. Bernadette and Bill felt terrible about it all and sought a way to cheer me up and, via me, my mother.

It hadn't occurred to me until then that I might, in small and unexpected ways, benefit from Iris's crisis. So each family was trying, somehow, to cheer the other. Was it working? My cheer had faded nearly as quickly as it came, but the others seemed to be in slightly improved spirits, at least for now, all except Athena, who was indifferent and elsewhere in her thoughts. Behind me I could hear Iris explaining everything to Bernadette: *lymph nodes, carcinoma, radiation, Mass General...*

I turned to the small living room bookshelf.

A volume about famous disasters disclosed the gruesome details that followed the sinking of the *Essex* by an enraged nineteenth-century whale. This, in turn, led to the sorry fate of the *Mignonette* and came up to date with the grim, snowbound survival tale of Uruguayan Air Force Flight 571. And as I read these enumerated miseries, a familiar weight began tugging my thoughts down through soil, rock, and emptiness, until they fell upon that underground sea.

I DON'T know how long we've been sailing away from Nolan and his island. Long enough not to feel sick about it anymore. All we think about is where we're going. At least, that's all I think about. I point, Captain Severn sets a course, we sail. But I feel doubt behind me. The crew doubts me. Nobody says anything. If they say they doubt me, then they're lost on an underground ocean, following a kid pointing nowhere. I'm glad. If they're scared, they're quiet, and I need them quiet because I doubt too. City still pulls me, but in the dark nights I wonder why. Maybe I'm wrong. Maybe when we get there we won't find anything. Then the magnet in my bones will pull me overboard and drown me if my crewmates don't. That's a fear I can't allow above water. To think about the consequences of what I do will slow me to a stop because I won't know how or if I should go on. And I must go on.

hot bread
gunshot ghost
wall rainbow
blue snow
sinking boat
light bursting in darkness
betrayed girl
snow battle
book of my life

Thump! Our boat shakes, almost flips. Something big and smooth and shining wet slides out of the water and back down in a long, lazy curve.

Silence in its wake. We make no sound. No screaming, no yelling, no whispers, no breathing.

Thump!

The same long, smooth body breaching the water, then disappearing back into it.

Then nothing again. Seconds pass. Minutes. Is it gone? Can we fight it? Severn digs in his pack and pulls out a small, old gun and a hunting knife—what good are they against a beast this massive? Might as well shoot spitballs at it. This is what comes of adventuring with pacifist utopians.

The water bubbles, pops. A huge, smiling, furry face

emerges from below. Unbelievably, it's a face we know. And yet we don't.

It's Lutra. But Lutra grown into a giant, a nightmare otter.

Chisolm shouts her name and Lutra sees her and starts chattering—I say chattering, but actually it sounds like cannon fire at close range, or at least what I imagine cannon fire to sound like. What I'm trying to say is that it's incredibly loud, although Chisolm doesn't seem to mind. We cover our ears and watch Chisolm reach out to touch her otter's huge wet nose. From that nose to the end of her tail, Lutra's as big as our two boats placed end to end. Her whiskers alone are longer than me, and she's close and trying to get closer, much too close. When she puts a paw on the gunnel of Chisolm's boat, it tips. She wants to climb aboard. Now, at last, our silence breaks and everybody starts shouting and screaming because the boat's about to flip. In the chaos of Lutra happily squirming up and Chisolm shouting to her to stay down and the crew yelling at Chisolm to control her animal, there's a shot.

Gunshot. Severn stands in the second boat, my boat, gun smoking.

Lutra turns her giant head and stares at him. The little bullet did nothing but sting her and she's not happy anymore, she's mad. She swims close to Severn, who's busily trying to reload his stupid single-shot pistol while Chisolm screams at him from the other boat to stop.

One swipe from Lutra's paw knocks him overboard. She grabs him with her claws and takes him down.

Now the water's flat as ice. Quill wails and falls in the stern. In the other boat Chisolm stares at the water. It explodes.

Lutra's twisting and turning. Severn's knife is in her side. He's holding on to the handle. Water raining off his face, hair flat wet to his forehead, mouth wide, arms white muscle rope. Gone.

Lutra dives again.

Quill's crying is the only sound except for the gulls. They're coming, waiting for a kill to eat. Then their calls turn into gull screams and they dive onto something coming up. But the something moves. It's Severn and he's alive.

But when we pull him back on board the look on his face surprises me. Not happy, not mad, but what?

Quill towels him off fast and hard, brushing Rook aside when he tries to help. Poor Rook. And over his head I see Severn look at Chisolm and Chisolm look back at him. The strange look on both their faces is the same. Disappointment.

Severn wanted to drown with Lutra. Chisolm wanted the same thing, or at least she wanted Severn to disappear.

Can the others see what's going on? No, they're not even looking. They're all looking off the port side because that's where Lutra is. The knife didn't kill her, how could it? It was a pin to her. She dives.

Then our boat flies up and crashes back down, almost flips. It'll flip next time.

No yelling, no screaming this time. We know what's coming. She's enraged now. She's coming for us and there's nothing we can do.

Shout from the other boat, and we look over in time to see Chisolm in the water swimming to Lutra. They both dive and when they come back up Chisolm is riding her beast, hands grabbing the neck fur of her giant otter, who is swimming away so fast they're almost out of sight before we understand what's happened. Chisolm looks back once, but if she says anything she's too far away to hear.

Captain Severn calls out to the other boat. I look and see

why. They're following Chisolm and Lutra. They'll never catch up, the otter's too fast. But they're going anyhow. Severn looks at me, face drained of all authority. I shake my head.

We can't follow them, I say, raising my voice so everyone on board can hear me. It's the wrong way. They've made a bad choice.

There's no argument. Everybody on board is too tired, too scared to argue.

Quill doesn't seem to care that her mother is gone. No surprise there, I suppose. I don't think I ever saw the smallest sign of affection pass between them. If anything, they seemed to physically repel each other. By contrast, Severn's near death has suddenly made him visible to Quill, or at least present in some new, more valuable way. She holds on to him so tightly there's no air between them. Rook, looking completely miserable, tends the sail and steers the boat where I point.

MY MIND's eye blinked, and I slid back from that subterranean world to the faded pastel carpeting of the hospital waiting room. Despite the presence in my muttered vision of Monsters! Escapes! Jealousy! Myles appeared to have dozed off in the middle of writing it down, and so I jotted a rough outline of the ending before nudging him. He stirred, his eyes opened vaguely, briefly he saw me, and briefly smiled before nodding off again. Well, I would let him sleep. He'd been up early to drive into Boston and here we were at Mass General, waiting for Iris on the stained upholstery of the waiting-room chairs: the gum-stuck, fluorescent interior from which all volition, all humanity, seemed to have been siphoned, leaving only us, drained captives of procedure waiting powerlessly, thoughtlessly, for, at best, a temporary reprieve from inevitable loss. The hours in such places are vast and hollow chambers through which adults pace or slump in mute regret with improved intentions for a future that dwells in a suspended medium awaiting the good, bad, or indifferent word, after which one's life ends, or limps on or begins again. Mind you, I didn't feel like that at all, at the time. At that age a waiting room was a place where I was licensed to daydream.

Daydream, read, sleep, and distract my father from his suppressed dread. Down a long, sunless corridor I saw Iris being wheeled in a gurney from one room to another. She waved anemically in my direction and I waved back, but by the time Myles sat forward to look, she had disappeared. Years later, when I recalled this image, Iris had no memory of it and denied that it had happened, even when I attributed the lapse in her memory to anaesthetic—she swore that she wasn't even on the same floor as the waiting room. Who then had I waved at? Some mother-double? A hallucination? I maintain that I saw her, whether she was there or not. Or maybe I just saw her out of habit. Afterward, the hours went on ringing hollowly by.

Myles had a single dollar in his wallet, and we debated for some time which items to purchase from the vending machine, deciding eventually, or rather Myles decided, that day-glo orange crackers with peanut butter provided the most nutrition at the lowest cost and with several of these we fortified ourselves sufficiently to carry on waiting. Peering over Myles's shoulder, I saw that he had flipped the pages of his legal pad away from the record of my pre-birth adventures and was intently constructing a poem. I wandered away and examined the intricate braids of a ficus plant for a time. Of the others waiting in that room I have no memory—a series of multi-hued heads bowed over crossword puzzles or staring vacantly out the window. But what was out the window? That too remains obscure to me—or rather opaque—great squares of plate glass so overexposed by the bright exterior that nothing of the outside world appears to me but vague impressions of buildings flashing in the lengthening afternoon. Idly I picked up an abandoned, tattered *National Geographic* and looked wistfully at fantastical animals painted on the rock walls of ancient caves. An anthropologist imported a shaman from Botswana to give his professional opinion of the work done in French caves tens of thousands of years ago. Low quality, said the shaman. Its purpose? asked the anthropologist. Stone is the veil between the visible and the invisible, said the shaman confidently, The painting pierces the veil. Would you say, then, the anthropologist went on, That the cave painting is a kind of window through which to view the supernatural? The shaman said, No certainly not, the painting is not an opening in a wall, it is what makes the opening—it is a spear, a knife—No, the shaman interrupted himself, to be precise, the painting is the *thrust* of the knife. I flipped the pages to a black-and-white photo of two men in hats and jodhpurs posing with some pack mules in a jungle clearing. Percy Fawcett and Raleigh Rimell shortly before they disappeared in the Amazon during one of Fawcett's doomed expeditions to find his lost city of Z, a fabled pre-Columbian metropolis.

Zed, Myles corrected me when I read the caption to him. The last letter in the alphabet is pronounced *zed*, not *zee*, I don't know why Americans insist on getting it wrong.

I knew very well his position on this, but my name, my

looks, my hand-me-downs all marked me as far too eccentric in my grade school to get away with using Commonwealth pronunciations.

But Myles never let go. It was one of the emblems of his difference. Ireland had taught him zed, Canada had reinforced it, and he was not about to succumb to bland Yankee locution just to fit in.

Now an orderly came to lead us by corridors and elevators to Iris's room. What use to describe this repeating scene? Iris's pallor, the bloodless room, her wracking pain, the morphine lull. Such hours would come and go again and again, staining that year with patches of clinical green, bleached linoleum, and stool samples—each time the same sentiments and gestures expressed by the same doctors and nurses, the same indecisive prognosis, the same unpayable bill added to the others in a growing pile when we returned home. So identical are these scenarios in my memory that the same dark shapes fall swiftly past Iris's recovery room window, followed by the same commotion and sirens, the same nurse's voice explaining that two workmen had fallen from a scaffold and perished. But surely it was only once that this could have happened. Only once that Iris sank back into her pillow as though the news were a physical blow. She insisted on leaving immediately and checked herself out against the advice of her doctor.

We drove straight from the hospital to the home of our friends Simone and Jack in a nearby suburb. I say 'drove straight' because that was the intention. Navigated by an experienced commuter, the trip should have taken half an hour, but for Myles and Iris it required a minimum of two hours. Accustomed to this delay, I settled down for a long nap, using my coat to muffle the noises of increasing agitation in the front seat. For some reason, my parents were never less than stunned by how lost they became in their efforts to navigate Boston's suburbs.

The house where Simone and Jack lived was an unremarkable structure on an unremarkable street in an unremarkable neighbourhood. But in a side room was their study, a bohemian lair ornamented with bookshelves that covered every inch of wall, and it was here they received visitors like Myles and Iris, fellow travellers in the the counterculture. With couches draped in exotic caftans low-lit by hanging paper lanterns, the place looked to me like a library from the Arabian Nights. A record player spun the latest LP from Alain Stivell at low volume but rich quality from hi-fi speakers placed strategically about the room. Jack was an audiophile who dressed like an urban fiddler, in leather vest, newsboy cap, trim goatee, and gold earrings, although he played no instrument.

Iris sighed with relief as she sank into an armchair and accepted a pint of homebrew stout. This was her element. All her pain seemed temporarily to ebb as she sat back and listened to Simone spin one yarn after another of her childhood on the beaches of Brittany, playing in the shadow of her family's ancient chateau, collecting geodes filled with glittering purples and blues that sparkled in the high sunlight when cracked open like stone coconuts using the wooden clogs slung around her neck by her teacher as punishment for speaking Breton instead of French in school. Tragically, she'd had to leave everything behind, along with her collection of first-edition theosophy texts, when her diplomat father was posted to Argentina, but then at least she'd had the chance to learn tango from master dancers, as the near-blind Borges, a great friend of her mother's, looked on. Yes, sad now that her lupus affliction prevented her from practising those exquisite steps although even if she could there would be no dancing with Jack who was the worst she'd ever met. And here she smiled indulgently at her husband, twenty years her junior, who basked in her gaze.

I was surprised to learn recently that there's a sizable Zen centre in Buenos Aires, said Myles, gamely leaping into the brief pause, but he was up against a formidable talker with decades more experience in maintaining control over a colloquy, which is what she called such evening conversations, only half in jest, and as she shook her pitch-black locks I caught sight, for the first time, of their white roots.

Zen is everywhere these days, she said, Which means it's done for, as far as I'm concerned. Orthodoxies are already beginning to hamstring it. Orthodoxies and imbeciles. I read your letter about Willard's latest tomfoolery. I was suddenly overwhelmed with guilt. It was I who convinced you to join me at New Pond. Only to abandon you to your fate when I could see that it was nothing but another sham—I told you so at the time, do you remember? You laughed—you're not laughing now... Another sham, another disappointment. I think I can safely say that I have practised with more so-called teachers of Buddhism than any other individual in North American over the past twenty years—and I, for one, am through with it all... Meditation—yes! The dharma—yes! But teachers—no, no, no, and no. If there's no poison in their hearts at first – and which of us is poison-free?—the trust their students lend them, the trust they demand, is injected into their souls, where it infests... Until they invert from ego-free angels—so they claim—into demons... I'm not exaggerating—I've seen the demon-fire in their eyes (I saw it in Willard—I told you so at the time, do you remember?

You laughed...). To tell you the truth, I've grown suspicious of anyone willing to instruct the souls of others. I see the sinful pride in their hearts—too old not to see it. Hell, I can smell it—smell the evil (and there is evil in the world, no matter what they say). Listen to me, with all my heart I strongly urge you to leave Willard. Leave that place, come to Boston or go to New York. Go anywhere with enough people to jostle your beliefs. That cesspool in the woods will drown you.

Yes, yes! said Iris. We must leave, we must.

But Myles smiled vaguely and shook his head, saying he knew Willard was flawed, deeply flawed, yet he still had good qualities and there was much yet to learn.

Which you could learn anywhere, said Simone, interrupting sharply, I learn more from the Transcendentalists—remember them? Sometimes what you're looking for is right in your backyard—than I ever learned from Willard. Find a Native American elder to teach you about happiness, hatred, love. Have you read *Black Elk Speaks* yet? You must. How to be a human being—that's the question. Who cares about attaining nirvana if it means you go on being an asshole? Or go back to your faith—investigate the Gnostic Gospels, Origen, Eriugena, Hildegard of Bingen, Meister Eckhart, Teresa of Avila... Have you read *The Cloud of Unknowing*...

And as she spoke, Jack roamed the shelves, pulling down the books in question and stacking them on the coffee table in front of Myles and Iris, who leafed through them with beer-infused delight.

Do you, Simone asked, suddenly looking at me, Want something to eat? A book to read? A game to play? You'll be bored here listening to us jaw all evening.

No thanks, I said, I'm fine.

He's a sponge, said Myles. He likes to listen.

And I did. Although I also liked to talk and had something to add on the subject of geodes, or rather a question to ask, as in where could one find them? And what exactly were they? But by the time there was enough of an ebb in the word flow to insert a phrase, the subject had drifted so far from the beaches of Brittany that it would've been disruptive to bring them up. Instead I maintained my hush and drew a cloak of silence around me so as not to be noticed again, and sat and listened to the torrent of talking and talking with occasional eddies and now and then a contribution from a tributary brook (my parents or Jack) that served only to raise the waters of the flood even further.

Yes, even Myles was (mostly) silenced by Simone. Here both he and Iris disappeared, and I could feel their relief in doing so. Simone's deluge of words calmed them, washing away their distress for the time being. And I could see that this was part of Jack's attraction to her. Her speech was a balm to whatever personal wounds he suffered from. And in being neutralized by her, the three of them joined me in my natural state. For I had already learned years earlier that people who can disappear and disperse themselves into the surrounding atmosphere, tailoring their wants and worries and wonderings to the direction of flow, are highly valued (if subconsciously) by the authors of the flood. I did my best to go along, for to voice objection, to resist, was to invite notice and critique. I wanted neither. I was too lazy. In any case, there wasn't any room for me, qua individual, either in this conversation or any other held by my parents and their friends. And why should there be? Who wants to hear the inner life of an eleven-year-old? Siblings can develop their own subcultures separate from their parents wherein they can forge their selves. An only child with a passive temperament assimilates to the parental culture or rebels utterly. I chose the former path, a willing prisoner. But none of that was on my mind then, I hadn't a glimmer of self-knowledge at that age as best I can remember. No, back then the anaesthetizing effect of Simone's talk and my parents' temporary happiness, made me happy. And drowsy.

IT's LATE afternoon when we see an island on the horizon over our port bows. It's off our course but not by much. City pulls me straight ahead, but the crew is tired. They want land under their feet. I can't force them on.

After I saved everybody from Nolan, Rook started talking to me. But after Lutra came he whispered that it was my fault. My fault she'd turned into a giant and almost killed us. My fault we'd lost Chisolm and half the crew. What he really means, I know, is that it's my fault Quill and Severn are together. Now he says we have to go ashore. He says we need water, we need supplies, we need a rest.

Okay, I say, For one night.

Severn points the boat at the island. It gets bigger, and the bigger it gets, the stranger it looks.

It's a fortress, says Severn.

He's right. The whole island has a big wall all around it made of dark red stone, and high on top of the wall there are crowds of people.

We see a bright flash at the top of the wall, and a few seconds later we hear a bang, followed by a strange whistling sound. Then the water explodes near us. Waves throw the boat up, up, over. No, not quite over. We're back down, full of water. We're bailing, we're yelling.

Another flash, another bang, more whistling, exploding water. Flash, bang, whistle, boom. Flash, bang, whistle, boom.

They're shooting at us! says Captain Severn, and he slams the rudder starboard. We come about and head away from the island. In a few minutes we're out of range of their cannonballs, or whatever they're shooting.

Why? Everybody on the boat wants to know why. Who cares? They don't like strangers. Or they don't like our boat. Or they're in a bad mood today. We have to go on. There's a thing coming. My Follower is still after me. I can feel it back there but can't see it. Night falls.

Captain Severn is in the stern getting ready to drop anchor when I crawl back to talk to him.

We have to sail all night, I say.

He looks at me and it's too dark to tell if he's smiling or angry.

Can't do it, says Severn, No light. No stars.

I have a candle I've been keeping in my pocket. I hand it to him.

Use your compass, I say. We keep moving.

Why?

We're being followed.

He stops what he's doing and stares at me. At least, I think he does. I can't see his eyes, just black shadows. What's following us? How do I know?

I know, I say. Also, we're nearly out of drinking water.

Silence.

We have to keep going, I say.

And so that's what we do. In the stern, Captain Severn sticks the candle on the seat in front of him to light his compass and keeps his hand on the tiller while Quill shifts the sails to catch the night winds.

We sail like that for three days and nights, switching hands at the tiller and sail. Whoever's off-duty naps if they can in the light, in the dark. I sleep sometimes, but wake up again and again, feeling my Follower somewhere behind us. Closer? Maybe. Bit by bit.

But the lack of rest dulls our senses, and more than once I catch myself nodding off and see whoever's at the rudder doing the same. And that's how and why we run aground on an unforeseen beach one night. There's a soft scraping sound and then the boat jolts to a stop and we're suddenly wide awake. Severn was sleeping with his hand on the tiller but he jumps up, as do we all, up and out, and minutes later we've hauled the boat out of the water and anchored it to a rock we find by the light of the candle. Then we lump together some bedding on the sand, schedule people for watch, and black out. I wake up with first light and get close to Rook, who's morning lookout. He wraps a blanket around me, although he doesn't need to. It's warm. It's always warm down here.

Slow light leaks out of hidden pockets like it's been hiding in the water, in sand, rocks, and grass all night. We're in a lagoon. One side is a high, long cliff topped with pearl-grey scrub, and the other a low, curving spit of dark orange sand. Behind us there are hills covered with trees. More orange sand under our feet and all along the long beach. Every growing thing is pale. Pale grass, pale trees, pale bushes. Paler even than the water, which is bright green.

No direct sun, says Rook. Little chlorophyll.

After days at sea, any leaves are good to see. To our right, at the base of the spit, a loud splashing comes from a geyser blowing water a hundred feet in the air. The water is burning hot, says Rook, he investigated last night. There's a loud sound in the bushes above the beach. For a second, I think my pursuer has finally caught me. I grab Rook. Then we laugh. The thing making the sound comes out of the bushes and it's nothing but a huge bird.

It's as tall as me. Huge, lumpy beak and pale grey feathers.

The bird doesn't look at us. It waddles away down the beach and then disappears into the bushes again. It almost seems as though the bird's walk is some kind of signal, because as soon as it disappears, the island wakes up with birdcalls, howls, chattering.

Amazing! says Rook. I wonder...

But he trails off as Quill wakes, stands, and stretches, looks around and smiles vaguely at us. Since the battle between Lutra and Severn, Rook and I seem to have faded into her background and she appears not to notice that Rook avoids speaking to her.

Eden, says Quill, It seems we've stumbled on paradise.

That's what it feels like for the next few days. We find bright blue pools so full of fish we can pull them out with our hands. There are wide, low, sprawling trees heavy with white apples, not very sweet but crisp. We eat and sleep and swim. Even I, who must go on, am tempted to stay. But I have to go, I have to go—every time I lie down to sleep and collect my images, I can feel the gap where yet another one has disappeared. And out there, over the water, back the way we came, my Follower is closing in. I can almost smell the foul hot odour of its wings beating the breeze.

But the others might stay here forever. I must do something to shake them free of this place.

I DIDN'T realize I'd fallen asleep on Jack and Simone's couch until Iris woke me at dawn and shuffled me out to the car, where I conked out again, half-slumped in the front passenger seat, for Iris took the back, lying down with her head propped on pillows, staring out at the unfurling miles, the ocean constricted by appearing and disappearing bays.

They had talked all night and now Iris was anxious to be home, so Myles drove, drove, coffee, coffee, tea, coffee. And was the soup from the lobster pound halfway home more flavourful for her pain? Or was it much the same as the previous trip and all the ones that would follow? Let's say she enjoyed it and I think she did. Of sensory pleasures, of thick stews and small flowers and noisy crickets, of clear mornings or swollen tides or sudden rains, she is an enthusiast, and so, dim as my memory is, I will choose to believe that the delight she took in the material world was only sharpened by her illness.

There were, on the other hand, many elements of the world that did not please her. The unexpected arrival of Pierce Jones shortly after our return home was one such. Pierce materialized, as he would at random intervals throughout my childhood, as though he were an emanation of the road in his uniform of scuffed denim. An olive-green army surplus sack was always slung insouciantly over his back. Pockmarked, handsome face slender from low rations, knife sheath at his hip threaded through a wide leather belt with a buckle depicting Mr. Natural urging all to Keep on Truckin'. Always too, in my memory, a hand-rolled cigarette dangles from the corner of his sly mouth. He would step down from a passing transport truck, or saunter up the drive, the precise image of a charming drifter. Too precise, according to Iris who was as aggravated by Pierce as she was fond of him. She was scornful of his pose, for he lived in a city where he worked as a garbageman and he was in the union, made more money than Iris and Myles combined, and owned his own art deco house, which he had meticulously restored. None of this mattered to me. If he was playing dress-up, his costume was convincing, although perhaps the aura of wandering romance with which I have imbued him in my memory is influenced by the gifts of exotic comic books that he always had for me, stashed somewhere carefully in the interior of his sack, from which they would emerge crisp and miraculously undamaged, and I, thanking him shyly, would retreat to my bedroom to read in full colour of the further exploits of Asterix and Obelix or of yet another incarnation of Siddhartha, the future Buddha, in which he was invariably the king of some species for whom he would martyr himself in yet another act of selflessness to save his people.

Such afternoons remain carefully shelved in my memory, to be pulled down and opened when under duress—they emit a long glow of comfort. In the memory I half sit, half lie in my bed, Shadow curled behind my knees; through the window, dusk creeps out from the forest and settles on the vegetable garden—on the dying tomato plants, on the low-lying sprawl of the pumpkin plant, the lettuce withstanding the frost; crows cry hoarse elegies to summer (Gone! Gone!); smoke from the chimney whips down the roof, eddies briefly on the windowsill before scattering with the last light. Wood-stove heat is particularly well-suited to this vignette—intense and friendly, it cooks the chill from a body inside out. And it saturated the interior of my room with an invisible colour that glowed against the blue frost on the grass outdoors. So, wrapped in this warmth, made warmer by my peripheral awareness of the cold outside, I read my comic book while the murmur of adult voices rose with the scent of cooking.

And yet, what part of this is accurate? For Shadow was dead and buried under that frosty grass, the heat of the stove was too far from my room to reach it with any conviction, and Pierce Jones did not murmur but recounted his exploits in a loud Kentucky drawl punctuated by guffaws. As I tried to parse a Latinate pun in Asterix, I could picture him below with his boots propped on a stool, leaning back with his flask of bourbon perched on his stomach while holding forth about his latest love affair—a befreckled young thing from a massive family—a peach, a straightforward, uncomplicated working-class peach with dirt under her fingernails, just the sort of girl he needed, so unlike the high-strung, posh mother of his two children. And here he would kick down his boots, rummage in his sack, and produce a bottle of some rare liqueur for Iris and a first edition of William James's *Varieties of Religious Experience* for Myles. Then, settling back with a look of high satisfaction, he would resume his soliloquy. As previously noted, the arrival of a visitor with fresh stories was one of the few instances in which Myles listened with interest rather than holding forth himself.

But what of Iris? In this scenario she usually stood at the counter chopping and stirring, interjecting exclamations of interest, launching queries about old acquaintances. And here, no, that could not have been the case. Here she must have sat wrapped in a blanket by the stove and perhaps the pain of her wounds diminished her courtesy, perhaps her face even revealed the displeasure she felt in Pierce's unexpected arrival. Yes, I think that's quite possible. Quite possible that she sat and from time to time nodded coldly or smiled a particular smile in her arsenal wherewith she turned up the outer corners of her mouth an immeasurably small distance while the rest of her face was suffused with pain and reproach. When delivered in my direction, this particular smile had a devastating effect. But, if Pierce noted it, he seemed immune.

Myles too, I imagine, failed to notice Iris's discontent and busied himself with cooking. He was an excellent, if erratic, cook. With the help of neither recipes nor training, he would launch into the matter with an experimental, not to say frenzied, zeal reaching wildly varying results: sometimes perfectly caramelized carrots, tender fish, and roasted potatoes, but sometimes burnt rice, gritty salad, and greasy broccoli. I don't remember if the meal that night was delicious or inedible but certainly it was one or the other.

The next morning was a Sunday, and Artemis called to ask if I wanted to come over. By this time, I had finished the Asterix and was now reading *The Lost World* by A. Conan Doyle. The day was cold and grey, a thin coating of wet snow had fallen in the night. Cross-legged and hunched over my book in bed, with a blanket draped over my shoulders, I felt certain that I didn't want to venture outside. It would involve a cold mile to Artemis's house, followed by snowballs. I declined, but Iris was displeased and exhorted me to pull myself from my book and go see real people. Personally, I thought her concern for my social life was a ruse designed to cover her unspoken sentiment that I should visit the Krimgold-Gragnolatis because they needed visiting. And I found her exhortation unfair, as after issuing it, she herself retired to her bed with a novel. But I knew better by now than to invoke fairness as any grounds for complaint.

Pierce said he would walk with me and so together we set off. From a maple branch that hung over the road, Pierce cut a section with his bowie knife. As he reached up, I was startled to see the butt of a gun stuck in the waist of his jeans. He saw me looking, pulled the weapon out, and handed it to me and continued walking. Whittling as he strolled, he muttered that I should be careful because the gun was loaded. I nearly dropped it but didn't and instead held on to it with both hands, as though bearing something made of glass rather than wood and metal.

Beautiful piece, ain't it? Black walnut stock, silver inlay, single-shot 5.87 manufactured by the Henry Deringer Company in Philadelphia, PA, more than one hundred years ago. Do you know who John Wilkes Booth was?

I did, of course I did. Every schoolchild in America knew the name of the actor who shot President Abraham Lincoln in the back of the head at Ford's Theatre in Washington, DC, in April of 1865.

Last year, said Pierce, I worked weekends renovating the home of a neighbour. It was eighteenth-century colonial. Got it perfect, even made myself some curved copper plastering tools to repair the crown mouldings. When I was done he said he didn't have any money to pay me. I was pulling out my knife to gut him when he said to wait because he had something better. Then he showed me this gun. Now I happened to know that this guy was the nephew of a bigtime burglar. He boasted that he'd been in his uncle's gang and they'd gone into the Ford's Theatre museum in broad daylight, stole the gun, and put a fake in its place. This was it, the gun itself. That thing you're holding is an agent of fate. Because of this pistol, or at least the fucker who used it, the North came down hard on my people, they hammered us into the dirt after Lincoln died. Don't get me wrong, I'm no Confederate, I don't fly the Southern Cross, that's all horseshit, but history's got hinges and this gun is one. Course it may not be the real thing, but it sure looks like it and it's pretty. I liked it, I took it. I used it to pistol-whip the bastard and left it at that. It's not a good idea to antagonize low-lifes too much. You've got to cut your losses when you're dealing with crooks. Keep that in mind when you grow up.

As I pondered the meaning of the term *pistol-whip*, Pierce handed me the stick he'd been whittling. It was forked. A slingshot, he explained as he hauled from a back pocket a wide elastic ribbon, which he swiftly knotted to the two tines of the fork.

Then, maintaining his sardonic gait, he stooped, caught up a stone, fitted it to the elastic, and drew back, saying, You aim through the fork, then let it fly. The stone in question shot from its sling at invisible speed, the only sign of its passage a thwack on a distant trunk. Pierce turned to me with a sly smile and, handing me the slingshot, said I would never know if he had been aiming for that tree or not.

Gratefully I hefted the thing in my hand and tried to follow his example, but my stone, ill-fitted or ill-flung, flipped skyward in slow and wobbly flight before coming to earth a few feet in front of me. I was downcast, but Pierce said gently, Practise, that's all, and it was then that he caught a snowball in the ear. He crumpled, cursing with stunning fluency, and as he did so I received a stinging blow to my thigh, followed almost immediately by a second and third, one winging me in the arm and another grazing my forehead. We were under attack from both sides of the road. I shouted to Pierce that it was an ambush, and we turned and sprinted back and to our left, diving into the woods for cover.

Panting behind a scrubby, narrow maple, Pierce dug the slush out of his ear while I brushed myself off. There was no question who our assailants were. I explained to Pierce that Artemis and Apollo specialized in strategic assaults, or rather it was Artemis who masterminded them and Apollo, her faithful adjutant, who obeyed. Pierce slid off his jacket and wool cap and hung them on a dead branch that he pulled from the snow. Then, instructing me to keep a sharp eye for the provenance of the incoming fire, he slowly slid this facsimile of himself out from behind our sheltering tree. Almost immediately three snowballs came flying for it. Pierce retracted the stick, then inched it out again. And again came the projectiles, this time flying like bullets from both sides of the road. From my vantage on the other side of the trunk, I saw both of our assailants as they stood to fire before ducking back down behind their blinds. Artemis was in a stand of cedars on our side of the road, while Apollo had little more than a large tree stump for cover on the opposite side. Pointing out to Pierce that Artemis was the more formidable of the two, I proposed that Pierce should take care of him while I attacked Apollo. But Pierce demurred—there was a simpler way, he said.

If you cut off the head of the snake, the snake dies, he explained grimly, and I looked at his knife with alarm. They're just kids, I whispered. Pierce snorted that it was a metaphor. Then he explained his plan. Once I'd absorbed the strategy, we set to work quickly packing together a small arsenal of snowballs. Then, as Pierce crept off into the woods, I began flinging my ammunition in the direction of our two attackers. What ensued appeared to be a classic standoff with neither party gaining ground as we exchanged fire. Once I heard a muffled cry from Apollo as one of my missiles must have connected. And once a ball from Artemis nailed my hip.

The dull sky carved by naked maple branches or pierced by spruce trees seemed to have cancelled out all woody echoes—the sounds of our battle flew briefly through the air before dropping dead into the shallow snow. My cold, wet fingers grew bitter red and numb from launching the snowballs and my toes too had lost feeling and my socks were wet for I had worn nothing but canvas sneakers. Winter had begun, yet I refused to dress for it. I knew that, like me, Apollo was becoming distracted by these discomforts, and by the quality of the winter sounds, and the dark crows bursting at strange intervals from one tree to another with rusty cries. He too would be sidetracked by the angularity of the stripped forest, by the peculiar flexibility of the snow layered over the unfrozen sheath of dead leaves.

But on the other hand I also knew that the cold and discomfort only sharpened Artemis's attention. I knew that she currently thrived on the numbness in her fingers and toes, that her vision grew clearer, her ears more alert. And for that reason I concentrated my barrage on her outpost, for if she was not distracted, all would be lost.

And then, as I watched one of my snowballs sail wide of Artemis's cedars, I saw a sudden darting motion followed by shouts, scuffling, flying snow, and shortly Pierce emerged with Artemis in his grip. He called to Apollo to surrender; his captain had been captured and he was now all alone. But Artemis shouted to Apollo that honour demanded he stand firm and fight to the finish. From Apollo's stronghold there was silence. Would he fight on? Or was he frozen, hesitating in a panic of uncertainty. Pierce had been right—cut off the head of the snake and the body dies.

I gathered up my remaining snowballs and charged out from behind my tree. With a reckless scream I dive-bombed Apollo's redoubt, firing missile after missile as I went. But when I topped the stump with my last snowball I held my fire because Apollo was crouching, hands up, surrendering.

I pulled him from his grotto and marched him out to join his brother, while Pierce and I congratulated ourselves on a fine victory. Apollo seemed glad enough to have it over with, but Artemis loudly declared the unfairness of Pierce's superior age in the contest. Pierce rejoined that Artemis should put a cork in it and take her defeat like the immortal huntress for whom she was named.

Now we retreated together to the siblings' tiny house, where it stood tucked into its swampy stand of trees. It was hot inside, woodstove at full tilt, and Bill was there busying himself with paramedic paperwork, his scant red hair standing on end, a thick odour billowing out from under his powerful arms, blue eyes round and buzzing with frantic energy. His voice, always soft, had dialled down to a nearly inaudible pitch in recent weeks. Distracted and unbathed as he was, he welcomed us in warmly. He served us hot cider and fell to muttering mournfully with Pierce, as Apollo and I followed Artemis into their room, where we played cards and discussed *The Count of Monte Cristo*, which they had recently borrowed from me and read immediately.

Both of you?! Pierce's voice suddenly spiked in the other room. One after the other? Or all at the same time?

Bill shushed him and their voices dove back down to a murmur.

But Artemis and Apollo were now glowering at each other, and then Artemis accused Apollo of farting, and when Apollo denied it, Artemis attacked him. As they rolled in a death grip, cards abandoned, I lapsed into my habitual neutrality by picking up *Tintin and the Calculus Affair* and, making myself comfortable, let the gasping of the siblings and the woeful murmurings of Bill fade into the background.

Later that night, at home, Iris tucked me into bed, while below I could hear Pierce and Myles talking as they would go on talking far into the night, until their conversation came to rest over a game of stalemated chess. As Iris kissed my forehead goodnight, I asked her what it was that Willard had done to Bernadette and Bill. Iris drew back and looked at me unhappily until at last she said, So, you did hear. I was afraid of that.

No, I said, I haven't, that's why I'm asking.

She stood and said remotely that when I was older she would explain, but not now. Then quite suddenly a spasm appeared to shake her body and she abruptly seated herself in the chair near my bed. I could see the sweat shining on her face in the moonlight coming through the skylight and thought that maybe the mention of Willard's transgression was enough to wrack her, but then I remembered she was trying to stop taking drugs for her pain.

She rocked in the chair and began to apologize in advance for what she was about to ask. Her tone was so deprecating, so regretful, that immediately it triggered a deeply embedded guilt. It would require decades to learn of its presence and ferret it out. But guilt it was—a conviction that even though I knew not yet what she needed of me, whatever I provided could never fill that need, nor yet could I possibly deny her an attempt to fill it for she was already half-withdrawing her request even in the very act of making it, so sensitive was she to its importune nature, indeed to the importunity of *any* request ever made by her. But at last, strangled and disassembled, half-dead in fact, the request limped out, tacked onto the end of a long series of subclauses and caveats: would I, could I, tell her more of my horrible memory, my gruesome vision of my expedition to this life?

Ah, could I? It was a hard thing to call up at will. Usually a few scattered images tumbled into view unsought and I could then train them into the story. Yet here was Iris battling, not with Myles or the forces of the world at large but with herself, her own body. And although the mutiny of self was unknown to me at that age, still I looked hard in the back corners of my mind for the entrance to that subterranean world. And it seemed out of reach, for it was a curious feature of the place that when it overtook me it filled my mind to the brim, but when it receded, its effect dispersed like vapour and nothing was left but the faint outlines of people and landscapes, colours faded as though exposed to the sun for years.

But there, there now, a still life of explorers in a pallid jungle, because the desire to please my mother must have been an animating force in itself, the texture of their clothes (degrees of threadbare), the cocktail of curiosity and dread in their eyes, the rigidity of the pale grass through which they moved, all took on a shocking presence, like the sudden immanence of the side-lit paper on which I write these words, because it happens to all of us, I think, when sometimes our thought-fog rolls back and the naked world is there below us, free of us and our concerns. Just like that, those explorers begin to move and I hear the rasp of boots through grass, the chatter of subterranean birds.

IN THAT jungle, on that island, I walk with Quill, who keeps stopping to collect bugs and flowers and to take pictures of the strange plants we pass. There are white flowers as big as her growing on top of tall trees. Hawk-sized silver butterflies fly from one to the other. On the ground we see tiny, golden snakes shining through stiff, azure grass. There's a vine that climbs all over the trees like a pale green blanket. To make up for the plants, the birds are striped and spotted and feathered in every colour possible, so bright I can barely look at them. They're everywhere. One looks like a heron but its beak curves long and black as it pokes through vines to watch us.

Quill spends a long time holding a magnifying glass up to a metallic-purple beetle crawling on a leaf. I look at the view through binoculars. We've been climbing for half an hour and are in a clearing. Below us stretch the lagoon and the water.

What do you see? Quill asks, still peering at the beetle.

I look at the horizon and the water. No sign of my Follower, but it's out there—what's that black speck in the distance? Heat steels up my arms on its way to the back of my head, but the speck resolves itself into the shadow of a wave. I let go of a breath I didn't know I held. But that sudden burst of fear is enough to harden my resolve. Darkness pulses in my chest. I move the binoculars and find what I need.

I see Captain Severn, I say. He's sitting on the beach, looking out to sea.

May I look? asks Quill, leaving her beetle.

I hand her the binoculars and she takes them, scans around, and then settles on the beach. I can see her smiling affectionately to herself as her gaze finds Severn.

The sailor longs for the sea, she says warmly.

Is that all he longs for? I ask, heart skipping.

Quill smiles slightly, mistaking my intention.

What do you mean?

I just wondered, I say, trying to maintain an innocent, neutral tone, If he was watching for Chisolm.

133

Quill frowns slightly, puzzled.

My mother is long gone, Severn knows that.

Probably, I say, But sometimes it's hard to give up on the people you care about.

Care about? snorts Quill. My mother is a grasping, manipulative snake. Why would Severn care about her?

Keeping my face carefully blank, I say nothing and stare out to sea. I can feel Quill's gaze hardening on my cheek.

What did you see? she demands, her voice rasping slightly.

Nothing, I say, shaking my head.

What did you see?!

She grabs my arms and stares into my face. There's a sudden, wild look in her eyes that makes me regret my plan. Again I deny seeing anything, but it's too late. Her gaze drills into me with a frightening, lunatic force. Reluctantly, hesitantly, I describe seeing Chisolm summon Severn to her cabin, his expression of despair as he gazed at Quill's back. And I tell her of the look that passed between the two of them after Severn nearly drowned battling Lutra—the look of mutual disappointment that he resurfaced alive.

Quill lets go of me and backs away slowly, eyes wide, face hollowed out, shaking her head with disbelief. Then suddenly she turns and crashes away through the forest.

What have I done? I drop the binoculars and run. Straight through the trees and bushes in her wake, calling her name, telling her to stop, that I was wrong, I saw nothing. But she knows, she knows. Once I said it, she knew it, she always knew it, but couldn't.

Tiny bears, birds with hoofs. No time to stop for these surprises. No time to turn back. I feel like I'm going to throw up, but at the same time pressurized with a force that surges me under, over, around, and out of the woods in a few minutes, in time to see Quill yelling at Severn, Severn trying to hold her, Quill breaking free to run down the beach, Severn in pursuit. I chase them. Can't believe how fast they're going. In no time, Quill's at the end of the beach and scrambling up the bluff toward the clifftop, Severn close behind. I follow, sprinting up through the tall, white grass as fast as I can. Can't see anything ahead until I stumble out onto the clifftop.

Please, Severn says quietly.

He's talking to Quill, who stands at the edge of the cliff looking down at the waves far, far below. She doesn't seem to hear him. She leans out into the wind. If it drops, so will she. My heart falls at the thought. No, no, no, no. This isn't what I planned. I just wanted to rattle the cage. To get us going again.

Severn starts forward but stops when she turns her head and looks at him. I would stop too. The look is the worst I've ever seen. It isn't angry. Not sad either. Disgust.

Rook staggers out of the grass behind me—he must have seen the chase. Severn doesn't look at us. Quill does, but she looks without seeing. Then she does. She sees me. She gives me a short, strange, nod. Severn reaches a hand toward her. She glances blankly at him, then turns and steps into the air.

THERE WAS a time in my life, says Myles, when I too was in such inner turmoil that I contemplated ending my life. This Quill character strikes me as somebody suffering from deep psychological conflict. But what is the source of this conflict?

Love, obviously, said Iris. We were eating a late Saturday-morning breakfast. On the couch nearby, Pierce snored lightly.

Love? said Myles, puzzled.

Yes, of course, said Iris. She's in love with Severn and just discovered he had an affair with her mother.

How do you know?

Weren't you listening? Would you please stop slurping your oats?! You eat like a peasant.

Well, I *am* a peasant! Where do you think my people come from?

Your mother doesn't eat like that. I feel like I'm in a barnyard. It's turning my stomach.

So don't listen!

I'm trying not to!

Pierce remained undisturbed by all this. Last night's bourbon had shut down his ears. I could barely hear the exchange myself, so often did food etiquette feature as mealtime debate that it receded into my background. I turned from my underground vision to breakfast, which was cooling rapidly. Must fill up on oats, as Myles and I had plans. Some weeks before, he had come across an old wooden dory in the barn of a house he was painting. The owner had no interest in it, so Myles loaded it onto the top of the car and brought it home. To me it looked in bad shape, but Myles insisted that with a little attention it would be seaworthy again. He'd been worrying away at it since, plugging cracks with caulking, scraping and repainting the hull. Now, he was convinced, it was ready for its maiden voyage, despite the fact that winter was settling in. Iris considered the expedition crazy and dangerous. She insisted I squeeze a life jacket on over my thick coat.

Down at the bay, we slid the dory over the thin coating of snow into the high tidewaters and there she floated reassuringly. Once in, we tipped out our oars and began to row. Myles was in the bow and I in the stern. It was a calm day, the air cold, water colder. We were warmly dressed for land, but out on the waves the wind began to seep in. As did water. Slowly at first, then with gathering speed.

Ack, ack! to my left. I looked over to see a river otter, head just above nearby waves, peering at us and yelling in an unfriendly way.

Reminiscent of your Lutra, said Myles. Don't worry, otter. We're not here to bother you.

The otter paused at his voice but then, startled by a splash at the shoreline, vanished underwater. The splash revealed itself to be Bear, a neighbour's black Newfoundland dog that was so excited by the unusual sight of a boat in the bay that she decided to investigate. She closed the distance to us quickly and began to paw speculatively at the gunnel. Speculation turned to pleading, then a determined attempt to climb on board. Letting her up would have capsized us definitively. I found a stick floating nearby and threw it for her by way of distraction. Bear headed off to retrieve the stick. Meanwhile the boat was taking on more and more water. I gave up rowing and began to bail, suggesting to Myles that we should bring the craft about and head back to shore before she sank.

Not at all, said Myles, rowing valiantly for the far side of the bay. She's perfectly seaworthy. Shipping a bit of water is normal.

It's more than a bit, I said, grimly bailing.

The bay was forest-lined, but the leaves had dropped with the deepening winter. That muted colour scheme (grey trunks, green conifers) under a cloud-blocked sun was getting me down. That and the fact that our boat was sinking. Here we lived a minute's walk from the water and had never owned a boat until now and no sooner did we put to sea than we sank. Between Myles's energetic rowing and my increasingly frantic bailing, we managed to make it to the far side of the bay. By then we were ankle-deep in freezing brine and had to tip the boat over to empty it.

Remarkable synchronicity with your story, said Myles cheerfully between gasps of effort as we flipped the dory over and propped it on our heads to portage back home. He seemed undaunted by the boat's performance, as though the attempt alone were sufficient to call the mission a success. He was talking about the appearance of otter and of Bear and Bear's attempt to capsize us and was proposing Lutra as a fusion and magnification of the two animals we'd just encountered.

And don't think he hadn't noticed how my tale of stowing away on board the *Lizzy Madge* was later echoed strangely by Bayo's account of his flight to North America.

As he said that, I suddenly remembered the image collection.

two people up to their ankles in a sinking boat

A patch of heat on the back of my scalp began to spread, and I fought dizziness to keep the boat upright on my head; cold salt water dripping from it into my hair failed to cool my skin. What about the other pictures?

an old building full of music
an accident on the road
a refugee

Was I or was I not making up this story?

Makes you wonder, said Myles, heaving the boat back up over his head, If art imitates (inhale) life or it's the other way (exhale) around (inhale).

What do you mean? I asked, startled. Had he been reading my thoughts?

Aristotle, he said. Art is a mirror held to nature. Famous (inhale) philosophical (exhale) dictum.

But this is a memory, not art, I said.

All stories are forms of art, even if they're memories, he said.

Anyway, I don't like it, I said, trying to shake the hot uncanny. This dictum. What a waste of (inhale, exhale) time. Why would nature need a (inhale, exhale) mirror?

Nature might be vain, he laughed. But even if it doesn't need it, *we* need the mirror to see nature more clearly.

This seemed ridiculous to me. Why not just look at nature instead of mirroring it? Myles said this would be ideal, but for some reason the human mind needed to mediate experience to grasp it. The mirror frames the world's chaos, organizes it.

What chaos? I asked. I don't see any chaos.

But Myles was on a train of thought and wouldn't be shaken from it. As it happens, he went on, The whole point of Zen practice is to experience the world here and now. Not in a mirror.

Did this mean, I wondered, that if you were practising Zen you wouldn't need art?

Maybe. But I prefer to think you could use art as practice, said Myles. Take Basho for instance,

> Year after year
> on the monkey's face
> a monkey's face.

or,

> How admirable,
> to see lightning and not think
> life is fleeting

or better yet

> In the field
> attached to nothing,
> the skylark singing.

That's good, I said, I like it. But what, I went on as we heaved the boat up the driveway and hoisted it back onto the sawhorses for further repair, What about Jules Verne? Or Robert Louis Stevenson? Or Lord Dunsany? Or Poe?

Escapism, said Myles. Delightful stories that elasticize the imagination (to paraphrase Yeats), but they won't lead you to any deeper understanding of the things that really matter.

What really matters?

Suffering and death.

There's a lot of suffering and death in Poe.

Hmm.

This last uttered in the skeptical, indeterminate tone that signalled the end of the conversation or, at least, of conversation on the subject at hand. We had, by this time, entered the house, and Myles put on the radio. When not reading or sitting in meditation, he loathed silence. It came, I theorized, of growing up in a household full of siblings. His brain required background babble or it became lonely. On the radio was *Morning Pro Musica* with Robert J. Lurtsema, who had by this late hour diverged, to Myles's disgust, from the usual

Baroque fare and plunged into the atonal world of twentieth-century composition.

That. Was, intoned Lurtsema slowly, Concerto. Grosso. 1. By. Alfred. Schnittke.

Schnittke, Myles muttered. Why is he always playing Schnittke? It's unbearable.

But now, to his relief, the news came on. As usual, it wasn't very good and, as usual, it seemed to give Myles morbid pleasure, perhaps because it confirmed that we were indeed dwelling in the vale of tears about which he'd heard so much since infancy.

Tikhonov replaces Kosygin in the Troika, he muttered, turning down the volume, Thatcher tests another nuke in Nevada, and the Cold War rages farcically on.

It was hard for me to see the farce of it. At school one day a group of anti-nuclear activists had arrived to give us a workshop in the gym. They spread a gigantic map of the earth over the concrete floor, split us into groups, and assigned each group a continent. Then they spilled bags of red tiddlywinks on each continent and proposed that we spread them out over the land masses. By the time we were done, no more than occasional specks of land showed through blood-red dots.

Each tiddlywink, declared one of the activists, Represents the radius of destruction from a nuclear bomb. The number of tiddlywinks on this map is equal to the number of warheads in existence right now. As things stand, nuclear bombs could obliterate us all.

In *A Canticle for Leibowitz* I read about a world after nuclear war, and it wasn't hard to draw the link to the yellow-and-black sign riveted to the wall of my school's basement cafeteria designating it a Fallout Shelter. Occasional drills sent us down there, where our teachers were tasked with trying to extract calm from a hundred children, in a confined space, with nothing to do. That school is long gone now, demolished the year after I graduated and replaced with a basement-free building (because the Cold War is over or because everybody now acknowledges the uselessness of bomb shelters?), but I can still see the cinder-block walls painted glossy beige, the steel posts positioned to support the floor above, and the crowds of shaggy-headed children in hand-me-down bell-bottoms yelling and cursing and hugging and shoving. That's how we were to survive the bomb. I knew better. I knew only one location was safe come nuclear armageddon: underground. *Under* underground.

WHERE WE stand looking at air. Quill is gone. But I still see her there, giving me a nod like she's going out the door.

Then Severn runs for the edge. Rook and I tackle him before he jumps. Severn howls—I've never heard a sound like it: horrible, long, wretched. But Rook makes no sound at all. He lets go of Severn and rises and begins stumbling around in circles, talking to himself very fast and low and alternately clutching and violently shaking his head. I can't stand it. I jump up and race down the hill, not stopping to look back up.

What do I think about? I don't think. Or I do. I think of a broken body, a crushed face, blood in sand. Or maybe nothing. Just blank water.

I slide through the tall grass at the edge of the cliff. Between the stalks I see the bright green lagoon. I hit the beach and knife right. Far ahead of me I think I see something on the sand and slow down to put off getting there. The afternoon light begins to change. Now evening makes everything beautiful. In the last light I see the towering chalk-white cliff to my right, calm turquoise water to my left. In between a thin strip of orange sand, turning red and then black faraway where Quill has fallen.

What will I do when I see her? Have I seen dead bodies before? Not dead but on the edge of death.

Unbidden, one of my pictures surfaces.

a woman, ill, in pain, in bed, reaching her arms for me, she is trying to heal, for me

And that image makes Quill's end worse—a cold blue death she freely chose. When I see her body I'll fall on my knees and start hitting her like she's a locked door.

But when I reach the spot where she must have fallen, there is no body. There's nothing but blank sand. She must have landed in the water and disappeared. And now that I'm here, all the anger leaks out of me and I sit abruptly on the wet beach. How can I be angry with her? I should be angry with myself. This is my fault. All my fault. I should have kept my mouth shut like Rook. This was why he wouldn't tell Quill what I told her. So now there's a new secret to keep. Rook can't know what I did. If he finds out, he'll drop me and never look back.

A little later I see Severn sitting on the sand, staring out at the sea, Rook pacing back and forth in front of him, weeping, sometimes stopping to shout.

Why?!

Severn says nothing, his gaze fixed on the waves. Rook goes back to pacing, then a thought seems to occur to him and he rounds on Severn again, but this time his voice is quiet, intense.

I know why. She found out.

He crouches next to Severn, talking low and fast for a minute, and I can't hear what he says but as he speaks Severn's face seems to wrinkle and fall around his staring blue eyes. Then Rook stands abruptly and walks away fast in the direction of our camp. I trail after him, leaving Severn where he sits.

Back at the camp Rook prepares a meal for me without speaking. His movements are automatic, sharp, stunned. Once he stumbles slightly and then sits down hard on the sand and can't seem to move after that. I find a blanket and drape it over him and without looking up he pulls me down next to him and wraps the blanket around us both. Do I say I'm sorry? Does he shush me? I don't know because I'm falling asleep.

Then, on the edge of sleep I remember the sudden fear that froze me at the top of the cliff just before Quill fell. What was it? Not Severn's hand reaching for her or the look she gave it.

The nod.

It makes me shiver again to think of it. Because she looked at me as she tilted her head and stepped into nothing. And now I know why, and where my fear comes from.

When I walked with Quill in the woods, she was happy. But I was not and so I decided to change everything by telling her the truth. It was a truth everybody knew, and Quill must have known it too but didn't want to believe it. And when I made that impossible, she ran to Severn to make him deny it, but he couldn't deny it so she ran again.

Running, her mind came apart. At the top of the cliff there

was nothing left. And where there's nothing, something can move in. When she nodded to me, it wasn't her. It was another. It was a greeting. My Follower. It caught up to me. It took her over the cliff. It's here.

TRAGEDY? SAID Iris. Does there have to be a tragedy? Isn't there's enough sadness in the world already?

It's what happened, I said. There's nothing I can do about it.

And this seemed true. More and more my story was making its own way forward, and I was starting to fear that interior force it was gathering. I still didn't know what to make of the appearance of those images in my life. The images from her—my—invented past.

Well, that's tragedy in a nutshell, said Iris, laying her head back down on the couch where she was stretched out under a blanket.

Was my mother recovering, or was she not? To her great frustration, she appeared to be hovering in some indeterminate zone, in danger of becoming a permanent invalid. And with every passing day the money that she was not earning piled up on the wrong end of her mental scale, adding to her worry. This, in turn—according to her doctor—delayed her recovery. At one point I remember her declaring to Myles that there were thirteen dollars and sixty-seven cents in the chequing account and ten in savings and somehow he would have to buy groceries for the week from this amount, and Myles muttered that the car needed gas as well. Also the electric bill was due. Not to mention the impossible enormity of the medical fees. The money raised by Willard's concert paid not even a portion of a fraction of a segment of the amount required. Iris's composure stalled and broke down. What, she wanted to know, her voice rising to such a pitch that it nearly passed beyond audible range, Were they going to do? To which Myles, with an abrupt bark, said what *could* he do? Now that house-painting season was over, he was driving a boat for a scallop diver. He rose at 4:00 a.m. every day, came back at three, did dishes, prepared dinner and tended to Iris. And yet the few dollars that he earned bled from the bank account at an inexorable pace.

From this discussion I absented myself and went upstairs to my room, and although their bitter voices rose clearly through the sizable gaps in the floorboards, within minutes I could no longer hear them, for I was lost in the depths of my old costume box.

To call it a box is an exaggeration—actually, it was a large broken-down basket piled full of old hats, masks, bolts of threadbare muslin that served as capes or togas, or flying carpets, as the case demanded. It had been some years since I had largely abandoned that basket for books, but late October had come and Halloween was that very night and I was unprepared.

Halloween meant a great deal in our neighborhood and its rituals and repetitions over the years gave it special gravity.

We would gang up, Artemis and Apollo, the blond twins Rinzai and Soto, and half a dozen others, at my house, for it was at the bottom of the road. Haunting westward through the dark frost and rags of snow, we would pass the empty farmhouse where the gibbous moon wobbled in old window glass, and reflected too off the slick ice coating the mud flats as we crossed the bridge. And on we would troop, over the brittle, half-frozen gravel, performing our costumed parts even between houses as we walked.

That night Artemis and Apollo planned to be two of the three musketeers, while Rinzai and Soto were to dress as elves. There was also Poe, who would paint on a goatee and wear a dented tin pot on his head at a rakish angle, his wheelchair would be Rosinante and every house that we approached a windmill. His older brother, Herbert, an aspiring actor, liked to make himself up as a ghoul—fetid flesh drooping and peeling from his ghastly jowls. Their sister, Emilia, was always a scarecrow.

For my part I found little inspiration in my old costume box and went rummaging in my parents' closet, where I discovered a hooded cape of dark purple velvet. Throwing this on I went back to my room and dug out a wire-mesh fencing mask given to me by my aunt Olive along with a rapier and white gauntlets. With hood pulled up over the mask and the cape draping to my heels, I was a blank spectre so anonymous I frightened myself when I looked in the mirror.

While I waited for my friends, I walked out to the road to test the costume. My vision, although slightly impaired by the mask, was fine under the bright moon. I walked a little way down the road and felt myself more curiously embedded in the night than when in ordinary clothes. No longer a human superimposed upon the inhuman world of invisible beasts and silhouetted trees, I was a creature of the night, more frightening than anything with tooth, claw, or root. Up the hill I saw headlights appear and then the hum of an engine as a vehicle came down the road. Feeling myself newly hostile to that other world of machines that now intruded so noisily on our chill and quiet phantom wilderness, I froze myself into immobility on the shoulder of the road and waited, a hooded stone, a faceless tree, a being from a sphere alien to the headlights that now suddenly lit me. The headlights slowed briefly, as though the driver had temporarily lifted his foot from the accelerator in shock before slamming it back down. The truck jumped forward and shot down the road. Pleased with myself for having run off the intruder, I strolled farther down the road, enjoying the renewed silence as the engine noise died away.

But not for long. Moments later I heard it slow and as I turned to look, the headlights pulled into the driveway of the empty farmhouse. Then the truck began to reverse onto the road, and I realized it was coming back for me. The tables had suddenly turned, and before those monstrous headlights could touch the road again I fled deep into the trees. Stock-still behind a trunk, I hid and watched the slow wheels roll by, the headlights plying the dark, lighting the shoulder where I had lately stood. It went by and carried on back up the hill, and I sagged with relief against the tree. But only for a moment. Just as I was working up the nerve to venture back out, I heard the truck once again turning around. Panicked, I retreated even farther into the woods, the half-frozen moss giving way reluctantly to my step, twigs dragging across my mask. I moved fast, protected by my disguise, invulnerable to the woods but a soft target for the shotgun I imagined racked behind the driver's head. Deer-hunting season was about to begin. Then I froze, for the truck was driving by again, more slowly than before. It stopped exactly where I'd been when the headlights first lit me. And it crouched there, wheels im-mobile, engine vibrating, clouds of exhaust curling into red brake lights. Blood-fog. I waited for the door to open, for a giant, angry hunter to step out with his powerful jacklight and fell hounds who would come eagerly baying for my blood and corner me and loudly, joyously call for their master to shoot me down and prove ghosts didn't exist.

148

But nothing happened. The doors remained sealed, the windows black, the driver as anonymous as I behind my mask. For all I knew there was no driver, or he was himself a phantom who had little patience with the play-acting of hippie kids. Then the truck revved again and shot away up the hill.

Moments later I heard the ruckus of my friends come between the trees and I bolted out to meet them. Their hubbub died at the sight of me but I was tired of being frightening. I ripped off my mask and showed my face.

Once they had congratulated me on my costume and I admired theirs and joined their fantastical society, my earlier dread faded—I donned my mask and got down to spooking the neighbours. House by house up the hill we ghosted past Emily Marco, who, once she'd terrified us by emerging from her chicken coop as a very authentic-looking witch with a candle under her long face newly ornamented with warts and blackened teeth, proffered cookies; past the brightly lit miniature home of Herman and Susan Bojanowski, both sporting frizzy wigs and clown noses as they maintained a slapstick patter and handed out fudge squares individually wrapped in wax paper; past Willard's, where he allowed us to take wormy apples from a basket while he inspected and approved or disapproved of our costumes with a joviality inspired by vodka, judging from his breath; past the home of Rinzai and Soto, whose father sang "Over the Rainbow" to us as his wife fed us teacups of chocolate mousse; past the sophisticated and strange-angled domicile belonging to Celestine Francoeur and her husband, Theo, the documentary filmmaker, both dressed in skin-tight black leather from head to toe and linked to each other by fur-lined handcuffs as, with their free hands, they loaded into our bags gory chocolate eyeballs imported, I later read on the foil wrapping, from Lichtenstein; and finally we arrived at the house in the swamp wherein Artemis and Apollo dwelt.

It had been transformed into a chateau fit to accommodate musketeers and their allies. The doorways were newly arched with meticulously sculpted cardboard. And cardboard unicorn tapestries draped the interior walls, crenellated battlements silhouetted the windows. We toasted each other with tankards of frothing cider, and the games began; one room was populated with lifesavers suspended from strings, and we could only pass by chewing our way through ten of them. Next we were obliged to bob for apples before identifying, by feel, slimy organs recently extracted from a fresh corpse.

But through all the games we looked forward anxiously to the final show, when the lights went out and by the low radiance of a single candle Artemis and Apollo's mother, Bernadette, read to us a horrifying tale of a murderer loose in Madame Tussaud's wax museum. And just as the protagonist had wound our nerves to their breaking point, just as the wax statue of the killer may or may not have blinked in the dim gaslight of the deserted museum at midnight—from the next room a blood-curdling scream tore our ragged nerves, and we screamed as well.

The front door slammed, we heard pounding footsteps, Bernadette leapt to her feet as Bill rushed in, red hair on end, eyes receding into their hollows as he whispered in her ear, she seemed to collapse, but unlike Bill who was turning into crumpled paper, Bernadette's face darkened as she grew smaller, as though her energy, compressed into a tighter space, threatened to explode. She snapped her book shut and moved from the room, and an instant later we heard the front door slam again. As we milled, hopped up on sugar and speculation, our various parents showed up—the Bojanows-kis' their clown wigs askew, face paint smeared from weeping; the Francoeurs, their handcuffs unlocked and limply hanging; Myles, uncostumed, grim, and distracted. In the car on the way home, he broke his silence only briefly to explain that Pierce had been badly injured.

Will he die? I asked remotely, because in the wake of Shadow's death and Iris's illness I was beginning to expect the worst. Myles said that he might, and then he stopped talking. At our driveway he paused long enough for me to get out and then said he was going to see Pierce at the hospital.

I found Iris huddled and weeping next to the stove in which unseasoned alder logs were feebly smouldering as their sap bubbled at the edges. The house was cold; the plastic windows snapped in and out with the rising wind. Iris held me tightly in her arms for a time, but when I pressed her for more information she could not, or would not, say more than what Myles had told me.

In bed that night I thought of Pierce and thought that I felt nothing at all. It seemed strange I'd tried so hard to suppress my grief over Shadow and yet here was a member of my species, and one I liked, in mortal danger and I seemed immune to sadness. I didn't yet understand that stowing away sadness can lead to habitual grief-storage so immediate it's packed and stashed before you can feel it. But though I didn't grieve, or didn't think I did, I felt heavy and I wondered. And thoughts of injury, thoughts of death, led me down with my sinking feelings underground.

TWO DAYS after Quill's death, Rook and I set to sea. When I look back as we tack out of that lagoon, I see Severn building himself a hut where our camp had been. He doesn't look up to watch us go.

Somewhere close, very close, my Follower is hiding. Maybe it's in a fish under the boat. Maybe one of the gulls above. Why doesn't it just dive and take me like it took Quill? It makes no sense. Unless it plans to break the expedition apart—first Nolan, then Chisolm and half the crew that split off. Now Quill. And Severn staying behind. Only Rook is left to complete the expedition. Yes. That must be it. It's getting rid of my crewmates. It wants me alone, unprotected. But why?

We need to keep moving. If I can get to the city, I'll be safe. Not sure why, but it's true. Rook doesn't argue when I push to go. He's in pain and wants to leave the pain behind, if possible. We have enough smoked fish and fresh water to go far, even though I know it's close.

In the following days Rook and I barely speak. We sit alone on either side of the boat, Rook broken by grief, me stabbed with guilt. I want to confess but don't dare, and I can tell there's no point telling him what really happened. How could he believe me if I say my Follower took her? In the silence between us, I take my little picture fragments from the box in my mind and look them over.

bushes and trees alight in a snowstorm, bursting through darkness
a dark-haired girl betrayed, eyes swollen with hate
a pale woman in pain, reaching for me from her bed
two men battling in snow, yelling at each other

I had more. Where are they? There was something, a smell, warm, buttery, and there was blue air, but where, where?

I slam my fist into the side of the boat and Rook looks up, startled. I look away without speaking. He has troubles enough—no need to hear me rage against disappearing memories, such as they are. It's not fair, I think bitterly, to lose so much when I have so little. But what's fair? Rook has lost a whole person. And who's to blame for that? One sorrow makes another.

I WOKE suddenly, sweat-drenched and terrified. Then relief as the autumn sun outside my window brought me back to the world above ground. The world of Myles and Iris. It was the morning after Halloween. But with that realization my good spirits fled as quickly as they came. Pierce was hurt. And how he had been hurt was stranger than any dream. So strange, no adult would tell us children the details, and we had to piece it together collectively from eavesdropped conversations. This is what we found:

Long after the last trick-or-treaters had passed by, a knock came on Willard's door. Thinking it might be a late straggler, he threw open the door with the same drunken gusto he had greeted us with earlier. But what stood before him was an apparition from another century, or so he at first thought. It was a tall man (had Pierce worn lifts in his shoes?) made even taller by the spindly stovepipe hat that rose precipitously from the pale head upon which it perched. The face sported a fulsome dark beard beneath which Willard discerned Pierce Jones.

But gone was the sly grin, the mischievous air. It seemed Pierce had been so fully animated by the costume as to be possessed by it. Even his diction had the cadence of the early nineteenth century. The pallor of his face, the consumptive cough, the waist and tailcoat and tarnished pocket watch all contrived to give the impression that he had stepped out of a daguerrotype into Willard's living room. Surely Willard felt in that moment, beneath the amusement that he later professed, disquiet at the peculiar strangeness of his visitor's stilted, eccentric behaviour. But he chose to take Pierce's get-up as an elaborate joke, for it was well-known that Willard's old farmhouse had been haunted in the past by just such an apparition—a top-hatted man who knocked on the door late at night asking the way to the cemetery. It was a haunting that had reputedly led the previous owner to vacate and sell the house and property to Willard for a preposterously low sum (naturally, there were those who suspected Willard of posing as the ghost in order to scare the owner into selling).

And did Pierce repeat this spectral demand for directions? What, in fact, did he say? This, no one—not even the adults closest to Willard—knew, for on that subject he remained silent. What story did he later give the police? For surely, given what occurred, Pierce must have confronted Willard—but about what? About the Gathering? Or one of the other whispered secrets on the periphery of every conversation in the neighbourhood? Whatever it was he said, the gesture that followed them was of greater consequence. Pierce drew from inside his coat the antique pistol that he had earlier shown me and pointed it at Willard's head. Was Willard's response truly, as he related it, one of samadhic calm? Did he really join his hands in meditative contemplation and enter a state of oneness with his own impending death? Or did he, as Pierce would later claim, beg for his life? Maybe both. Maybe neither. Whatever Willard's response might have been it triggered in Pierce a startling response. He pointed the pistol at his own body and fired.

Old guns are notoriously unreliable, and it was due no doubt to the misfiring mechanism, in tandem with Pierce's sudden and inept (or was it inept?) aim, that he did not lose his life that night. Nor had he, by the time the ambulance arrived twenty minutes later, lost much blood, for it appeared that the heat from the muzzle had cauterized the wound as swiftly as it made it. Yet it was a serious injury, for the bullet had lodged in a muscle and delicate surgery was required to remove it.

Myles brought him home a week later and installed him on the old trestle bed that normally served as a couch. Now there were two invalids in the house, and with Myles at work and me at school for the bulk of the day, the task of caring for the most recent invalid fell to the other. Iris was able now to hobble to the kitchen with her cane and deliver, with a complex mixture of asperity and solicitude, soup and medications to Pierce's bedside. Next time, she said as she handed him a cup of tea, Try champagne and sleeping pills—less bothersome for the rest of us. Pierce smiled weakly and drifted back into his morphic haze.

Jokes aside, Iris refrained from asking the questions to which everyone wanted answers—why the absurd getup? The ancient pistol? And most of all, why the confrontation with Willard? Well, maybe not the latter question, for it seemed that there were, in fact, a surfeit of answers available, none of them, however, voiced in the presence of children.

That the adults did not lack for answers we inferred from stifled arguments in tones not of questioning but assertion— yet the difficulty lay in the variety of possible answers. It was, some ventured, the action of a maniac. Or it was the desperate act of a deceived idealist, a romantic who had discovered that his leader was flawed, by extension the petulant act of a child who must destroy his father as we all, purportedly, must do. But others darkly muttered that it was jealousy that drove Pierce. But of what Pierce might have been jealous remained carefully shrouded, for no one would speak it aloud.

And for my part I wondered, and wonder still, if Pierce knew himself what it was that led him to enact such a strange scenario. Had it all made some obscure sense to him at the time, as he carefully outfitted himself in antique costume and loaded his pistol? Was I the only one who knew the supposed origin of the gun? Did I alone note his costumed resemblance to Lincoln? Bound up in all his other motives, was there a performance intended to reverse the past? A latter-day Lincoln shooting a performer (was that not Willard's true vocation?) with the gun that felled him? Did he know then, and would he ever become aware, of the tangle of impulses that drove him to his action? Could he? If they came as much from outside of him as within? Who can?

Meanwhile, as though spent by his singular explosion, as though having served his purpose, he had extinguished that part of himself that had intrigued me—the self-conscious rogue, the knife-wielding pseudo-drifter.

No, he was not even pseudo anymore—he subsided into blank convalescence. He apologized to Willard, claiming to have temporarily taken leave of his senses. He accepted the drugs given him to prevent another such incident, and as he lay on the trestle bed, contentedly receiving Iris's convalescent ministrations, while others declared him to be recovering, he grew daily greyer and more distant in my eyes.

Many came to visit despite what he'd done, despite the fact that he had nearly destroyed the Teacher—indeed, perhaps because of the gravity of his offence, he was all the more attractive a candidate for forgiveness. Willard arrived with a full murder of retainers, some stinking of the cow barn, some brushing the mill's sawdust from their knees while eyeing the house's posts and beams that they had themselves milled some years earlier. And as Willard, in his benevolence, teased Pierce for his silliness, denim-clad courtiers chortled appreciatively and all was apparently forgiven.

But what of Willard? If Pierce could be forgiven, could not Willard too? The problem lay, it seemed, in the nature of the wrong committed. It was evident that what Pierce had done required either condemnation, approval, or forgiveness. But since no one could agree on what it was that Willard had done and whether or not this contested act was even an offence, it remained in its nebulous, unacknowledged nook in the consciousness of the neighbourhood, growing daily more septic until its putrid stench infected our house to the degree that Iris began to speak of moving. Why, she would demand of Myles's retreating back, Do you wish to remain in thrall to that foul dictator after what he's done?

Dictator? said Myles. Let's not exaggerate.

Fine, said Iris, voice rising, he's your priest, shaman, guru, personal druid... He's some kind of sacred monster for all of you lost children!

Oh for christ's sake, not another one of your bloody fables! Do you really think I'm going to throw everything to the wind? Give up years of practice, all based on nothing more than rumour and innuendo?

To which Iris would cry that he didn't want to know, didn't want to believe, that his precious Roshi could be so deeply flawed, such a manipulative asshole, because to do so would be to reveal himself a dupe. Instead he chose to believe that Willard was a transcendent being, when in reality just like a spoiled child he had his gnarled little world of yes-men revolving around him, anxious to do his slightest bidding.

It's pathetic! she yelled as Myles slammed the door and stalked out of the house to his tool shed. And she followed him, demanding that he not walk away from her, that he turn and answer her, and so he turned, his face glowing with rage, and shouted that he would not argue with someone who wound herself up into hysterics over shreds of gossip and nonsense concocted by fools.

And as Iris began to weep with anger and injury, I, who had followed them out, began to speak. Their reaction I don't recall. In the midst of their fight, were they relieved by the distraction, or exasperated with my saga? In any case, it was enough to knock them off their rails. They stopped shouting. They found paper, pens, typewriter. They took notes. I have them. And from them I've written this:

WE SAIL through the night toward the red light. The magnet in me seems to pull the boat faster. Even though I've lost so many of the images that dragged me forward, the few I still have become stronger, harder. And City is still there, its cataracts growing closer in my mind, so close I think I can hear water crashing into water, and the scent of lilacs drifting over the spray. I'm so near my destination I think my body will burst. But it stays calm. Calm and tired. So tired I sleep, and the city lights might blink in a dream. A dream I wake from to see the blinking continue.

We don't cheer. In the light from the city, I see Rook's face, red and hollow and tired. We're quiet. No sound but flapping sails and waves hitting the boat. Then maybe I sleep again, because the next thing I remember is sailing in the middle of lights floating as though strung on bushes in a snowstorm on a dark winter night...

It takes a while to shake this thought. I can almost hear the low voices of people I know—my parents?—talking about the lights, the snow. Then I wake. There's no snow, no bushes, the voices don't belong to my family but to strangers in the water all around us.

We wait for shouts, for alarms, none come. Passing close to a light, we see there's a man in a boat that looks like a basket. It's so small his legs dangle over the edge. His light is a candle stuck onto the gunnel of his basket-boat. There are dozens more like him.

What are they doing? I whisper. Is it a ritual of some kind?

They're fishing, says Rook. The fish come to the light. It's a lure.

Like the city's light lures us. I look carefully at the floating men and see they're tugging on fishing lines wrapped around wooden sticks. I think of how strange it is to finally see other people down here. These are the first humans we've met since coming underground.

The fishermen are hard to see. Cheekbones and shadows. They're less interested in us than we in them. As we pass, they raise their faces to watch, then go back to fishing. It's an odd way to arrive. We seem to be sailing between candlelit ghosts. And I feel like we're ghosts too, ghosting to a dead city.

But that feeling fades, the closer we come, because this city lives. I thought we were going to find crumbling walls, sad old people in sad old buildings. We come with daybreak, which seems to make the city lights brighter.

The closer we sail, the stranger it looks. In places huge

buildings carved from red-rock cliffs. Then there are stacks of metal rainbow cubes and columns that could've grown in place. Maybe they did.

Bismuth, says Rook.

No glass in the windows, maybe because it's always warm and there aren't any bugs. A bridge made of green stone and dark purple bends over us.

Porphyry, says Rook, his eyes big in the lighter light, And malachite. He's hanging off the bow of the boat to get a better view. He's waking a little from his sorrow. Then he sits back suddenly in the boat and his eyes darken, and I think he's wishing Quill were here to see this. I do too.

I do too, I say, abruptly, too loudly.

He looks at me sideways and after a pause smiles a little, his old snarl-smile.

We sail around yachts and ferry boats, bumping waves in their wake. The wind leaves, so we row on under another stone bridge covered with people on foot, on bicycles. Nobody looks down, nobody notices us. Their clothes are drab, some ragged. Used to quiet, I jump at bike bells. Shouts in the crowd.

We're on a river or a deep bay that leads into the city. The waterway is lined with buildings and their balconies full of pale flowers and vines hanging down so far we can almost touch them.

Deeper and deeper we go, until we come to a huge stone wall, broken and patched in spots, with water gushing over it. And above that there's another wall, another big waterfall, and another above that, and so on up beyond where we could see. Are these the waterfalls from my memory? No, they don't match—they're coming from too high up, or they're not wide enough. But my memories must be off. They're in pieces after all, and maybe I've put the pieces together wrong in my mind. For now, we can't go any farther so we row to one side, find a tree to tie our boat to, and go ashore.

What a beautiful park, says Rook as we walk along wide paths. Big trees with black bark and pale green leaves shade us from thin light. Where are the lilacs? The place is grassed very short. Couples sitting on benches and cyclists going by. Some of them look at us, but most don't. Very often we see young men and women eye-scrape us from inside their clean, black uniforms. Small, round hats sit at an angle on their heads.

Police, says Rook.

Suddenly he pulls me over to a large sign near the water-front, where we see the image of a woman riding on a giant animal, an otter, climbing ashore. There's writing next to it. Writing we understand.

In this place, it reads, She came ashore.

Chisolm, says Rook. She's here.

I walk to a nearby policeman and tell him we need to find the woman on the sign.

Kphh! says the policeman. He calls a policewoman over and tells her what I said. They both laugh. It's a joke to them. I'm not joking. I'm losing my memories, I'm losing my mind, myself. I can't even control my own body. It moves by itself, faster than me, faster than thought. While the policeman laughs, my hand slips under his arm, pulls the gun from his holster, and points it at his head.

Take me to her, I say.

We're in a funicular. That's what Rook calls it. The police don't call it anything. They say if we want to see Chisolm, this is how we get there. The funicular is a glass-and-metal box. It's squeaking up a track. The track runs next to the waterfalls, all the way to the top. From up here I can see the underground ocean we sailed across. It's getting higher and higher the higher we go. Now it looks like a big wall of metal water in front of us. Down below, the city gets smaller, wider, more beautiful. Roofs, towers, bridges, trees. All wrong. All completely wrong.

Rook is as quiet as the police. He looks at me strangely. He's scared of me. Of the gun, I suppose. I don't say much. I don't feel like talking. All I feel is rage. The policewoman lifts her hand to scratch her nose. I aim the gun at her eye.

Don't move.

Be careful, says Rook quietly. Be very careful.

The funicular squeaks, jubs, and stops. We're at the top. Rook opens the door and we get out. A very big, wide place paved with flat stones, and there are some small trees in spots. On the far side is a large set of steps up to another level of paved stone. Behind that is a big building, a palace, a castle full of towers and windows and porches, and stone steps up and down. It's made of gold, granite, ruby, silver, and it all flashes in the sad light of this mistake of a city. After all we've gone through, all we've lost to find this place, and find it's wrong. It's not City. How could I have made such a mistake? The answer is obvious. I believed in something that doesn't exist. There is no City. And my pictures, my memories, are just tricks played by my empty mind. My stupid mind. My non-mind. I have no past. I have nothing. I am nothing.

Just below us there's a giant hole in the rock. A huge river of water pours out of it loud and fast and falls down the waterfalls one by one into the city.

A giant creature slides down the steps. Lutra. She looks at

me, then dives into the river and slips like liquid from water-fall to waterfall to the city below.

A group of people stand up above us on the second level in front of the palace. It looks like they're waiting for us. I march the police in front of us, pointing the gun at their backs.

I hear music. A dozen men and women separate out from the group above. I recognize them—the piano tuner's wife, the ship's carpenter, the doctor. They were all on the boat that followed Chisolm. They're in black uniforms and they have rifles, which are pointed at us. But when we get closer, they move apart. Behind them I see a piano. A single figure sits at it, playing big and complicated notes. She's wearing the same black uniform, but anybody can see she's more important than the rest. She stands and walks toward me. It's Chisolm. I barely recognize her. She's old.

She doesn't look back at the people behind her, but when she spreads out her hands and moves them down, the rifles go down too. Then she turns her hands over and holds them out to me.

Here you are at last, she says.

NEVER USE this poison, muttered Willard, snorting nasal spray from his cushion, where he sat in full lotus, each foot lapped over a knee, as did we all, since we were children and still supple and had been trained to do so since our earliest years.

It's addictive, continued Willard, referring to the spray. But, of course I addict to everything. Anyway, he continued, squinting at the fine print on the back of the bottle, You're all too young for it. So if you get a cold, just blow your nose and stay away from chemicals.

He uncapped the bottle and absently took another snort. Where was I?

Where? I'd no idea. I'd been underground. Seated next to her blond twin Rinzai, Soto raised her hand to say we'd been talking about the Heart Sutra. That made sense since we began every Zenday School session by reciting it.

Iris hadn't wanted me to keep coming to Willard's house on Sunday mornings after what had happened on Halloween and at the Gathering before that, but I defied her wishes and snuck out of the house to attend. There were two reasons.

Despite all the strangeness, I still liked Willard. All the kids did (even Artemis, who wanted to kill him) because he provoked and intrigued us into liking him every Zenday. It wasn't that we were oblivious to our parents' struggles with Willard, it's just that we had our own friendship with him and it was going well. We were still under his spell, and the other business was grown-up stuff.

Athena would be there and I'd become attached to the strange dizziness I always felt in her presence.

And also, I liked learning how to bake bread, which is what we spent the bulk of our sessions doing, since we were too young to work the sawmill. Willard believed in teaching through action. He had created two enterprises: a sawmill and a bakery. He ran the bakery out of his kitchen, to which we would shortly adjourn. But we started out each Zenday morning with a short meditation session on cushions on tatami mats on the floor of Willard's sunny living room, which was permanently infused with the smells of incense and baking bread. He sat facing us. And when he rang the bell to end the meditation, we recited the Heart Sutra. And then Willard chose a line to expound upon. That was his word for it. *I'm going to expound now, listen up.* We thought the self-mockery was hilarious. We thought it meant what we were supposed to think it meant.

The Heart Sutra, he began, Says, *all things are the primal void, they are not born nor destroyed, nor do they wax or wane.* So what the fuck does that mean? said Willard, It means your boogers won't stay boogers *(laughter).* Soon they'll turn into dust and join the dirt. That dirt will grow the plants that give you oxygen and the food you eat. That food becomes your bones and liver and lungs and also your shit and farts *(appreciative snorts).* That shit goes into the ground and those farts disperse in the atmosphere and feed the plants, which give you oxygen and food and so on. And so on. Ad shiteum, ad farteum *(guffaws).* It means there is no chaos and no order, only change and other stuff grown-ups cry about *(louder guffaws).* Change is the only constant. It also means there is no past, no present, no future, no world or time out there but what the mind makes. Reality is an illusion, a shared illusion, a real illusion, but still just a fart from the depths of your soul. That's because all of existence is really a primal void, a soup of particles that could do anything, anytime, anywhere. It is our mind that decides where and when everything goes. Just like we take flour, water, oil, salt, yeast, sugar, and make them into bread, so our mind takes the ingredients of life and bakes what we call reality. Speaking of bread, let's make some. Enough talk. Talking gets you nowhere, kneading dough gets you food.

We rose from our cushions and moved to the kitchen, which was outfitted with a big wood-fired oven. Since it was a tiny old farmhouse kitchen, there was barely any room leftover, but we squeezed together at the narrow counters, pouring flour, adding water and yeast and oil, mixing, kneading, shaping, baking.

Yes, change is the only constant, Willard continued as he

moved among us, adding calibrated doses of instruction and suggestion, teasing and encouragement.

And because everything changes, we need to let go of stuff as it changes. We can't hold on to it. If we do, we'll just end up feeling shitty. We have to let go of everything, even Zen. Because what is Zen? Zen is bullshit *(titters)*. No, it is. It's bullshit. I know it, you know it, your parents know it. Sitting on a cushion for hours at a time, *following your breath*, reciting sutras, asking yourself these stupid fucking riddles called koans, like does a dog have Buddha-nature? *Does a dog have Buddha-nature?* Who cares? Who gives a shit *(shocked laughter)*?

He stopped behind Athena, who was kneading dough.

We don't want any hairs getting in the bread, he said, gently pulling her long, tea-coloured hair back from her slender neck and tying it with a ribbon. She looked back at him and smiled, and the smile had a strange look to it. Or did I imagine it? A strange secret smile that I couldn't understand. And Willard smiled back, the same smile.

I was suddenly drowning in jealousy and mentally joined ranks with Artemis and Pierce in desiring Willard's death, even though I still loved and admired him. *Because* I loved and admired him, but above all because *he* loved and admired Athena, who loved him back. I began to understand the rage of Artemis, who had, in this instance at least, seen nothing as she was too busy pummelling her dough.

I don't think we're doing it right, I said suddenly. This isn't the way my mother makes bread.

Iris baked bread on the weekend, two loaves for us and eight more loaves for a restaurant in Frothingham. It was one of the several ways she made some extra cash for groceries. Willard knew all about it—he knew everything that happened at New Pond, and he viewed Iris's side business as competition with the New Pond bakery. But since she wasn't officially one of his students, there was little he could do about it.

Is that right, he said acidly. And how does Iris make her bread?

She uses more water, I said, And less yeast, and she lets it rise longer before punching it down.

A different recipe, said Willard, his voice mild but his eyes narrow. There are many kinds of bread. And anyway, recipes are bullshit, just like Zen. Because change is the only constant. So all things change, even bread recipes, even Zen, which is why we can't get bogged down by shit that was said in the past. Breathe your breaths, that's all you can do. And bake your bread. Light the fire in your belly and follow where it takes you...

He trailed off as he stooped to peer at a book sticking out of Apollo's jacket, which hung with all the others near the door.

What's this crap you're reading? he muttered, pulling the volume out and leafing through it. *The Hobbit*? You fill your brain with this escapist bullshit? Dragons and elfs and blablabla?

Elves, said Apollo quietly, Not elfs.

You make my point for me, snorted Willard, Arguing the name of a non-existent species. How is that going to help you understand how to live? How to be here, on this earth, in this life?

Uncapping and snorting some more nasal spray, he leafed through the book.

Wizards, dwarves, hobbits. What the hell is a hobbit, anyhow?

It's a small person, Apollo began, Who—

Bullshit, snapped Willard, stuffing the book back into Apollo's coat.

Apollo likes it, Athena protested gently, slowly, smiling her sweet, tranquil smile, the smile of a divinity intervening with indifferent, celestial warmth in the affairs of mortals.

Hmm, said Willard returning her smile, mollified. Yes, but should he?

The sun came around the corner of the house and suddenly shot into the kitchen. A giant patch of rainbow light appeared on the wall.

Now, there's a true wonder, said Willard. Where's it coming from?

The rainbow flew around, disappearing and reappearing as we twisted and turned, trying to pinpoint its source.

Freeze! said Willard. We froze. The rainbow hovered on the sink, trembling, pulsing colour. Willard walked to it and waved his hand around, until a shadow-hand appeared, obscuring purple and red. Then he turned and asked where an imaginary line from the rainbow through his hand would lead. Our eyes swivelled across the kitchen, until they met something flashing in the sun. A ring on Soto's hand.

If I may, said Willard, gently removing it from her dough-encrusted finger. He brought it to the window and held it up to the sun. Shards of rainbow scattered across the room as he turned it.

Cut glass, he said. A prism. Isaac Newton used one of these to figure out that white light is actually a combination of all colours. All things change, right? When sunlight shines through a prism, it refracts, it bends, it changes, it breaks up into a rainbow. And you don't need a prism. Look through a glass of water and what do you see? Bent colours, that's right, Soto. What Newton saw became part of the beginning of modern science. That's what happens when you look, really look, at what's around you, what's right in front of you, instead of dreaming about dragons.

Maybe, I thought, but maybe a dragon is a refracted dinosaur. Maybe quiet country people went through Tolkien's mind and shape-shifted into hobbits on their way out onto his page. Maybe Aristotle was wrong and art is a prism, not a mirror held to nature. Or maybe the mind is the prism and the refraction is the art that emerges on the other side. And if so, good thing, because without art's prismatic effect, dragons and their kin would be homeless. Where would the fantastical live if it weren't for books and drawings, sculptures, movies, and the brains of daydreaming schoolchildren?

Willard had a talent for getting under my skin like a splinter and forcing me to dig him out with a mental needle. For his part, he'd clearly grown bored of Zenday and did what he always did when bored. He wandered over to his piccolo, where it waited on its stand, picked it up, and began to play. As always, we groaned and yelled and covered our ears.

Dexter Gordon! shouted Willard, pausing briefly. Open your ears! Here's a koan for you—how did ex-slaves invent the greatest music of the modern world?

Jazz is bullshit! I said.

There was a pause—everybody stared at me. Then Willard laughed.

Now you're catching on! he said, and went back to playing.

We groaned louder and clamped our hands more vehemently in place. All children hate bebop.

Myles and Iris were slumped over coffee at the kitchen table. It was a cold, grey later-November day, but that was just the backdrop to their mood. They couldn't believe Ronald

Reagan had been elected. It was unthinkable. The polls claimed a tight race, and my parents and all their friends scoffed at the idea that a no-talent actor turned right-wing ideologue could possibly win the White House. But Carter lost in a landslide.

Who elected this clown? demanded Myles, his face scrunching with cognitive pain. They're like lambs being led to the slaughter. And they're taking the rest of us with them. He's the Pied bloody Piper! How could this happen? *It's morning in America*—what horseshit! People just want somebody who will tell them what they need to hear. It's some kind of suicidal game of follow-the-leader.

Are you so different? murmured Iris. Sticking with Willard despite everything?

What are you talking about? There's no connection at all. Willard's pursuing spiritual insight. Reagan was a pitchman for GE, for christ's sake. He's nothing but a salesman.

Willard's a salesman too. He just wears a costume you prefer and sells a product you want to buy.

I don't understand what you're saying, Myles said bitterly, putting on his coat and hat. I'm going to get water.

Iris sent me to help.

Outside, Myles and I stood on the frozen surface of our well. I held the bucket while he chopped a hole in the ice with the big axe. But just as he was enlarging it with an angry swing, the handle slipped through his fingers and vanished from sight into the dark water. Myles said Fuck for the first and last time in my childhood memory and sank to his knees on the ice. He crouched there for a long time, his head in his hands. The well was a hand-dug hole no more than five feet in diameter, ten in depth, but there was no question of retrieving the axe until the following August, when the water would dry up.

But an axe we must have, for the sake of the wood that must be chopped and fed into the rusty stove, a relic whose difficulty burning the sap-laden young trees that we fed it now was the source of the curses and complaints that my parents directed at it. Myles searched his bedlam shed and found an old, rusty axe head, then matched it with the handle that had come loose from a pickaxe. The combination was ill-fitting but serviceable.

In the meantime, I hauled in the white plastic bucket that was flooded to the brim with cold, blue water. Chunks of ice rattled on the surface, miniature bergs in a portable arctic sea. From the bucket Iris ladled a kettle full and placed it on the stove to heat for Myles's shaving water, because tonight was his first night of teaching a continuing education course at my school and I was to accompany him for moral support.

Myles wasn't used to public speaking, and his disquiet grew and radiated from him all along the rutted, twisting length of Middle Pond Road as he nervously anticipated lecturing, even if it were to an appreciative and uncritical small crowd of retirees eager to hear about Buddhism from a genuine practitioner here in the backwoods of Maine.

The room deep within the snowbound building was too bright, and I could see the sheen of sweat on Myles's suddenly red face as he anxiously, haltingly introduced himself and me, and began rapidly laying out the four noble truths, the eightfold path, the five moral precepts, and the five skandhas. But before his bewildered audience could get in any questions, Myles launched into an account of a young Indian prince named Siddhartha who lived a coddled, isolated lifestyle on the grounds of his ancestral palace, until one day circumstances exposed him to the three unavoidable horrors of humanity: old age, sickness, and death.

I knew the story by heart from bedside reading of Buddhist storybooks, from the famed Jataka tales and from Indian comic books. I remembered how Siddhartha promptly dropped everything and set off to find a tree he could sit under and try to come to terms with the sad, grubby shittiness of life on earth. How it took years of ascetic practice, but one day he woke up. Really woke up right inside his waking life, to the true reality of all things, achieving a transcendent serenity called nirvana. And having burnished that serenity to perfection, he got down to the business of teaching others how to wake up too.

Having warmed somewhat to his task, and choking only a little on the homemade cookies that one of his students had proffered to the group, Myles was saying, But how did this Indian prince achieve nirvana?

Yes, I wondered. How? Was it by unveiling the four noble truths and following the eightfold path while adhering to the five precepts that he was able to pierce the five skandhas and dissolve their hold on him? Yes, Buddhist math is weird, because four plus eight plus five minus five is said to equal not twelve but the zero point of enlightenment.

Still, that's not the whole story, because the Jataka tales maintain Siddhartha had a leg up on other seekers, of whom there was, and remains, no shortage in India. This advantage had to do with his personal karma, a kind of bank record of past actions. He'd accumulated some truly excellent karma, the very best, so they say, due to the nobility of his actions in past lives.

I narrowed back in on Myles's lecture, only to realize I'd

been thinking in tandem with him, and I wondered, for neither the first nor last time, whether my mind was little more than an extension of his preoccupations.

Past lives, Myles was saying, Yes. American Buddhists don't really like talking about reincarnation much—it's too awkwardly metaphysical for secular skeptics who just want to sit on a cushion and find nirvana at the end of a breath. But that's like saying you like Christianity, just not the Resurrection. It's all of a piece. Some Buddhist traditions go into detail about it, saying, for instance, that after death, the spirit enters an intermediate state called antarabhava (a.k.a. the bardo in Tibetan), where it experiences a powerful flash of pure understanding, only to have the rug ripped out from under it by a series of truly ghastly hallucinations generated by its karmic actions in previous lives. Finally, after enduring these terrifying visions, the soul gets housed in a womb from which it will be reborn. For the practitioner, this intermediate state can be a moment of great opportunity in which to truly wake into a state of liberation, but for those with shoddy karma it can be a perilous experience from which they can topple into a terrible reincarnation as, say, a slug or a serial killer.

Myles paused briefly, took another cookie, and accepted a mug of coffee poured from a thermos likewise provided by a student, and said that one of his teachers told him reincarnation is not necessarily limited to earth. There's nothing to stop the soul from travelling to and from distant worlds...

I needed to pee. Slipping out as quietly as possible, I wandered the dim and empty halls until I found a bathroom.

On my way back, the spookiness of the place began to worry me. It was a creaky old building with high, water-stained ceilings and walls gone wavy from a century of standing still.

A strange muffled banging was coming from somewhere in the shadows up ahead. I turned a corner and saw a dim glow from under a doorway. The bangs were banging from the same place. I eased open the door. It was an empty classroom. The noise was louder here—not just banging, but crashing, explosive, mad. The room itself was dark, but from under another door in the far wall there glowed an awful red-orange light. I crossed the musty carpet and received a shock from the door handle as I gripped it and slowly opened it to find, instead of a broom closet, a quiet, spare room with an open window overlooking a city in a vacuum. A city on the brink. I slammed the door shut and returned to Myles's class, where I sat not listening, but worrying about my story, which seemed to be invading. That night I tried not to sleep, for fear of underground dreams. And in the end, the dreams didn't come, or if they did I don't remember.

The next day, Myles stuck the last good logs into the stove and sat sharpening the teeth of his chainsaw with a thin file. It was my task to locate the toboggan.

Together we moved out into the foot-deep snow that blanketed the backyard. Myles broke the trail while I dragged the toboggan behind me with such apathy I fell well behind, until Myles turned and exhorted me onward, reminding me that I lived in the house as well, I too benefited from the heat (so-called) thrown by the stove, did I want to freeze in the night, did I want my poor mother to freeze? I caught up and followed him sullenly into the woods.

It was mid-afternoon and already the meagre winter light was beginning to fail, but while the trees obscured the light, the snow that had managed to drift down through the needles and branches laid a slender coating of iridescence over the roots and frozen puddles of the forest floor, and by that thin light, together with the pale grey sky trickling from above, we threaded the tree trunks, looking for our victims. Since this was not our property and we were poaching wood, Myles felt morally obliged to abstain from taking living trees (although, he pointed out, the owners lived on a Caribbean island and had probably forgotten that they owned this land, if land can truly be owned). Nor were old and rotten logs flammable enough. Thus the search was for blowdowns, the recently deceased casualties of the wind sagging miserably in the arms of their neighbours, roots torn from the ground but unable to fall.

The trees were dark, dimensional streaks against the pale blue snow, the hard sky. My toes were numb, cuffs of my corduroys already stiff with ice; and now Myles was cursing over the chainsaw that refused to start as he yanked it and yanked and yanked, yanked, yanked with mounting outrage until at last, impossibly, it sprang to life. To life? No. To death. Heartless, lifeless, angry teeth blurred by speed screamed death to the panic-stricken trees unable to escape, cursed by fate with immobility before the rapacious cyborg that my father had become as he fused with the machine.

Many years later, when I first used a chainsaw, I understood, or rather experienced, that strange transformation. The power of the saw demands to be used as it vibrates eagerly in your hands. Within the cocoon of brutal noise, all objects transform into things that must be cut.

Soon it was no longer merely blowdowns that Myles was aiding in their descent, but trees that looked *as though* they might blow down imminently, and a short time later, trees that really ought to come down to allow more light to their neighbours. It seemed to me, as I trailed that path of destruction, that I was moving through an arboreal slaughter-house—the raw, blond ends of the logs that I loaded into the toboggan bled sap and the torn chips of their flesh littered the ravaged snow that was greased and blackened by the chainsaw exhaust.

When at last the machine sputtered out from lack of fuel, the sudden inrush of silence (as of a breath after minutes underwater) was both an overwhelming balm and a tearing of the veil that revealed the forest as an echoing mortuary, a place of sorrow that I felt I must escape as quickly as possible, dragging the heavy sled through a maze of resentful trunks, until I burst free into the open and saw the warm lights of the house in the near distance.

Now the early winter evening was upon us. After stacking the wood, I collected a flashlight and headed back into the woods for the remaining logs. Why, I asked Myles as we loaded the toboggan in the blue gloom, Are we here? He paused and looked at me, but it was too dark to see his face. Only much later did I understand the tone of his voice when he replied: it carried the sound of budding interest.

I think we're here, he said as he piled some brush to one side, To find out why we're here. A friend of James Joyce drew a portrait of him in the form of a question mark, because for Joyce life was an open question to be experienced rather than answered.

How do you live a question? I wondered. From there he expanded at length, but I recall nothing of what came after. He had given me the answer I needed from him, and I've never forgotten it. Did I thank him? Probably not. I should have. I thank him now. Even as my search for meaning has waxed and withered, become richer or more despairing, lazier and more confused, I guard that moment in the woods. My father's seal of freedom.

Myles stacked the chainsaw and its fuel atop the wood, and together we pulled the toboggan back to the house. The night was warming and the snow had grown wetter and less accommodating. Gone was the satisfyingly dry, bottled squeak of flakes compacted under advancing weight. It was replaced by a slithering that lasted only a few feet before humidity overcame inertia and the wet snow stuck and halted our forward movement, until we jerked free and advanced a few feet farther.

When we finally stomped the caked slush from our boots and entered the house, it was to find Iris making dinner for the first time in months. And for the first time in months there was colour in her face and her eyes had shed their tarnished sheen. Brandishing a spatula, she gestured at the trestle bed.

Peering through the bunches of drying herbs that dangled from the ceiling joists, we saw Pierce sitting up propped on pillows, chatting with a stranger who sat next to him in a rocking chair. Myles, delighted as always to encounter new people (as though each stranger represented the possibility not only of new and intriguing stories, but also of the perfect friend—a possibility eternally doomed to end in disappointment when he discerned character flaws), advanced with a broad smile and a broad hand extended, his interest piqued, no doubt by the stranger's shaven head and robed figure and the Asian cast of his features.

This, said Pierce triumphantly, Is Yoshida Roshi.

Yoshida Roshi—a fable come to life! For years we had all heard tales of Willard's dharma brother, of their training

together back in 1950s Kyoto, of Yoshida's legendary booz-
ing and whoring of which Willard spoke with such nostalgic
sentiment that everyone who heard his reminiscences was
left with the intense desire to have accompanied those holy
rakes on their progress—to have imbibed with them the
crazy wisdom of their cigar-chomping master as they sat in
excruciating full lotus recovering with vicious concentration
from yet another sake-fuelled all-nighter staggering through
the antique streets of Kyoto.

And here he was in the flesh, summoned apparently by a
letter from Pierce. But of that, neither he nor Pierce, nor my
parents would speak, at least not until I went to bed after
dinner.

So for now Myles had regaled Yoshida with tales of his visit
to Japan years before my birth, while Yoshida listened with a
bemused smile and, from time to time, nodded or murmured
agreement with some detail that Myles described: the rice-
papered screens; the swooping rooflines; the scalding baths;
the efficient towels; the superlative noodles.

Then Yoshida responded with stories of his wartime experience. Inspired by his Zen master, he had enlisted and,
failing the exams for the air force and kamikaze glory, had
ended up a foot soldier fighting brutal rearguard action on
Okinawa as the American troops advanced up the island
shoulder to shoulder, shooting anything that moved. As his
knees trembled and he pissed his pants, he had tried to recall his master's instructions for wartime action—unite with
his fear, use his meditation practice to erase the barrier between himself and his gun, between himself and the bullets
he fired, between himself and his enemies, between himself
and his death.

He had been shot in the arm, and as he lay there slowly

bleeding to death, an American soldier had stumbled upon him and, against orders, tied a tourniquet around his arm and saved his life. That soldier was Willard.

After a moment of respectful silence, Myles said in troubled tones that surely the teachings of this Zen master were corrupt.

How so? Yoshida asked.

Myles responded hesitantly, heavily, that to employ a philosophy of peace to practise war was an outrageous blasphemy.

Yoshida shrugged and said that if Buddhism taught anything, it was that peace was to be found everywhere, in every moment, even behind the barrel of a gun.

That's sophistry! Myles cried. Or rather, I know now that's what he wanted to cry, what he should have cried, but he was face to face with an ordained Zen master, a Roshi, a man who must necessarily have experienced Enlightenment since he had received Transmission from his master who had received it from his master and so on and so on and so forth for thousands of years back to Shakyamuni Buddha himself.

Who was Myles to debate pedestrian ethics about war and peace with an enlightened being, a man who had experienced the All. And so instead he even-handedly noted the well-known fact that Christianity, despite being founded by the Prince of Peace, had managed to contort its theology into doctrinal support for wartime atrocities whenever Christians wanted to shed blood, which seemed to have been, and continued to be, often.

But (he wanted to say) I'd always thought, always hoped, that Buddhism was not likewise corrupted.

He didn't need to say it. Everybody, including Yoshida, understood what Myles was thinking. It was the thought of so many Western Buddhists of his generation. But Yoshida did not respond to the unspoken. He clearly had no further interest in the topic.

Instead, he broke a brief lull in the conversation by saying, apropos of nothing, Tell me of Willard, it signalled the end of my time at the table, and I was instructed to ascend to bed.

There, lost in *The Lost World* I muted the rise and fall of voices, the outrage and resignation, the pained references to exploitation, corruption, power games. But I was pulled from the book by the slick, loud whisper of winter coats, the hasp of zippers, and moments later I heard the loud knocking echo of the Han through the woods. And as the voices and boots downstairs shuffled out the door and the hammering outside increased in volume and speed, I knew that these interior and exterior audio signals taken together signalled that Myles was bringing Yoshida Roshi to sit Ruhatsu, the week long meditation that preceded the birthday of the Buddha.

Far up the hill, the great, thick plank of wood suspended from the eaves of the zendo was struck one hundred and eight times each morning and evening, summoning aspirants to converge upon their cushions and there to perch in snowbound silence and herd their minds, leashing their thoughts to their exhalations as they sought to pierce delusion, banish concept, abandon imagination, and dissolve into the passing instants until the instants ceased to pass, for how could time pass one by if one were one with time? The delusions of old age, sickness, and death, of form, feeling, thought, choice, and consciousness itself, would fall before the power of the breath. And as the rhythmic crack of the Han echoed out over the moonlit snowscape, over the trees quaking with cold, as it coursed down the hill and into my ear, I discovered

I was counting and my gaze slipped to the baseball on my shelf and I took it down and counted the stitches in time to the hammering of the Han, and just as Pierce had promised, the number was the same.

As the last echoes died away, I turned wearily back to my book, where I found that Professor Challenger and his companions, having escaped the dinosaurs on the great basalt knoll, had stumbled down into a lost city led by a goddess in human form.

THEY CALL her the Delegate.

The Delegate came ashore on her great beast.

The Delegate is the Voice of the People.

Her Voice has spoken for a Thousand Years.

The Delegate will see you now.

We're in big apartments with big open windows and big curtains. Chisolm sent us here. We've had baths. We've got new clothes. They're green-black uniforms like the ones everybody else wears. Now that we're rested and clean and changed, somebody's come to bring us to Chisolm. To the Delegate.

We walk through the long, tall halls of the palace. There are mirrors on all the walls with gold frames. We come to a huge room full of people, all in uniform. Chisolm walks out of the crowd. She takes my hand and guides me to the far end of the room. We walk up some steps and turn to look at everybody.

This, says Chisolm, Is our Seer. It was she who led me here to the City, the City that was lost. The First City.

But it isn't, I say.

Chisolm looks at me strangely.

This isn't it, I say. This isn't City.

There's a long silence. Nobody moves. Chisolm's face is going bad in a very strange way. Like something ancient suddenly exposed to air when it shouldn't be. I don't care. I look away. I was angry before, but now the anger is gone. I feel wrung, grey, nearly invisible.

Down in the crowd there's one person who's not in uniform. He's got white hair, a long, brown face. He's tall. He smiles at me.

Take her away, says Chisolm quietly. And two people grab my arms and lead me out of the room.

From the window of the jail where they lock us, I can see a big painting of Chisolm coming ashore on Lutra's back. The picture's on the wall across the street. There are words written underneath. The Delegate Is Eternal, they say. I hold the window bars and look through them at the painting, at the street. The people going by look sad and bored, tired. Behind me, Rook slumps on a stone bench. The cell is a cave carved from rock. We're not alone. Thin, sick, ragged people, long greasy hair in their faces, sit or slowly pace. Some crouch in the corners in the shadows. Rook stands and paces too and talks—why did I have to piss off Chisolm? Who cares if it's City or not?

I can't lie, I say. I learned that from you.

That's noble, says Rook, But there's such a thing as withholding the truth.

I didn't say it was noble, I say quietly. And I know about withholding truth. There's something I haven't told you.

What is it?

I'm the one who told Quill about Severn and Chisolm.

Rook sits down heavily, suddenly.

Why? he asks after a long pause.

Somebody sitting in a back corner moves, speaks.

She was afraid she would be stuck on that island forever, says the stranger.

Her voice is familiar. She stands and walks into the half-light. I know her face. It's old. Not as old as Chisolm. I still recognize her.

She was afraid she would never make it here, says Quill, And now that she's here, she finds that it's not what she was looking for after all.

You're dead, I whisper.

Obviously not, she says.

How is she alive? She says it's simple. She never hit the ground. She couldn't look at Severn anymore so she stepped off the cliff. Halfway down, she landed on the back of something with wings and feathers.

A bird? asks Rook, trying to pull himself from shock.

Large bird if so, says Quill. It carried me for days over open water.

An angel?

Strange angel, says Quill. The wings had black feathers. Greasy.

And that was all she ever saw or knew of it. She passed out, and when she came to she was on a hill overlooking the city.

That was a long time ago, she says. A thousand years ago, some say.

Hardly, says Rook. It's not a thousand hours since you walked off that cliff.

He means, since he lost her. He doesn't say that, but his voice is shaking.

If you say so, she says. She doesn't notice how pale Rook is, or how he's staring at her like she stepped out of another world. She's lost track of time, she says. When she came, there was nothing here. A swamp. A river. Mountains.

Then Chisolm arrived with her beast and soon the second boat followed. Finding no city, they built one.

Why are you in prison? asks Rook.

I'm often here, she says, Because I rebel. And Chisolm jails rebels.

Later in the night I wake Quill and whisper to her that I remember the clifftop. I remember the look on her face and that it wasn't her that jumped. Something took her over. I want to know what it was.

You, she says.

Not me, I say. It was a creature. Something dangerous. It's been following us.

It was you, she says again. Great black wings grew from your back. I looked in your eyes and saw I must jump. There was no other way.

That's not right, I say, Not at all.

It is, she says. It was. You were right. It was what I had to do. You made me jump and then you saved me.

I saved you?

Who else?

Not me. I'm not a bird. Not an angel either. I have no wings. I was on the cliff. I ran down to the water. I thought you were dead, just like everybody else.

You saved me, she says again. And now I'm going to save you.

I don't understand what she's saying. She must have had some kind of vision. It's hard to read her expression because her face never changes. It's flat and hard, like the faces of people who've been hurt and hope they won't get hurt again

184

as long as they make their faces into shields. I know that because my face is the same. And that's also why I think she's shaky underneath. I think that because of the way her eyelids flicker at the wrong time and how her words bounce to a stop too fast. I know she needs to believe something and so she believes everything I say. And also maybe it's because her mother doesn't. Doesn't believe me, I mean. So Quill believes me when I say this city isn't City.

And when she says she's going to save me, she means it.

Very early in the morning two days after coming to jail, we hear shots in the hall. Then shouting, more shots, running steps. A lot of smoke, then four people come through it wearing bandanas. I've never seen anybody like them. They look good. Really good. They've got velvet hats with brims, pocket watches, big sunglasses, bigger guns. There are two men and two women. They take off their bandanas and they're beautiful. One of them is holding keys and opens our door. We walk out over guards. They're tied up. Some of them are moaning, some are bleeding. Never be a guard, that's what I think. When things go bad, it's the guards who get it first.

We walk down alleys. I can hear sirens, but we don't run. Some people look out their windows at us. They wave. We wave back. We turn corners. We fade down streets. The streets are made of stone. So are the buildings on either side.

Carved from stone, says Rook. He sounds impressed. I'm not. The stone is falling apart. The buildings have cracks in them. White-green bushes in the cracks. White-green vines hang from the roofs. Chickens on the roofs. I think Rook sounds impressed because he's happy. His crooked face is wide open again. He looks like he's dancing a little when he walks. Quill doesn't notice Rook, but Rook doesn't care. He's happy she's alive. I want to be like him but I can't. Everything around me looks like it's falling down. Everything is broken. I'm broken. Breaking. I can barely speak anymore, barely have any words. I try to pull my pictures together but they slip out. Only a few left now. I'm almost all gone.

book
girl
snow
fight

We come to a canal. It smells like fart and rot. Piles of garbage float, some swans grease by. We cross a footbridge to the other side. Then there are steps going up a steep hill, small, stone, slippery. They go back and forth and up and up, up, up. Clumps of white grass on either side. The buildings are worse and worse. Then they're just caves with doors. Then the doors start to look a little better. Some are open. Some look nice inside. Warm, messy. Quill stops, we stop. We look around. We're on a different hill than the one with the waterfall and Chisolm's palace. We're around the corner from the bay.

Beautiful, says Rook.

In a monochromatic way, says Quill.

The city is below us. We can't hear it. Or we can, but it's quiet. The place we came from, the jail, the dirty stone streets and buildings, are all tiny under us. I feel a little better. Why does it feel good to be so high above things?

Quill takes a pair of binoculars from one of our rescuers. She looks out to sea. I see nothing. Some specks maybe, on the horizon. Boats? There are boats in the harbour. Big, small, in between. Farther out is the huge stone post we passed. The column. It goes from the water to the rock ceiling. Clouds drift around it.

The Gun, says Quill when she sees what we're looking at. That's what people here call it.

Why? asks Rook. It looks nothing like a gun.

Quill's busy with her binoculars again. She doesn't answer. One of her beautiful friends does. He takes off his sunglasses. His eyes are big and dark.

They say in ancient days there was trade between planets, he says. Merchants travelled inside comets. They say the Gun pokes out of the ocean above like a volcano. They say it is a volcano. Comet spaceships landed in the mouth of the volcano above and came down the tube like a ball sliding down a chute. Then, when they were ready to leave, a vent released volcanic energy, forcing the comet up through the chute like a bullet going up the barrel of a gun and shooting it into space.

Garbage, snorts Quill.

Well, says her friend, There's the man who's been claiming he's a comet rider. Says he came here from a distant galaxy. Wants to re-establish trade.

Snake oil, says Quill.

Your mom doesn't seem to think so, says the friend. She's been photographed with him.

Tabloid trash, says Quill. Let's go.

I DON'T remember the phone ringing, nor Iris picking up. What I remember is a fresh loaf of bread sitting on the kitchen counter with one end sawn off. The end lay on its back, a pat of butter melting into its exposed crumb, steam rising. And I remember my mouth closing on that heat, salt, fat, crunch. But then the phone must have rung. A heavy black plastic phone with a rotary dial and a thick curlicued cable twisted into unresolvable knots. We shared a party line with strangers and so, if not careful, might hear the gossip of an unknown family, salacious, meaningless.

This phone call, however, was for us—for Iris, I should say. What I remember is her pacing, her fingers further twisting the cable while she stuttered some form of explanation—an explanation she clearly did not feel it her duty to provide, yet which she nevertheless provided because it was in her nature to do so. Like many people, she disliked, above all things, the sensation of failure, and it was this dislike that the person on the other end was exploiting. *Person on the other end*—why beat around the bush? It was Willard, I could hear him, and he was calling about bread.

Caught off guard at first, she soon found her feet in the conversation.

But it's not your recipe, she said, her voice rising. I got it from *The Tassajara Bread Book*.

Espe Brown?! Willard's voice shouted down the line now. That hack? Most of the recipes in that book he stole from me, did you know that? That asshole robbed me and now he's getting rich off my work. So yes, you're using my recipes and you're doing it wrong!

Iris began to deny culpability, indeed to deny Willard's right to accuse her, and in so denying, she began to weep tears of outrage. The tears got in the way of her words momentarily and, choking slightly, she paused, and in the pause she listened, because Willard had seized the opportunity to speak. Listening, her mouth tightened, her face turned white and upon the receiver she slammed down the phone.

Then she stopped crying altogether and in a silent rage went about preparing dinner. When Myles came home, she took him outside, and through the kitchen window I saw her explaining with violent gestures what had happened. Then he turned abruptly and walked quickly to the car. Iris rushed inside and ordered me to go with him.

I suppose she reasoned my presence might have a civilizing effect, and this was probably a wise decision, for it seems unlikely that Myles would have assaulted someone in front of his own child. He didn't acknowledge my presence in the passenger seat but seemed preoccupied with arriving at his destination as quickly as possible. This was the sawmill where Willard and the others were ripping tree trunks into boards. It was a picturesque spot overlooking a forested valley, and now in early winter the stone sky sank into snow and everything was anchored heavily to the earth, especially the mill itself, its giant blades rotating in a blur under a long peaked roof, and within the open walls the men in torn, stained, heavy working garb fed logs into the shrieking machine and manipulated its levers, the cold muting the ordinarily powerful odours of sawdust and sweat.

Willard turned when he saw Myles stomping toward him and smiled disdainfully, as though he were expecting the visit yet was disappointed to find his expectations fulfilled. Myles was either insensible to, or disinterested in, this disdain. He stalked up to the sawmill motor, reached in, and switched it off mid-cut. The blade quickly, unhappily, ground to a halt in the middle of a log.

Ignoring the protests of the other men, Myles stood inches away from Willard and informed him that he was never again to speak to Iris as he just had. Willard raised his eyebrows dismissively and said that Myles's ego had been wounded, he understood, but this was an ongoing problem, he must practise, practise, to subdue his pride.

Go to hell.

Myles said this loudly, abruptly, then turned and stalked back to the car. Behind him I saw Willard's stunned face and his followers standing in various states of awkward shock.

There is no hell, called Willard, recovering enough to inject a mocking tone into his voice. Only the one you make.

You've made one! shouted Myles as he got in the car. And you're in it. Up to your neck in burning shit.

Somewhere in the mute tangle that constitutes a son's feelings for his father, bound up with the resentment, the love, the awe, and the disappointment, lurks always a desire to see your old man bring down another old man.

All the better that it be a principled stand in defence of one's mother. Whether this is due to some atavistic need to see one's leader lead, or to see loyalty and honour displayed, I can't stop my heart from swelling when I remember this moment. And any love I had left for Willard was snuffed out or maybe transferred to my father. I envy Myles's whiplash reaction, so unlike my own passive, prevaricating, hairsplitting penchant for appeasement, for rational discussion, for compromise. Mine is a useful attribute in nine-tenths of interactions, but useless, even cowardly, at rare but important moments. This was one of them. Willard had spoken of Myles's pride as an impediment, but if my father's pride drove him to defend my mother and if my pride in him is a sin, it is one that I embrace. Like my namesake, far rather would I be in hell with my loved ones than lonely in heaven.

My pride overwhelms memories even of Myles's regrets and recriminations when, a week later, a note arrived formally accepting his resignation from the New Pond. He had been cast out with a letter of juvenile punctiliousness registering outrage against the collective in coldly affronted, quasi-legal terms (whose pride had been wounded now?).

Myles laughed at the note, but it was a bitter laugh and later he would blame Iris for having provoked him to confrontation, thus causing his banishment from a world he had worked so hard to help build. And Iris would say acidly that if it were her fault he had been forced to free himself from the clutches of that tinpot tyrant then Myles ought to thank her, and it was a fault she regarded as a virtue.

Myles would shake his head regretfully and mutter how strange that it had all come down to a few loaves of bread.

The timing of Willard's phone call was suspicious, or so my mother reckoned. Willard had known about the bread recipe since I'd mentioned it at Zenday School, but had waited more than a week to call. Why? Iris parsed the situation with some relish over the liqueur that Pierce had earlier brought. Her drinking companion was Bernadette. Together they deduced that the phone call had been calculated as an intolerable provocation with precisely the purpose of causing Myles to resign (although perhaps not in so explosive a manner). Again, why? Because of the presence of Yoshida Roshi, who had, since his arrival, been interviewing Willard's disciples one by one and during late-night drinking sessions with Willard had confronted the latter with his findings. In a rage, Willard had thrown his dharma brother bodily from his house, and Yoshida had limped down the road to the little shed on our property that he was sharing with Pierce, and there he had installed himself and carried on his investigation.

You see, Yoshida explained drunkenly one evening over dinner to drunken Pierce and my drunken parents (for a time after Myles's expulsion, his potent home brew flowed freely), When Willard left Japan, our master enjoined him not to teach for ten years—he knew that Willard was weak, that, given authority, his ego would swell to a dangerous degree. And he was right—look what has happened.

We did not know, said Pierce. We thought he was enlightened.

Enlightened! scoffed Yoshida. Enlightenment is nothing—it's a bolt of lightning in the night: you see the landscape and then it's dark again. It is, he went on as he opened another bottle of beer, Merely the opening of a bottle. But you must drink the bottle. He poured himself an amber glass and illustrated his point. Indeed you must drink *many* bottles before you can see clearly for any length of time.

It appeared that this came across to Pierce and my parents as the deepest wisdom, for they swayed and nodded with bleary profundity.

But! announced Yoshida, abruptly raising a long bony index finger and shaking it at them admonishingly. Willard alone is not responsible for all this—it was you, you and all of your needy friends, who begged him to teach, who pleaded, who browbeat him into doing it. It was you, he said, head wobbling, Who destroyed him. He was a man before you made him a monster.

He was a child, Iris said harshly. And yes, his disciples (and I'll say again that I was never one of them) bear some measure of the blame, but it did not require much browbeating, if that is what he told you, to induce him to become what he became. You can't make an omelette from an orange. He was ready and not so secretly willing to fulfill his destiny as the leader of a pathetic cult of personality.

But by the time she finished her sentence, Yoshida was

nodding off and Myles had passed out with his head on the rickety table and Pierce alone was wide awake. His only comment was that he was ready for a cigarette and he duly stepped outside.

And where was I throughout this interchange? At my usual post on the wooden bench next to the stove, sitting silently, absorptive.

I wonder now if I was the cipher I thought myself, an anonymous listener, an eavesdropper, pleasant, attentive, but otherwise void of personality. Who knows how others saw me. For the most part they didn't see me at all, other than my mother, that is, who saw me now and ordered me to bed. Fifteen minutes later I was under the covers when she climbed the stairs and, swaying slightly from inebriation, came in to kiss me goodnight. The kiss landed on my lips and stayed there an instant longer and a fraction softer than the usual peck, and I did not like it, but she seemed not to notice that I wiped my mouth with dramatic disgust as she stood and ruffled my hair, smiling benignly and saying that if my father and she had done nothing else right, at least they had made me.

But, I thought, was it not I who was supposed to have chosen them?

Tell me more, she said as she cast her eyes about for the chair and sank into it, still smiling with unfocussed warmth in my general direction. Tell me more of your tale. Have you, she blinked rapidly and yawned, Had any more visions?

Had I? So she could not, in fact, read my mind as I had always feared, for if she could she would have known I was losing track of that underground adventure. It seemed to be dropping further and further away from me and all the while becoming more significant. And to call up the sequence of events on demand required an effort that seemed, in some obscure way, to undermine the nature of the story, as though to relate it in a series of episodes, with one action following the next in tidy progression, might reduce its power. Yet the need, the need in my mother's smile, the need for distraction, for respite, for an echo of magnitude, compelled me to set events in motion and so I drummed up City.

A WOMAN blows into a black stick with silver buttons and makes music I like. We're in a bar on a side street at the top of the hill. Everybody drinks and eats. Rook dances to the music with one of Quill's beautiful friends.

The bar is full and very loud. For some reason there are people holding big cameras and looking at everyone with them. The stone ceiling curves over us. I mean, the stone walls go up and turn into the ceiling and then come down and turn into wall again in one big curve. In some places pale vines grow up the walls and across the ceiling. The heads of strange dead birds look down from the curving walls. They're old. Sometimes feathers fall off them. There aren't any windows. Long lamps hang from the ceiling. Their light barely touches the floor's cracked tiles. Actually, they make the place seem dark.

We sit at a big booth. Quill is in the corner, talking very close and fast to her other friends. I walk to the bar and try to ask for water, but the man behind the bar doesn't hear me. Rook has stopped dancing and is standing nearby, talking to a tall man with wild white hair, brown skin, and a pointy white beard. Black eyes, black eyebrows. He raises his hand and the barman sees him and he orders water for me and hands it to me when it comes. I recognize him then. He was in Chisolm's court. The only one not in uniform. The only one who didn't look shocked when I said this wasn't City. He smiled at me then. He smiles at me now. Big gaps between his teeth.

Charmed, he says, holding out a hand. Call me George. Very deep voice. I shake his hand. He turns back to Rook. I was just telling your friend of my travels, he says. His breath bites my nose. He's drinking something that looks like water, but isn't.

Gimlets, he says, holding up his glass. Not bad here. Had worse. More for my friend, he says to the bartender, and points at Rook. Rook says No, but the barman doesn't hear him. When the drinks come, I have a few sips of Rook's before he sees me. He hits my hand away and slides his glass out of my reach. The drink is very sweet and it burns my throat, then my stomach. My head starts to float and the room shines. I hear George talking from close up and far away at the same time.

...slingshot my comet from star to star and read, he is saying, A vast pile of books as you can fucking well imagine. When your arse is locked up for a hundred years you plow through more than a few pages. That said, it wasn't a hundred year's worth—to ride the comet, we snort a dust that slows you down, down, down, down—he slides his hand down through the air—Till you're practically fucking catatonic; metabolism, movement, perceptions all glacial. If you'd been able to peer in through twenty feet of alien rock, you'd've seen me looking like a goddamn statue; probably took me a day to hobble from one room to the other.

The gimlet in me seemed to be doing the same thing George's slowdust did. It dusted my mind. My eyelids took minutes to blink. George kept talking:

...sent by a consortium of merchants to open up an old trade route. This place is en route. Not sure what the fuck happened in the old days but there was a fight over tariffs or some shite like that, trade stopped, this place obviously went to the dogs for a couple of millennia. But somebody needed a batch of your more exotic metals, and so here I am, trying to make a deal. What a circus, what a piss-shit circus. Mind you, he said, swallowing his drink and calling for another, You have to be as patient as a stone in my line of work. It takes a special type to shoot around, fuck. We're a strange bunch, to be honest. I won't go into the shitty details, but suffice to say that if there's a rock-rider type, there's usually more than a dollop of personal tragedy mixed in with general fucking misanthropy. There's a guild, can you imagine? That's because we need someplace to lurk between missions. It's a sad spot—the atmosphere, I mean—the furniture's plush, the windows big, the sherry dry, but what a mood, what a sorry mood. We slump around in armchairs reading and drinking, completely fucked, completely out of place and time, family and childhood friends all dead for centuries. Technically I'm a thousand years old, for instance, did I mention that? I've seen things, you couldn't possibly imagine—twin moons, rainbow nebulae, butterflies the size of eagles—but what do I have to show for it? Who can I tell? Hapless fucks like yourself that I buttonhole in alien bars so I can bend your ears till they're broken. No, we're assholes for the most part. Lonely old wretches. That's why we drink so much. Or maybe not. Some say the alcoholism is linked to the dust, which is chemically addictive shit and so, when off-rock, we need some kind of depressive taken in lower doses. Who knows? Who cares, fuck?

He stops to drink. Rook isn't listening anymore. He's staring at the TV behind the bar. Our faces are on it. And Quill's. There's a picture of the jail we broke out of. There's somebody talking, but it's too low to hear.

Turn that up, George says to the barman.

No! says Rook.

Don't worry, says George, You're among friends.

The music stops then. I turn to see the musicians put down their instruments. Quill stands at the microphone.

No need, she says, To turn up the TV. We all know what it says, what it always says. What it will always say, unless we do something about it once and for all. You know me and know what I've done and why I do it. How many rebellions, and yet still my tyrant mother stands. Nothing changes. And yet it does. This time something is different.

Quill pauses, a long pause, I wish she would get on with it. But she's just slowly staring around. The people with cameras have turned them on her. Lights are flashing and clicking all around.

Her, she says finally, and then I see she's pointing at me. Everybody turns to look. The cameras too.

This girl, says Quill, Her sight led my mother to seek a city. The City. But when Chisolm couldn't find it, she built one. And now the girl has come at last and she has told me, as she told my mother, that this is the wrong place. This is not City, and it never has been, never will be. And for that my mother threw her in jail.

An explosion shakes the bar and bangs all the glasses together. Some crack. Some break. People shout. Quill doesn't move. She's looking at the TV. Chisolm is on the TV. She's talking. The barman turns up the volume.

...an invasion, Chisolm is saying, From the Isle of War. Once more the forces of chaos are at our gates. I am declaring an emergency and ordering all citizens to stay indoors as we mobilize our resistance to this aggression.

There's another explosion and the TV goes black. All the lights go black and we rush outside.

The city is burning. Flares and fires light the port. Explosions everywhere. Spires and rooftops suddenly white, then suddenly not. Searchlights shoot down from helicopters. Planes are dropping bombs. Noise rings off stone sky, stone walls, stone streets. Between explosions I hear screams. Down below us and out on the water a huge boat with big guns fires into the city.

This is my mother's doing, shouts Quill above the noise. This is what she does when her authority is threatened and she needs a distraction. She secretly provokes the Isle of War into attacking us. They live in fear of her aggressions, so it takes little to set them off.

Horns honk behind us and we jump out of the way. Army trucks run by us. One after the other after the other. They're full of soldiers. People in the street cheer as they go by.

Up above, different planes and helicopters shoot out of nowhere in formation. They attack the other ones and the boat. The air burns. Things flame down from the sky.

We try to run back into the bar but can't. The place is a pile of rubble. We run and run.

We? Quill, Rook, George, me.

Quill leads us to an old museum in a cave in the hillside.

This has been here a thousand years, she says. A few bombs won't hurt it.

Others have the same idea. The place is full of people taking shelter. They sit propped against huge pillars or crouched under exhibits. There's a model of the city. Somebody begins to mark the bombed parts. The fight outside goes on all night, then all day, then into the night again. Then all the food in the museum's restaurant is gone. Even the cream and sugar packets are empty. Some people leave to look for supplies, but they never come back.

A missile hits the east wing, and we pass buckets of water, one to the other, until the fire is out. I want to see the exhibits, but the power is dead and candles and flashlights have to be saved. In the short bits of light that come from outside explosions, I see stained old sculptures of naked people, paintings of women wearing wings, glass cases full of flashing jewels and jewels and jewels.

Bomb light sprays everywhere now and then. It lights the others. It lights up George. I crawl to him.

We need a safer place, I say. He has a bottle of liquor he stole from the bar. He drinks from it.

Yes, he says, Come with me.

We walk downhill all night. Down and to the right. Down and to the right. Crowds of people jam the streets, the parks, the squares. They don't want to burn alive or die under a falling building. There are people everywhere. They scream, they moan. Some are covered in blood. But it's hard to hear them over firetrucks and ambulances and planes and helicopters. The crowds push and pull like ocean water. They push and pull and the crowd scares me more than bombs or burning cars or jets or shrapnel or choking black smoke or the ripped-off legs and arms we sometimes step over. I know the crowds will squeeze me to death at any moment. My head will pop off like a cork and fly up, up, up above the jets. And from there, the eyes in my spinning head will look down on the whole mess. The wrong city, the wrong people, the wrong time. How could I have been so wrong when I knew I was right?

But I'm not dead. I'm squeezed but not to death. I can breathe a little. I'm holding George's hand and also Rook's hand who is holding Quill's hand.

We are barely moving, but we are moving, back and forth with the push and pull of the crowd and also a little bit forward. We inch downhill for hours.

Then there are no more people. We break free of the crowd and the streets are empty.

Good, says Rook, leaning against a lamppost and breathing hard. We're through.

No, says George. This is no good. No fucking good at all. This is the water sucked away before a tidal wave.

We're in a square. There's a pale green hedge around a park in the middle of it. And an old fountain in the middle of the park. The fountain is a tall green-metal statue of Chisolm riding on Lutra's back. Water shoots out Lutra's mouth and splashes into a pool at her feet. Battle noise, people noise, all are far away.

Far away for a little while and then they're not. Shouts, screams, shots, louder and louder. Soldiers come into the square. They run, trip, fall, run past us. There's blood on them. Their uniforms are torn. They look scared. They go by us and around us like sad wind blowing by as fast as it can.

George says we need to get out of here but it's too late. The other ones, the troops of War, come in fast and neatly and neatly square us and point their guns. We raise our hands.

WE SMUGGLED our refugee friend Bayo out of St. Mike's in the middle of the night. By that time, the Frothingham cops knew he was there, but under the customs of sanctuary he was safe, unless he left. Thus the coat and glasses in which we costumed him before bundling him into our car in the dark. He crouched on the floor of the back seat until we were out of town and I practised looking innocently out the window as we rolled away up Route 1a to Route 2.

Columbus! said Myles around dawn. There's a state trooper on our tail.

Where? said Iris.

Two cars back, said Myles.

In the rear-view mirror I could see his glasses glowing anxiously, and behind him, or rather behind me, the orange fire of the rising sun.

Iris didn't turn around but antennae seemed to sprout from the back of her head as she took in the situation.

Myles, who'd had unfortunate run-ins with the law during his draft-dodging days, loathed and feared all those in uniforms. Bayo, of course, had even more reason to panic at the thought of police. I could see his hand shaking as he adjusted his hat. But Iris, daughter of a colonel, stayed cool.

It's fine, she said soothingly. He's just on patrol. He's cruising for speeders. Look, he's passing us.

Get down! hissed Myles to Bayo.

Don't move! barked Iris before Bayo could slip out of sight. That'll just draw attention. Everybody stay calm.

The police car slid past; the trooper didn't even turn to look as he went by.

Worried that Myles would have a nervous breakdown at the border, Iris insisted he pull over so she could drive.

At the crossing in Calais, Iris announced the presence of Bayo and his desire to claim refugee status. Inside the Canadian border offices, we sat in the lobby while Bayo was interviewed. When he came out carrying some kind of official document, he looked relieved.

We ate lunch at a Tim Horton's in St. Stephen and then drove Bayo to Saint John where we delivered him to a church group that was sponsoring him.

Once he was safely installed, Myles turned the car and headed due west on the Trans-Canada highway. Was this deviation planned? If so, I remember no warning, just acceleration.

We drove for a night and a day and into the following night in a frenzy. I never looked up at the passing landscape but read and slept and wallowed in my lethargy and powerlessness. My parents were heading back to their starting point, driving desperately out of a world that seemed to be collapsing in their wake—the world they'd built in Cove, the world of New Pond. To escape it, we were heading for a metropolis unknown to me—yet no city could be more intimate—Rochester, New York, city of my birth.

It was just a road trip, they said, to see old friends, to see what had become of the place. It was in Rochester that they'd met as part of the group that built the great Rochester Zen Center from scratch. Not just a building, not just an organization, but an institution, the fabled *boot camp of American Zen*. And when, for reasons unknown to me, they'd broken with the teacher there, the break broke their hearts, so that broken-hearted they retreated and rebuilt themselves in Maine. Eventually, the teacher in question retired, and now, ejected from New Pond, Myles and Iris thought the timing *propitious* for returning to the source, *just for a visit...* For my part, I thought the timing extremely fishy.

I don't want to move to Rochester, I said truculently as its suburbs accumulated in the evening light and gave way to stately residential neighbourhoods over which Myles and Iris murmured and sighed reminiscently.

We're not moving here, said Iris, We're just visiting. Ah, do you remember Meigs Street? she said to Myles. That place we had? The staircase?

I don't remember it, I said, slumping in my seat to avoid viewing the tall, beautiful houses.

Well, of course not, said Iris. You were just a baby when we left.

We parked outside an odd domicile with unlikely curves. It looked to me like a fist with the index finger pointed straight up, the finger being the chimney.

It really is art deco, said Myles as he surveyed the facade before inserting a key in the front door.

It was Pierce's house, and since he was at our place, we had the key to his. This was the authentic period piece he'd been restoring for the past ten years. Hard to believe that he'd truly *bought it for nothing*, or that it had ever really been *in shambles*. The interior gleamed with curvilinear wood surfaces. It looked suspiciously jazz-related to me, but I couldn't condemn it on the strength of that alone. Actually, I thought it was beautiful. There was a spiral staircase, bright orange rubber tiling on the kitchen floor, magically undulating plywood walls. Every corner revealed a level of aesthetic sophistication so novel to me that I wanted to move in immediately.

I hate it here, I said, not even trying to sound convincing.

Pierce's house was within walking distance of the Rochester Zen Center and in the mid-morning light of the next day, the Boot Camp revealed itself to be a luxurious, old residence, replete with columns and verandas and refinished hardwood floors.

It's exactly the same! said Myles as we walked in.

Iris agreed, but it sounded implausible to me—there

wasn't a speck of dirt on the shining floors, not a single bump or scrape on the blindingly white walls. The wood trim was immaculately finished.

We became aware that a bony young man was quietly existing next to us. Had he been there from the beginning? He had short-cropped hair and skin that reeked of clean-living. He bowed in Caucasianese-style and we returned the salutation and Myles announced himself. We were expected, he said, and were looking forward to meeting with Peter.

The young man's eyes widened at this impertinent familiarity.

I will notify the Roshi's secretary, he said.

Sorry, said Myles laughing, Roshi. It's just that we're old friends. He wasn't a roshi when I left.

Five minutes later the young man returned to say the secretary regretted that the Roshi was extremely busy today, but we were invited to attend a meditation session, which the Roshi would be leading.

We followed him down a series of hallways until we joined a line of other, aggressively healthy-looking people with whom we filed into a sun-filled room lined with bamboo matting and the familiar, round zazen cushions. Also familiar was the reassuringly acrid scent of incense and the decluttering peals of a brass bell.

Peter, a.k.a. the Roshi, floated in fully decked in the rough brown robes of a Zen monk, replete with a square of fabric in a subtly different shade, which denoted his status. His head was shaved, his skin yogourt-white, his eyes bright blue, and he maintained a quiet, benign smile that he turned this way and that in greeting as he entered. The smile landed indifferently upon all, with only the slightest nod of recognition when it came across Myles, Iris, and myself. Then he sat on his cushion, cast his eyes to the floor, and looked about no more.

I sat on a cushion between Myles and Iris, brought each foot to the opposite knee, and sat, sat. Sat.

Zenday meditation sessions were adjusted for young attention spans, and Willard had tolerated our rustling and fidgeting with good humour. But this was grown-up zazen. There wasn't so much as a sigh from the little throng of meditators, not a sneeze or snort. Nobody scratched their noses, nobody burped, and if they farted, they did so with extreme discretion. My limbs soon felt as though they were twisting inside my skin, I tried to breathe through a sneeze for so long that my eyes watered, my throat began to smoulder and my entire nasal region burst into flames.

A few cars motored sedately by; there was a shout in the street. Otherwise nothing to relieve the monotony.

The bell ring was a cool wave over my burning joints and head.

The Roshi spoke. His voice thrummed in a soothing, hypnotic register.

What is Zen? he said. (Why were teachers always asking this?) It is this moment, right here, right now. It is the smell of incense, of car exhaust, it is that boy there aching to be anywhere but here (*general laughter*).

He smiled at me with deep compassion and friendliness— a smile so perfectly calibrated to express his sincerity, his benignity, his serenity, that I found it thoroughly untrustworthy. Willard had ruined gurus for me.

Zen is, he went on, patting the floor, Just this, just this.

He continued in this mode for some time before rising and leading the way to the dining hall.

There we knelt at the low wooden tables and deployed

the provided chopsticks to eat brown rice and fresh tofu braised with miso and garnished with toasted sesame seeds and chopped scallions. Myles showered the meal in tamari sauce, wolfed it down, guzzled the green tea provided, and headed for Peter the Roshi, who sat slowly, calmly, attentively consuming his food.

It was immediately clear to Iris that Myles was breaking protocol, and she hissed at him to come back, but Myles ignored the warning and squatted down across from the Roshi, extending his hand.

Good to see you, Peter!

The monks on either side of the Roshi froze, chopsticks vibrating in mid-air. Unmoving, Peter gazed at Myles, benign smile back in place, blue eyes freezing. Finally, he nodded slightly and his remarkable voice motored forth.

Perhaps tomorrow, he said quietly, We can talk.

And so we returned the next day, but the Roshi was once again too busy to see Myles and Iris, as he was the following day and the day after that as well.

He was just another one of those young drifters who started showing up before we left, do you remember? Myles's voice was aggrieved, incredulous, All of them gape-faced, wild-eyed...

Angelhaired hipsters yearning for the starry dynamo, murmured Iris, Or however that goes.

Yes, said Myles, That's right, and even Ginsberg kept showing up.

Ginsberg was always showing up, said Iris, You couldn't turn around without bumping into Ginsberg back then.

I could barely follow the conversation due to the ice-cream

sundae on the white tablecloth in front of me and the view outside the window, which, as advertised, kept changing.

To assuage their dejection over their non-reception at the Zen Center, Myles and Iris had decided on an urban expedition. We had travelled to the top of a downtown high-rise where the twenty-first floor was a disc inside which the outer ring of the floor slowly rotated 360 degrees, revealing to diners the entire panorama of Rochester.

After we built that place from nothing, Myles went on.

You think you should be the one in those robes? said Iris. You think you should be the one in charge?

I could've been, said Myles forcefully, If I'd been willing to lick some boots.

Sometimes that's what it takes to get ahead, said Iris.

Well then, said Myles with a crooked smile, I guess we never will.

No, said Iris smiling back, We never will.

They contemplated the view and sipped their coffees, which, together with my sundae, were the only items they could afford in a joint like this.

The Xerox building, said Myles, pointing to another high-rise. We'd never have gotten the Center off the ground without Carlson's Xerox money.

There's the hospital where you were born, Iris said to me, And Highland Park. Too bad it's winter. In the spring it's full of gorgeous lilacs. I remember when we brought you home from the hospital, it felt like we were driving through a lilac ocean. And the scent!

What's that river? I asked, pointing to a wide body of water winding through the city.

The Genessee, said Myles, pointing to a mist rising from a cataract. See the High Falls?

At a nearby table in the restaurant, a small crowd of men dressed in business suits was growing increasingly clamorous and unhappy, until all but three of them suddenly rose and strode out. One of the remaining three, a stout, dark-haired man with an air of authority and a very red face, jumped up and berated the passing waitress, asking if she knew that those men were from the federal government, asking if she understood that they'd been waiting for their meal for one and a half hours...*one and a half hours!* He was never, he said as he pulled on his jacket, Ever coming back to this dive again. And with that he marched out, followed by the remaining two men.

Who was that? Myles asked the waitress, who was now removing my empty sundae dish with shaking hands and swelling eyes.

The mayor, she said, voice trembling. It's not my fault! There's only one cook and I'm the only server. It's not my fault.

Of course not, said Iris soothingly, as she fished in her purse for cash to pay the bill. Don't worry about him.

As we put on our coats and began to leave, Iris glanced down out the windows and said, Look, you can even see the Americana Hotel where they arrested Bowie for pot. She sighed and added, Even his mugshot was beautiful.

He looked like an alien, snorted Myles.

A lovely alien, she replied gravely.

THE POLICE are gone. They were everywhere before, but now they're gone. Everybody's gone. All that's left are prisoners and soldiers. We're stumbling downhill with guns at our backs. We fall, get up, walk, fall, walk. The soldiers shout, they jab us with their guns. Quill goes to her knees. A soldier yanks her up by her hair. Quill screams. Her knees are bloody. Rook tries to help, but the soldiers whack him away. George swears non-stop. The soldiers don't care. The soldiers don't look angry. They don't even look mean. They look like nothing. Their faces show nothing. Even when they yell and whack and jab.

Things are quieter. Fewer jets, fewer bombs. But more yelling. We tromp, fall, tromp, tromp, cough, cough, cough, cough. Smoke everywhere. Thick smell of things that shouldn't burn. Thick poison smell. Finally, we stop. Then we go through a big metal gate. The gate closes behind us and I see where we are. It's the park where we came ashore. I see the plaque with the picture of Chisolm and Lutra. We're crowded in with others. Many others. There's not much room to move. The guards line the gates. To keep us from climbing over, I guess. It's getting harder and harder to breathe. Must be because we're packed in so tightly. Everybody's using up the air. The air! We're underground—where's the air coming from? There can't be enough for so many people. I can't catch my breath. I've been numb since the bombs started dropping. Numbed by noise and movement. We've kept moving, until now. We must start moving again! We have to get out of here!

The stench is horrible. People pee their pants where they stand because there aren't any bathrooms. Everybody is wet with sweat. Through the sweating bodies I see a military truck parked near the gate. I slide between sweaty, pee-wet bodies. Rook follows, holding my hand, and Quill comes too with George. They see where I'm going. Rook tries to pull me back. I hear him saying, Useless, through the crowd noises. But I keep going. Not useless if it works.

It must work. My pictures are all gone. Nothing left but the faraway idea of lilac. Waterfall sounds fading. I can't stay here in the wrong place. Not just wrong—fake. Anywhere else is better.

We jostle up against the truck and climb in. I'm in the driver's seat and my hands reach under the steering wheel by themselves and find the right wires and yank them free and cross the bare strands and the engine starts. I don't know why I can do this. I press the accelerator down and we start moving. People jump out of our way. A guard yells. More guards yell. They start coming for us and I press harder on the pedal until we're knocking people out of the way with our bumper. People are spinning away when we hit them, falling in the rear-view mirror. Two guards jump in our path and point their guns. I duck and floor the pedal. The guards jump out of the way and we crash through the gate behind them into the open street.

Turn left! cries George.

Gunfire. A bullet blows out the windshield. I yank the wheel, we skid left into an alley. The guns follow. More turns. Right, right, left. An unpaved side road stops at a waterfall. I hit the brakes.

Go! shouts George. Straight!

I don't. I don't want to slam headfirst into the wall of rock behind the falls. But bullets close in.

Now!

There's nothing to lose. I gun the jeep and we crash into the waterfall. Or through it. Soaked on the other side, we see nothing. I flick on the headlights and there's a big tunnel in front of us. Big enough to drive through? Bullets zurp zurp through the waterfall. I hit the gas. Truck sides scrape rock, but we fit. We drive through stone. We drive into nothing. Shouts behind us. I look in the rear-view mirror. In the middle of blackness the waterfall is bright. Dark bodies move against it. Soldiers are coming through the waterfall. They fire after us. Soon they'll bring a truck. Soon they'll track us down.

Faster! says George.

I speed up.

Somewhere behind us a truck roars. The soldiers are coming.

The tunnel turns into a giant cave. There are stalactites as big as big trees hanging from the ceiling. It's dark. So dark I can barely see anything. Can't see the ceiling. Only a shaky red glow lights the place. A crack runs from one end of the cave to the other. The crack is as wide as our truck. The red glow comes up from down inside the crack. Our headlights hit the biggest rock I've ever seen. It sits above the crack. We're ants to it. It sits on tall rocks. A stony giant standing on three stony legs. I can't see the top of it because of the darkness. Maybe there is no top.

My ship! shouts George. He yells directions. Our truck races toward one of the stone legs. Strange and wild shadows everywhere. Little light. Where light, it's dark red. Where dark, it's jittering, flaring.

I brake hard at the foot of the stone leg.

Up! shouts George, and I see stairs carved into the rock leg. They circle around it as they rise.

I jump out. Quill and Rook follow. But the soldiers are on us. George is up the steps, disappearing around the side of the stone leg. I run after him. A soldier grabs my ankle, then screams. Rook is biting his other hand. He's ripping his hair out. The soldier lets go of me to bash Rook in the eye. Rook falls, but pulls the soldier down with him, twisting to land on top of him. Rook hits the soldier and hits him, but then there's a shot and he slumps and rolls off. The soldier shoots him again. He doesn't move. The soldier gets up. He points the gun at me.

He falls over. Quill's on top of him. Hitting.

Go! shouts Quill.

I go.

A few steps up, I hear more shots. I look back. Three soldiers stand over Quill, shooting.

They look up and see me. Bullets come. I run.

MYLES WAS a deadly shot and a dirty player. That's why our team nearly always won. Our team consisted of Myles, me, Apollo, and Willard. Yes, Willard, despite nearly coming to blows with him, Myles was always quick to let bygones be bygones (unlike Iris, who nursed grievances for decades, possibly lifetimes). Anyway, Willard had come and he wanted to play and seemed oblivious to the likelihood of an awkward atmosphere. Certainly Bill wasn't happy to see him.

Myles and Bill, former high school basketball stars, always faced off. To have them both on the same team wouldn't have been fair. Thus, arrayed against us were Bill, Artemis, Buddy Johnson, and his giant of an uncle, Clyde. Where Myles was quick, Bill was methodical. The games were always close. But Myles had a singular advantage in this venue. The Town Hall had impediments: a pot-bellied woodstove in the corner and half a dozen steel cables running the breadth of the space at a height of twelve feet, their purpose to prevent the aging walls from groaning apart. Myles learned his basketball on a low-ceilinged court and was able to gun the ball into the net with virtually no arc. He'd also played a great deal of street hockey and knew how to throw artful elbows in ways that were painful, persuasive, and so surreptitious it was difficult for witnesses to corroborate the fouls.

Thanks to these combined skills he led our team to victory three out of five times most Sunday mornings. But usually Clyde wasn't there. He was in prison for drunk driving, illegal clamming, public exposure, or some other felonious activity. Massive, strong, and quick, he was very dangerous on the court, and on the few occasions when he showed up, Myles usually came away limping because Clyde paid my father back for his sly elbows with crushing body blows.

But none of that came to pass that day. The game ended almost as soon as it began.

Bill had just hammered in a bank shot and Willard was offering his ritual opinion that Even a blind hog finds an acorn once in a while, when the door opened and the police stepped in.

Clyde sprinted for the back exit.

We're not here for you, shouted the sheriff. The sheriff's name was Jim. He was the father of one of my classmates.

Clyde slowed and stopped, but lingered by the back door in case it was a trick.

Jim strolled calmly up to Willard.

I need you to come down to the station with me.

Why? asked Willard, dribbling the ball in an angry, dismissive way.

Let's talk it over at the station, said Jim.

Are you arresting me? Willard asked as carelessly as possible, and took a shot that swished.

Nothing but net! he shouted triumphantly.

Jim sighed and gestured to his deputy, a shy young man named Pat.

Pat pulled out a piece of official-looking paper and read that the charge was: Inappropriate sexual contact with a minor.

Willard slumped suddenly.

Athena, I thought, and looked over at Artemis, who was staring at the proceedings with wild, frightened eyes.

As the police took Willard away, his gaze turned on Artemis, oscillating at high frequency between guilt and accusation.

Change is the only constant. How many times had I heard Willard say that? He would boil Zen down to that single truism. It's a cliché, he would say, but a radical one. Nothing, not the hardest rock, not the brightest sun, not the purest truth, not the holiest god, nothing can dodge metamorphosis. This is the only piety worth its salt.

The defections of Myles, Bill, and half a dozen others damaged the edifice of the New Pond. But what brought it crumbling down in the end wasn't the endless humiliation Willard visited upon his disciples, it wasn't the manner in which he'd reached into every corner of their private lives, nor the sexual offenses, nor the emotional manipulation. No, under his spell, or at least under the spell of their collective dream, they had failed to stop him. Within his spiritual fiefdom, he lived with impunity, but the habit of power he exerted there made him careless and he had meddled in the world of children, a world he didn't own. He had molested a teenage girl, neglecting to account for the complicated jealousies he aroused. But if Willard thought Artemis was responsible for his arrest, he was wrong. Artemis took a dim view of the police, reckoning in her anarchic heart that it was ignoble to rely on officialdom—she still hoped and planned to personally assassinate him loudly, bloodily, publicly. No, a muffled, anonymous call to the police from a pay phone wasn't Artemis's style. It was mine.

I AM dull and empty. I'm in an empty tunnel, behind three doors. George hauled me up the steps, opened a big metal door in his giant rock, and pushed me through. Then two more doors after. Blood dripped down his sleeve, off his hand. I watched it drop in shiny drops and splats, then he left me and staggered away.

I can't hear the gunshots against the door anymore. Can't hear anything. Bright light bulbs light the tunnel. I sit on its floor, dull and empty. I'm thinking. How can I think? My heart ticks. My sight is cold and clear. Too cold, too clear. I'm alone again. As I was before. Or very nearly. George is dying. He'll be dead soon. Then what? I've lost my pictures. I've lost my friends. I've lost my city. I don't know where it is. I don't know what to do. I don't know who I am and never will. I'm disappearing.

CRACK

Did my skull crack?

Floor shakes. Soldiers bombing us?

I stumble down the tunnel. Musty, old, wet, hard, CRACK

I fall. Shaking tunnel. Lights shudder. Get up, go on.

Opening to my left. A cave with machines. George is there, sweating, bleeding, pop-eyed. Grey metal boxes, screens. He bumps from one box to the other. He cranks levers, twists knobs.

On a black-and-white screen I see the dead bodies on the cavern floor outside. Soldiers aim something at us from their truck. Bright light. The floor shakes.

George hits a button CRACK

215

I fall. George falls.

On the screen the soldiers run. Something comes. Something white rolls toward them, grabs them, runs over them. Lava.

CRACK

They're gone. Screen shivers.

That got rid of them, says George, gasping. His hand is on a big lever, but then he takes it off. No, he says, We can't launch. It'd bury the city in a giant fucking cave-in. We'll wait it out for now. We're safe in here. There's not a fucking thing they can do to us.

He stands. He looks shaky. This way, he says. I follow him down the tunnel.

Big round cave at the other end. Bookshelves all around, from floor to ceiling high above.

George rips off his sleeve and washes his arm in a fountain in the middle of the room. Round fountain. A green metal fish is jumping out of it. Water from its mouth pours over his skin, the black hole in his skin. I help tie his sleeve around it. He falls back on the carpet and passes out. There are couches everywhere. I grab pillows from them and stuff them under his head, his knees.

Then I go back to the control room. I feel the point of heat in my back, and it spreads, spreads. I'm boiling in my skin. Boiling out my last memories. Boiling out sadness, love, anger. Boiling out all pity. There's no choice. There's only one thing to do. I find the big lever and use both hands to shove it down.

CRACK!

Shaking again. This time worse.

I crawl back to the room of books. Can't stand up anymore. Air presses me down. Roar, roar, non-stop thunder. Chandelier shakes and stutters above. Head for a couch but can't make it. Invisible thumb crushes me. Black fog sparkles in, fills the room, fills my eyes.

When I wake, everything is quiet. The fountain splashes, thousands of books in their bookshelves still line the room. George is gone. Down the hall I find him in the control room. He hunches over a screen, wearing headphones. Sweat drips off his face. Bloody rag still tied around his arm. He turns when I come in and his eyes glitter.

You launched us, he says.

Yes.

You destroyed the city.

It wasn't City.

It was *a* city and you killed it.

I don't say anything. There's nothing to say.

Something out there, he says. His voice sounds jagged, wrong.

You're sick, I say. You should rest.

I can hear it, he says, And see it.

He points to dots and squiggles on the screen. They make no sense to me.

A being! he shouts. A giant fucking bat or something flying through space with us. I've heard of them, legends over drinks at the club, massive feathered bastards swooping along next door like some kind of colossal demon or angel or demon-angel or winged fucking fate itself. Fantastically exciting but also scares me shitless but also there's absolutely nothing I can do about it, and also I'm getting signals, the thing is fucking talking to us!

What's it saying? I ask.

I try to be calm. I'm alone inside a rock in space with a dying man. And the thing that's been following me is outside. What else could it be?

It says it's time to fucking feast!

George flips his headphones off, jumps up, and runs out the door. I follow. He disappears around a corner. Another tunnel, then stairs cut in the rock, then light, light. Giant wall of sunlight.

Foot-thick crystal, says George. Always facing the nearest star. This is the room of endless day. That's why we can grow these massive fucking trees.

Green everywhere. Palm trees, vines, trees with red trunks as wide as trucks, purple fruit hanging from them. Silver fruit, ruby, gold apples the size of boulders. Bush berries glimmer underneath. Vegetables below them. Corn, beans, squash, peas, potatoes.

Everything's a bit pale after weeks underground, of course, but I left a special light on, and you'll see it all perk back up now that we're flying again.

He leads me to a stone patio in the middle of the room. A meal waits for us on a round wooden table there.

Sit, he says. I sit.

He uncorks a dusty bottle of wine and pours two glasses.

Drink, he says.

I drink.

He empties his glass and refills it.

Drink! he says again.

I sip some more. I don't like wine. It smells of cow shit, potatoes rotting in the ground. Where have I ever smelled those smells? Maybe I have a few last memories left inside after all. Memories so far gone there's nothing left of them but smells.

George swirls the wine in his glass and sniffs and snuffles it.

His clothes and skin are wet with sweat, eyes twitch.

Now eat! he says.

The food is good. Very good. Cold soup, salad, bread. I eat and eat but then feel strange. Not bad but strange. George eats fast and then faster. He finishes before I take a few bites. He moves so quickly he's a blur and his voice speeds and rises until I can't understand it. Suddenly there's a letter in front of me and George is gone. Confused, I read:

My dear child, it says, Fear not, all will be well. Unfortunately, I have to go. The big feathered thing outside told me I need to join it. Probably won't be back—by the time you read these words, I'll be long gone. I drugged your soup and wine—nothing dangerous, promise—standard stuff to slow functions for a voyage. Can't tell you where you're going or how long it'll take. No idea where you'll land. It'll probably take a few years—usually does—but will feel like a week or so because of the drug. You'll be lonely at first, but might end up liking it. No shortage of books to read! Food pantry is down the hall to your right...

I look up. Something fast and green in the corner of my eye. Plant. A plant! Shooting from the ground. A leaf uncurls and stretches. Snail sprints across it. I stand suddenly. Spider spins a web where I sat in seconds. All around me the jungle gropes and grows and rots and grows and grows, grows.

I stumble out and down the hall to the library.

For a long time, I don't know how long, I sit in a big armchair, thinking about my luck. On the one hand it seems good —I've survived everybody I know. On the other I'm alone. Completely. Not just alone, but trapped, flying, or drifting, I don't know where. I knew once. I could feel it. I don't anymore. I'm lost in every possible way.

Air from somewhere moves a little, makes dustballs spin across the room. Silence. Silence. I've never heard so little.

After a while even spiders make noise. Thread squeaks stick-ily from their bellies, snaps onto other threads. A little later flies die-buzz over and over. Death, death, death, death, death. I'm mineralizing. Barely living. Rook, Quill, George, an entire city, all dead. All for me. For what? For a half-life in a comet full of plants and books and dying flies?

I move. I have to, just to prove I can. A book lies on a small table next to the armchair where I sit. I pick up the book and walk out. I walk down halls, down stairs, through caves and caves. Big rooms with big faces carved in the walls. Faces as big as me staring out. Caves of food. Dried grains, dried fruit, dried mushrooms, canned everything. Caves full of machines that pump and whistle and turn. I climb down a ladder, through a pink mist. I hear waves lapping below the mist. Then I'm through. Below is a giant cave. The cave is a full of lake. Bright lake. The ladder ends above a skinny beach that curves around one section of the water. When I let go of the last rung and step on dark sand, I see why the lake shines. Pale lilac flames burn just above the water. The flames aren't hot. I touch them. They make no noise. The quiet fire quiets me. I sit on the sand, open the book, and, by the light of the flames, read.

JOHN LENNON was dead. New Pond was dead. It was Christmas Eve, 1980, and everybody I knew was weeping and had been doing so for weeks. The heroes of my parents' genera-tion had been murdered when they were young, but then assassination moved back abroad where people weren't as surprised by it. The scions of the counterculture had kids and got down to making lives and livings and forgot about death.

Then Reagan was elected, Willard arrested, and, to add

horror to absurdity, a madman shot John Lennon. All was lost.

We'd never seen so many grown-ups crying at once. It was disconcerting. We brought our parents hankies. We made them toast. We didn't know what else to do. Were they crying for John Lennon or for New Pond? Both? Some of us cried in solidarity, or just because everything was so sad. And when we did that, our parents straightened up. They dried their eyes. They called a meeting.

From the podium at the front of the Town Hall, Bernadette was the first to speak.

Finally! she thundered. Finally we're rid of that sick tyrant.

The rest of us sat on wooden folding chairs, listening. The great pot-bellied stove was burning full-blast and together with the heat of the sixty bodies a stifling atmosphere was generated—such that the great windows had been opened to the snowy night. Above us at either end of the hall the basketball nets hung gloomily from their hoops.

Bernadette went on, saying that we all knew what Willard had done, what he was, so why had it taken so long to reach this point, why didn't we throw him out and broadcast his abuses? The worst of his crimes could have been prevented.

My family, she said, voice cracking, Has been laid low. We've been hit hard. Many of you have been screwed too, literally and figuratively. And whose fault is it? It's ours. Mine, Bill's, yours, all of ours. The damage he caused our hearts is on our heads.

Next came Blatsky, who questioned mournfully, our bitterness, after everything Willard had done for us, all the land he had given, all the time donated to helping us, to instructing our stubborn egos by whatever means at his disposal, and if we had chosen to misunderstand his methods, if we couldn't understand where he was coming from, maybe we didn't deserve to have him. But deserve or not, we should gather the money to post bail for him and beg him to come back. Certainly he would never survive in the outside world where simplistic moral conventions would grind him to nothing.

Iris couldn't stand it anymore and began yelling from her seat.

Is it a simplistic moral convention to protect your children from dirty old men!?

The girl was hardly a child, said Blatsky. In many cultures she would already b—

But he was shouted down before he could finish and slid away in a lachrymose huff.

Although there were a few sullen stalwarts who shared Blatsky's views, the consensus was against them. There could be no question of getting Willard out of jail nor of his return to New Pond—too much damage had been done and nobody was going to risk their children to Willard's wayward hands.

What we need, Bojanowski argued, is a new Roshi, a new, untainted centre of gravity around which the community might orbit and grow. What good fortune, he went on, that we have an excellent candidate for the position in the person of Yoshida Roshi, himself a properly ordained master.

Yoshida sat calm and dispassionate, apparently indifferent to Bojanowski's words—the very picture, in fact, of the Zen master oblivious to worldly ambition.

But here Myles rose and, red-faced, nervous as always when speaking in public, and perversely loquacious as a result, proposed via a lengthy analogy concerning the English Civil War, the regicide of Charles, and subsequent reign of that unmentionable monster Cromwell (may his name live in infamy for his crimes against Ireland), that it was too soon to appoint a new teacher, even if a new teacher were necessary. It was time, he thought, to take no action, to reflect rather on our previous inaction, which had led to Willard's crimes. It was time to wait and let the bruises heal and then perhaps to reorganize ourselves, perhaps even without a teacher.

Bruises! cried Ms. Lum. They're not bruises, they're festering wounds, they're chronic diseases.

Yoshida, meanwhile, had shown no reaction to Myles's words, but it seemed to me that his expression had altered from disingenuous indifference to stony irritation. And in the end no consensus could be reached between those who wished to recall Willard and those who advocated the appointment of Yoshida, and so, by default, Myles's proposal of actionless action was chosen with no ceremony to mark the event. The meeting dispersed with little friendliness and we went to Midnight Mass.

Midnight Mass! Not quite the high drama of Easter, but nevertheless entertaining, with its peculiar pageant and nativity enacted by toddlers—the miniature Mary and her Joseph stumbling over their robes as they made their way up the aisle holding a plastic baby Jesus hardly visible through the billowing incense. The off-key screeching of the choir and the dismal electric organ ordinarily depressed me if we happened to come off-season, but this was a festival! All the lapsed and lazy and regretful Catholics turned out here with their dutifully baptized children for this, one of their twice-annual pilgrimages to the mother church (not counting weddings, funerals, and baptisms), and in this we were no different.

No, do not think that my parents returned to the bosom of the church for solace in the wake of the dissolution of their community. Every Christmas Eve of my childhood was passed in the illuminated midnight of that church, listening to the genial platitudes of Father Malenfant, while kneeling and standing and sitting and kneeling, not taking communion, for we had not confessed, nor for that matter had I ever been baptized (although it was suspected that Evelyn —Myles's mother—had seized her opportunity when alone with my infant self to perform an emergency baptism and save my soul from perdition should death visit me early).

Perhaps Iris could have abandoned her native religion entirely but not Myles—through a tumultuous childhood of immigration and multiple dislocations, Catholic Mass had been a constant—a constant that stretched behind him (and behind me, as he liked to remind me) fifteen hundred years to the days of Colmcille and Saint Kevin, the latter being so friendly with God's creatures that flies did him the favour of walking under the lines of text he was reading to help him keep his place (these flies linked in my mind with the thoughtful snails who allegedly crawled onto Siddhartha's scalp to protect him from the blazing sun while he was sitting in full proto-Buddhic samadhi). Yes, Catholicism and Zen warred in Myles's soul—the apophatic and the cataphatic, the chatty and the cryptic, the riotous and the ascetic—and it's all very well to say that there's no need for this war, that no conflict must exist, but saying it does not make it so.

I think of Christ, Myles said as we drove home through a gathering snowstorm, As a Bodhisattva, an enlightened soul who chose incarnation to help sentient beings and suffered for us much as the Buddha suffered through his multitudinous incarnations. Martyrdom has a long and highly reputable pedigree, but really Jesus, if there ever was an historical Jesus, was a mere pebble upon which the oyster of Church history formed the pearl of Christ, building the nacreous layers from the pagan traditions of Osiris, Zoroaster, Wotan on the Tree of Life, the Dagda, etc....

Iris, meanwhile, was chewing her nails to the quick to relieve her anxiety over the wretched driving conditions occasioned by the snowstorm.

Slow down! she cried at regular intervals. To which Myles would scoff that it was hardly a blizzard, there was no need to overreact. Just slow down, she would repeat and then stare out the window caught somewhere between sullen irritation at his rebuke and an attempt to will the panic from her body.

Oh! she exclaimed with pleasure as we approached the radiance of the Whites' house, and Oh! An eruption of Christmas lights flung across the bushes and trees and lawn led to the double-wide trailer dazzled with illuminated snowmen and Santas, entire sleighs and even reindeer, and a great luminous crèche filled with donkeys and ducks, kings and their gifts, sheep and their shepherds. And then it was gone, a brief vision in the storm. At all other times of the year, the trailer squatted unremarkably on its little patch of immaculate lawn, biding its time for that brief annual winter bloom.

Our own house was more modestly lit, but Iris loved her lights. Christmas, as far as she was concerned, was itself a festival of light in the darkness of winter. Somehow, in spite of her health, she had managed to hang bundles of tiny white lights both outside and inside the house, where the small Christmas tree was nearly falling over with its burden of glimmering ornaments. Two days after Christmas we were to return to Boston for Iris's checkup, and she had apparently decided to counteract her mounting dread with decorations and photons. Bells hung from every doorknob, tin angels twirled above candles, and although I felt myself too old for the tradition, I let her read "Twas the Night before Christmas" to me before bed.

The gifts the next morning were as follows: socks, mittens, camel bells, fudge, a Dover reprint of Lord Dunsany's stories with hallucinatory illustrations by Sidney Sime, *The Crock of Gold* by James Stephens, and *The Complete Sherlock Holmes*, as requested, with the original illustrations by Sidney Paget. Myles received a book on etymology and Iris a volume describing the megalithic monuments of Europe, which she had ordered herself. She and I both unwrapped curios from Myles's habit of buying up remaindered books (to wit: *The Collected Letters of Rodgers and Hammerstein, The Complete Guide to Harness Racing, Rolls Royce: The Early Years*). Then we ate banana bread sent by Aunt Carolina and sat about in our bathrobes reading our books while listening to a church choir on the radio.

How Myles and Iris afforded any presents, given their flat-lining bank account and mounting bills, is unknown to me. Cheques from grandparents judiciously spent, I think.

We rested carefully and thoroughly, for we knew the next day would be strenuous and long and distressing. We had Christmas dinner at the Krimgold-Gragnolatis. Although Bernadette was of Catholic descent, Bill was Jewish, so there was a menorah on the table, fully lit because by that date, the Festival of Lights was already over.

Iris was subdued due to her imminent checkup, as were Bill and Bernadette due to everything else—Athena refused to leave her room upstairs, Artemis ate with a disturbing aggression, and Apollo tried to keep up, but his effort was forced and he was so forgetful that he would often lapse into a daydream mid-chew. I chose to follow Artemis's lead as well and ate with abandon, and Myles shovelled the excellent food down his throat with more than his usual disregard for nuance or flavour. He ate, as did all those of us who ate, as a way of forestalling dread and guilt. And also there was the matter of the delicious braided challah and the beautiful and multiple pies that sat in such splendour on the side table. Iris had little appetite—something I recall with chagrin since I only note it now in review; at the time I had little awareness of how fraught that time was for her, or I suppose I must have had some subliminal awareness that recorded the tightness of her shoulders, and the spareness of her appetite.

Halfway through my meal, I excused myself to go to the bathroom, which was upstairs. The hallway there was narrow and dark, and the door to the bathroom was closed, but just as I reached it, the doorknob turned and Athena came out.

She saw me and her eyes flickered away and down. I said hello and could barely hear her response. Her face, once incandescent, was grey. She moved as though drained of force. And I said nothing, did nothing but blush. I had always blushed when near her, always been speechless, but now my speechlessness was compounded by what had happened, what I knew, what I knew she knew, what everybody knew, and what I had done to bring it all about, and having no words seemed a further failing on my part. I wanted to speak, to ease her suffering, but it was beyond me. She stood aside, and I backed up muttering, Sorry, go ahead, but she shook her head mutely and waved me past.

The next day, St. Stephen's Day, as Myles insisted on calling it, we set out early, yet not early enough, for Iris was in the car anxiously waiting while Myles rustled about shaving and packing last-minute notebooks and pens, amulets and talismans, and Iris honked the horn and sent me back into the house multiple times to urge my father on. Meanwhile he, with increasing agitation, turned in circles searching for socks, his wallet, a shirt, and sent me back to Iris with orders to extract the locations of these items from her, and I, a hapless double agent relayed the request such that she, with a yelp of incredulity, shot from the car to deal with the matter directly, only to see Myles exiting the house at a clip. As he leapt behind the wheel, Iris reckoned at volume that we would be late for her appointment, at which Myles scoffed that we would be early as he peeled out of the driveway in reverse, nearly colliding with a passing truck, and then we were rattling over the dirt road's winter skin, with Iris informing Myles that she would far rather be late than perish in a car crash, and Myles slammed on the brakes, clapped his hand to his forehead, and said, Oh shit! I forgot to feed the stove. Iris said with asperity that she had fed the stove as usual and in addition, as usual, she had made the necessary arrangements for a fire to be started every day to keep the plants from freezing. What did she mean, Myles wanted to know as he floored the accelerator, by saying, As usual?

It had been, and always would be, one of Iris's complaints that while Myles planned parties, it was she who ended up preparing for them. And despite her still-convalescent state, this was the case once again. But when she complained, Myles countered that she was not including the time he had put into brewing the beer for the event, nor the countless phone invitations. She said that he loved nothing better than talking to people on the phone and that he had brewed the beer as a matter of habit.

Thus was I inducted into a pattern of family behaviour in which I helped Iris to compensate for Myles's failings (in my view), or in which I participated in the tasks and duties of household work that children should be obliged to carry out (in Myles's view). In short, I cleaned a motley assortment of wineglasses and beer mugs that had acquired a thick, sticky coating of dust from disuse and woodsmoke.

We had returned from Boston the day before, and the news was good. Iris was healthy and there was no sign of cancer. A jubilant Myles had said, as though it were the inevitable and incontrovertible conclusion to be drawn from the situation, that we would have a party.

Upstairs, Myles put in phone calls from coast to coast to each person he could think of. He even called Saint John to invite Bayo, who was glad to talk but couldn't leave Canada until he received landed immigrant status. In the meantime, he'd gotten his work permit and was putting in punishing hours at a bottle factory and had found a cheap place to live nearby.

Downstairs, Iris moved about methodically sweeping and scrubbing and tidying, and whenever Myles took a break from the phone, she put in yet another call to yet another government department to discuss how she could possibly pay her mountainous medical bills. She would be redirected elsewhere and given a new phone number to call, but before doing so she would return to cleaning for a while, pausing only to yell up through the floorboards to Myles that he must pull himself away from his piles of books and half-written essays, to which he roared back that she must calm down as there was no need to lose her cool over a party, but her words dug him out of his trench and he began frantically bottling beer while pondering aloud how they were to make enough Irish coffee and in what cups they would serve them, and Iris said with irritation that she had secured a coffee machine from the historical society/volunteer fire department/garden club and Charlotte and Jane were bringing paper coffee cups and this was just typical of him, always so last-minute, and if it weren't for her losing her cool then the party would be a disaster because he certainly couldn't be relied upon—Was he listening to her? No, he was tuning her out. To which he replied that he'd been tuning her out for ten years, why stop now?

Eleven years, Iris corrected. Eleven years since I put my life on hold to be your wife. Eleven years of art I haven't made because I've been too busy typing up your manifestos.

What are you talking about now? he cried, distressed as he ran about putting the beer under the counter. Why must you perpetually change the subject? Your mind's all over the place, I can't keep track, and anyway, if it weren't for me you'd be a hermit living alone and going quietly crazy.

Yes, Iris lamented at volume, And I'd quite like that instead of being forced to make small talk with the ten thousand people you invite whom I don't even know.

Well, you'd know them, shouted Myles from under the sink, If you got out a bit more and talked to people. How in blazes have I run out of bottle caps? And then he was rushing to the car with me behind carrying a shopping list from Iris, and away we jumbled.

In Frothingham, Myles mused at length over the selection of hops and malt at the tiny Seventh Day Adventist health food store. I excused myself to go to the library. He murmured a distracted assent, and I slid off down the icy sidewalk.

But I wasn't going to the library. Not at first. On my way there I passed a door at the corner of Main and Water. In an ornate brick portico, an old, handsome wooden door with a window in it and the words Down East Real Estate painted in gold lettering on the glass. Inside, I was asked indulgently by a woman with long, blond, immaculately feathered hair, if I could be helped.

I'm looking, I said, but before I could say for whom, the grey-black waves of Willard's hair hove into view as he passed from one office to another. Seeing me, he continued on his way, and I followed.

His office was tidy, spare, shabby. At his desk he sat and shuffled papers.

Well! he said too heartily, smiling too brightly. What a nice surprise. What can I do you for, young man?

I sat down, saying, You never used to talk like that.

A man's got to make a buck. This is an office and this is how office people talk.

I'm not an office person.

Yes, but then what are you?

Is that a koan?

Just a plain question. If you're not buying or selling property, why are you here?

I saw Athena, I said.

Willard leaned back and pondered the ceiling for a while.

She's not...normal, I said. She's like a ghost.

What have they done to her? Willard muttered.

I wondered who he meant—her parents? Society? Not him anyway.

I'm the one who called the police, I said, and waited for a bitter blast. A blast I somehow wanted, hoping it would cool my head and slow my heart. I was feeling dismal and confused. The room was hot, still; a radiator under the window churned out heat that roiled the air above it, making airborne dust sparkle heavily in the winter sun. Willard seemed not to have heard me. He never looked in my direction but sat forward, searched in a drawer for something, found a pencil, broke it gently in half, replaced it, softly closed the drawer, accidentally dislodged a pile of papers with his elbow, and watched without moving as they slid from desktop to floor in a heap. He went to his knees to retrieve them.

You hurt people, I said to the top of his head. You were supposed to help them.

Can you see how that happens now? he said from the floor, face hidden by the desk, voice constricted. You thought you were helping Athena, I suppose, but instead look what happened.

You're the one who hurt her! I cried, jumping from my chair and leaning over the desk.

Ask yourself why you feel guilty, he said without looking up. Maybe your motives were not so pure as you think. And even if they were, would it matter? He placed the stack on his desk and sat back heavily in his chair, looking into the middle distance above my head.

Do you know, he said reflectively, I didn't want any of it. I didn't want to teach. Didn't want the responsibility. All I wanted was to play my horn and bake some bread, saw some wood. But then they came, from their campuses, from their drugs, from the war, all those lost kids looking for somebody to tell them what to do, how to be, how to live in this fucked-up world. I said no, I'm not your man, look elsewhere. And do you know what happened? They wouldn't fucking leave, they camped outside my door. Teach us, they said, We need you. Our world is falling apart and you know the way out of it, we can see it in your eyes, you know how to exist here, now. They said the very fact that I refused to teach them was further evidence that I must. It showed how egoless I was. I wasn't egoless, I was afraid! Afraid to fuck them up even more. They stayed there for a month, two months, three. More came, there were dozens of them. And then the snow fell and they were shivering in the night and finally I opened the door and let them in. Out of what? Out of pity. I pitied the poor fuckers and that was my downfall. What should I have done? Leave? Move somewhere else? They would've found me. I told them they could stay, they could help me bake and saw, but I wasn't going to teach them anything. They stayed and did everything I did. *Everything.* They made a religion out of me. They started talking like me, dressing like me, even moving like me. *No,* I said, you're doing it all wrong. This isn't going to help you, and then I made my first mistake—I told them what they should do instead. And they did it! And then one thing just led to another. That's the truth, that's how it happened. I didn't make New Pond, it was the other way around.

For a three full seconds I felt bad for him. Yes, I thought, they tricked him into it, they made a monster from a man. But then I remembered Iris's words, and my heart hardened.

You can't make an omelette from an orange, I said.

What? he asked, climbing to his feet, puzzled eyes.

Why didn't you go to jail? I asked more sharply than intended.

Willard looked at me in surprise.

Probation, he said. A misdemeanour, not a felony. Luckily the local justice system still has a few reasonable types. Anyway, thanks for stopping but I have to get back to work.

So that was that. I rose and moved to the door, but before I left he said, Don't.

I turned, and he muttered quickly, Don't squander your gifts, as I have.

I stood and stared at him. Was he admitting guilt? What gifts of mine was he speaking of? He'd never mentioned them before. He nodded curtly, teacher dismissing student, and I withdrew.

At the library, I took refuge from my disquiet in an old leather-bound edition of *Kidnapped*, but even the thick pages with their uneven edges and the smooth, thinner ones that bore the illustrations by N. C. Wyeth failed to distract me. I put it down. The giant windows arched nearly to the top of the high, bone-white ceiling, letting in great quantities of brilliant winter sunlight. But no amount of sun could brighten the bookish gloom in that library. Dark lacquered wood bookcases, glass-encased model ships, ancient suits of armour, all conspired to absorb light and reinforce the interiority of that quiet world. On a window seat sat a cheap, aging paperback with a cover that featured a shooting comet. I picked it up and flipped through the brittle, sand-coloured pages. I saw familiar words. Too familiar. Whole phrases, whole pages were unfolding, already known, already spoken. With growing unease I fanned through until I found words I didn't recognize. The words were: I am dull and empty. I'm in an empty tunnel, behind three doors.

I AM dull and empty. I'm in an empty tunnel, behind three doors. George hauled me up the steps, opened a big metal door in his giant rock, and pushed me through. Then two more doors after. Blood dripped down his sleeve, off his hand. I watched it drop in shiny drops and splats, then he left me...

ODOUR OF proto-beer suffused the Buick all the way home. Dark malt and hops in bulk packaging bounced in the back seat. It was a soothing smell, and I needed soothing after my encounters with Athena and Willard and finding the book and reading my story in it and reliving the awful end of Quill and Rook. The book was in my lap, borrowed from the library, but I dared not open it.

Off on a comet? asked Myles.

Sorry, I said. Yes, daydreaming.

I meant the book, said Myles. You're becoming a real Verne aficionado. That's one of his more obscure ones.

I looked down. The book had a title. How had I not seen it? *Off on a Comet* by Jules Verne. I'd never even heard of it. And yet between its covers were words, memories, stories from the back galleries of my self. What of my expedition, of Quill, Rook, Captain Severn, Chisolm, the others—were they just the contents of a book I couldn't remember reading?

I flipped through the pages, skimming, flipping, skimming, and was even more bothered to find nothing. No names I knew, no expedition, no City. I'd had some kind of bibliohallucination. All this triggered by what? By guilt? I'd hurt Athena, yes, Willard was right, and my motives were not pure. And now there was nothing I could do to help her or assuage my guilt. I hadn't done the right thing. Not at all. But what was right? What was right?

When we got home, there was plenty to distract me from my distress.

At the kitchen table sat a strange ragged man, wild beard, crazed pupils, cheeks concave with hunger. Iris sat nearby, anxiously watching him eat a sandwich.

Jack! cried Myles.

Even then I couldn't see him. There was no Jack here, no

urbane audiophile with neat goatee and sleek leather vest. This creature looked like a missing cat rescued from the woods. But then I recognized his earrings and, just barely, his eyes.

Where's Simone? asked Myles, drawing up a chair.

No answer. Jack kept his eyes down and dedicated himself to the sandwich until there was nothing left.

That's his third, said Iris.

Simone's dead, said Jack abruptly, pushing his plate away.

Myles shouted disbelief. Iris slumped back in her chair. I stood dumbly waiting for more horror.

Breast cancer.

Jack said it came on like a locomotive, he barely had time to say goodbye before it took her. Mind you, he said, with all her ailments he'd been half-expecting her to die on him for years now, but it still felt like a catastrophe. She was twenty years his senior. Of course she would leave first, he'd always known that, but when it happened, with hardly any warning, it shattered him. He didn't know how to live without her. He'd gone feral. Walked away from her burial service and kept on walking, not knowing where he was going, heading vaguely north for no particular reason, into the woods, out of the woods, through subdivisions, across highways.

He said, It turns out December is a bad time for a grief-walk.

He wasn't sure how long he'd gone on like that. Days and nights of walking, until he fell beneath some trees, huddled under boughs and snow, and nearly died of exposure. That brought him back to life enough that he stumbled into a truck stop and found a driver willing to give him a ride. The trucker was headed for New Brunswick and went out of his way to drop Jack here. Even waited to make sure there was somebody home to let him in.

Crying, Iris said she was glad he made it, and Myles said with feeling, yes, yes, he must stay for as long as he needed, as long as he wanted. Pierce was gone, he'd moved into one of the cabins down at the Zendo and so his trestle bed was free. Jack thanked them and muttered that he should call Simone's family in Iowa. He'd abandoned them at the graveyard and they would be wondering where he was.

Iowa? said Myles. They're not in Brittany anymore?

Jack went silent for a long time at that. He looked down and looked down and clenched his toes and straightened them, struggling with a thought. Finally, he looked up and supposed it didn't matter anymore since she was dead.

Simone was never from Brittany, he said. She wasn't even Simone.

What did he mean, what did he mean?

He meant her name was really Sheila. Sheila Miller from Des Moines.

Fresh out of community college, she'd married an insurance agent, had three kids in a row, and suburbed through the fifties and sixties until two days after her youngest turned eighteen, when she took advantage of the new no-fault divorce laws to leave her husband and move to Boston, where she resurfaced as Simone Le Gall, daughter of a French diplomat, raised on the beaches of Brittany.

But the clogs around her neck! said Myles.

Invented. Or rather, borrowed from true stories.

Her children! said Iris. We met her children.

They humoured her.

And you, you humoured her too, said Iris.

It was the reality she wanted to live, said Jack.

He'd met her when he was twenty-five and she was a glamorous older woman. By the time he learned the truth of her history, he was so deeply in love with her that her world became his and he did everything he could to maintain the story she wanted to tell.

She was something else, he said, And when I was with her I became a part of that, and now it's all gone. The world is small. And dull. And empty.

There was a long silence while we all stared at the ground, absorbing Jack's news. Finally, Myles rose.

Well, he said, Then this party will also be a wake.

I WAKE in shock, read, sleep, wake. Outside, days go on for weeks. Or maybe just one long night of asteroids and competing moons. I close my eyes and see twin planets, green one chasing black around a broken star. I daydream to crowd out memory.

We must run too close to a sun that yanks us from our path. Coming round, we hit the sky of a strange planet and I rattle like a nut roasting in a shell as we burn down. We smash water. The comet sinks, I don't. I pop up on a raft, bruised but breathing, thrown on big surf in the middle of a storm.

Wind pitches me over huge water for a day and a night. Between the tops of giant waves, I see pieces of the sky on fire, and shake with each bang of thunder. Rain claws my face, waves punch me, and the noise splits my skull. I tie myself to the raft and give up.

When I wake the sea is a flat sheet to the end, and a red sun rolls up the sky. On the other side of the day, the last thunderclouds creep off full of water and lightning.

Now hunger takes over—the morning goes dark. Ration check: some jerky, a packet of nuts and dried fruit, a gallon of water. I swig and spit brine, and see the container's torn seal. Chewing the jerky, I look over the raft's speargun, which seems to be jammed. Can't fix it. There's a still. Following a manual, I set it up, but it'll be hours before there's enough water to drink, so must go on with a dry, dry throat and swollen tongue. Leaning my arm on the rubber gunnel, I look down for fish.

I'm the last surviving member of an expedition that logged a high count of strange sights, but here's a new one: my eye falls through numberless tons of clear water, past whale pods and schooling fish, to the lights of an underwater city lying there at the bottom of the ocean. I can see it as clearly as I see the little hairs on my arm. I see streets, towers, neon lights; I see a river all through and suburbs out beyond. I'm dreaming, I'm hungry, I'm thirsty, so I'm dreaming: or maybe not. I've seen so much that's strange. Or maybe not. Maybe those memories are just an ocean dream. The sun's coming up over an empty world. No life above water outside my heartbeat. Unless my heartbeat is a dream too, just water lapping, heard wrong, thought wrong, and I'm dying, or dead, or never was.

I look down again; the city still sleeps under me. Will they look up through telescopes to see my raft above them? Maybe the bottom of the ocean is closer than I think; maybe the city is very small and just below the surface. Maybe I'm a giant on a planet of tiny underwater people. Or I'm more than a giant. Yes, why think I'm dead when really I'm too alive? So much, I'm a god floating on the ocean of a world I made and this city shakes in my shadow!

Then I'm underwater, my raft upside down.

A few jellyfish in the bending light. Big shark nosing around my upturned raft, ten feet away.

To my right the jammed speargun hangs from a ball of cork tied to its handle. I run out of air.

I scramble to the surface, gasp, and heave myself, thrashing, to the right, grab the cork and dive under again. Too late, the grey monster is on me, jaws wide, teeth flashing. No time to position the gun for a jab. I swing my legs under me, kick, and nail the snout. Shark recoils, as do I from agony in my unused heel. No time for agony: it's circling back around. I wrap the cord of the gun around my wrist, hold the point rigidly in position, and wait. As though propelled by an explosion, it shoots toward me. I thrust with the gun, but the shark swerves up at the last instant, bites the cork, and dives. The cord cinches my wrist and jerks me down.

Within seconds we're far below, and my heart thuds in my ears, ribs crumple. I swing and bounce against the hard grey body. No point trying to free myself—the cord is a noose embedded in my wrist. I seize the shark's dorsal fin, climb onto its back and jab feebly at its gills and eyes, as instructed in survival manuals, but it's useless. If anything, the creature speeds up, and I can't find the gills anyway. My blood fizzes in my veins, lungs near bursting, and I know beyond doubt that I'm done.

Hours of near-death struggle and before that the outrageous adventures of the expedition, and now, an end I never saw coming: riding the back of a murderous fish to the bottom of the sea. And straight down I see the twinkling lights of my city growing closer. Will they collect my bones, the citizens down there? Place them in some museum they keep of the castaway corpses who fall from their sky? I need to breathe; I need to breathe, knowing, of course, that the water-breath will be my last. Yet the ocean is so warm it seems not water at all, but the thick air of a city summer. I have the sensation of riding the back of some great bird. I feel feathers under me, black and wild, the shark's nose is a beak, its head the head of a hawk; and looking down I see the wide waterfalls of a wide river washing through the middle of the city.

A lodestone in my belly lights and pulls. City. I gasp—inhaling a lungful of dirty wind. It smells of lilacs and gasoline exhaust, and I think I can hear cars honking far below.

Now the bird stops its headlong plunge and flattens out into a languid downward spiral. We're level with high-flying gulls. They wheel and fling themselves through columns of air around us as we drop, my creature and I, to the city below. Now I can make out a park, and as we sweep down under its treetops, I spot a young couple—a man and a woman sitting on the grass. I know them. And at the same time I understand that the creature beneath me is no longer a bird. Its wings beat too fast to see, and my hands grip exoskeleton behind spherical eyes that sparkle in the light. I'm skimming over blades of grass aboard a fly. We close in on the couple where they sit enjoying the spring air. And the fly and I keep shrinking, and as we shrink so does the speed of our flight and we are no longer two but merged into a single thing, a fleck of dust not flying but drifting forward as the man speaks; the woman throws back her head and laughs, and I am smaller and smaller still, nothing at all now but a speck of light barely moving, slowly spinning in the warm spring air between them.

OUR TINY house was radiant. Here was the hour I loved best—the hour of floor soap and new candles. They lit the shining floors and the dark, spotless, wavy old window glass and here and there were bowls holding narcissus bulbs that anchored slender green stalks atop which balanced small white flowers exhaling spring into winter night.

Iris and Myles were sitting, sharing a beer. I wandered up and down, absorbing the sheen of cleanliness draped over the interior of our house like a coat of fresh paint. Put on a record, Myles said, his voice dark and warm. Yes, said Iris, Put on the Dubliners. No, said Myles, the Wolfe Tones. No, I said as I sat down at the piano and began to play "The Well-Tempered Clavier." A knock at the door, and I jumped to answer it. It was Bill and Bernadette and Artemis and Apollo and, to my surprise, Athena. She was still pale, but less so. She stuck tight to Bernadette but accepted, stiffly, my parents' embraces. Then Rinzai, Soto, Poe, Herbert, and Emilia were piling in behind, and I took the kids upstairs to my room, where I situated them with a set of dominoes and taught them Mexican Train. I heard the hubbub growing steadily below and the tuning of fiddles and guitars. By the time I made my way downstairs, every step was packed with a minimum of three people and it took me twenty minutes to thread my way across ten feet of floor space. Bill was bowing wildly at his fiddle while Athena's fingers flew up and down the keyboard as Bernadette turned the songbook pages for her and there was somebody with a guitar and another with a ukulele, but I couldn't make out who in the crowd. Jack sat near the musicians, his face finally looking like him again— his sunken eyes were almost happy. Passing through a rare open space in the far corner on an elliptical route to the door, I overheard Herman Bojanowski lamenting to Iris that while he knew Willard had to be deposed, now the community was rudderless, adrift.

We were at the centre of the universe! he cried. Now we're in outer space.

No! shouted Iris over the noise. We were never on the map at all—we were nowhere, that was the problem. Now we're somewhere!

Uncomprehending, I moved on, noting that the pickled string beans I had disgorged from the jars where Iris had so carefully stowed them in August were not being eaten. People were sticking to beer. Gnawing on a bean, I squeezed my way outside, free of the stifling party heat.

Two extremely drunk men were heaving snowballs at each other, staggering backwards and sideways with each throw. A half-moon idled behind the thick curtain of cloud that covered the sky, and so I could not distinguish their faces, but they were yelling at each other in sharp staccato barks, and from their voices I deduced that it was Yoshida and Willard cursing each other in Japanese. Or, at least it sounded like cursing. They might have been having a civil conversation, for all I knew. It was characteristic of Myles to have invited Willard to the party in spite of everything—but inexplicable to me that Willard would have accepted. Had he no sense of shame? Maybe he had come in hopes of winning back his flock, maybe just to hold this snowy duel with his ancient rival.

I left them to their combat and wandered out to the road to marvel at the dozens of cars that lined its shoulder for nearly a quarter mile on either side of our driveway. Out here the volleyed shouts of the Roshis and the noise and music of the party were muffled. I breathed deeply, taking in the last, sharp lungfuls of the year.

Tomorrow, January 1, 1981, the decade would begin in earnest. At the stroke of midnight everyone would cut their feathered hair, taper their bell-bottoms, narrow their collars, and buy new stuff. No more repair jobs. No more making do. No more denim patches. All the big old rusty cars would be traded for small, shiny ones. In a few days, impossibly, Ronald Reagan would swear his oath of office. The ragged edges of happenstance and invention would continue their unsteady but ceaseless retreat before the radiant plastic tide. I could only hope this tide, like all others, would come and go.

A shadow in the snowbank. My Shadow? No, of course not, Shadow was dead, had been for months now. She retreated, too. Familiar welling in my gut, up my chest, my throat, my nose, under my eyes, where it pooled and pressurized. A practised flip of thought would deflate the sob before it burst. I'd gone this long without crying, why start now? But she was fading out, and I knew suddenly it was now or never because my cat, my cat, I wanted her back. If I didn't cry for her now I'd never cry again, I'd be as frozen as all this snow under which she lay, lost, my particular cat, my weird little cat who could only be held in one position (horizontally, with feet against my stomach) but would otherwise step from the fridge-top to my shoulders, where she rode fearlessly, growling at all comers until she leapt off and pranced and tossed her head like a pony or darted after toys with psychotic intent or clawed her way sideways across the living room rug or crawled happily under my bed's fitted sheet, loudly purring, no more, no more. I would never hear that happiness again.

Shadow was dead, Simone was dead, New Pond was dead, Willard rotten, Athena hurt. Iris lived.

Iris would live!

I gulped air and found I'd doubled over in the shadowed snow. My knees were soaking wet and frozen. So was my face. My tears slowed. To cry was to cry, nothing more. My mother was alive after all. And she was going to keep living, as she'd promised me she would.

Standing there in the snow, I looked up through freezing tears at the dark matted silhouette of pointed firs and spruce and beyond them the dimly backlit clouds through which I could see no stars, nor the blinking lights of jets, nor the fixed signal of a passing satellite. I wondered what else sailed past unobserved: how many planets carrying the bones of loved ones from another life, how many meteorites crashing to earth trailed by giant feathered ghosts, how many comets bearing children who sit in shock by burning lakes as they come flaming through the atmosphere to be born?

Colophon

Distributed in Canada by the Literary Press Group:
www.lpg.ca

Distributed in the United States by Small Press Distribution:
www.spdbooks.org

Shop online at www.bookthug.ca

Designed by Malcolm Sutton
Edited for the press by Malcolm Sutton
Copy-edited by Stuart Ross

BOOK
PRODUCTION
WAR ECONOMY
STANDARD

Acknowledgements

I would like to thank *Harp & Altar* for publishing an excerpt from an early draft of this book. I must acknowledge *A Brief History of Moonspring Hermitage* by Sarah LeVine and Morgan Bay Zendo, which was an invaluable resource. A grant from Arts Nova Scotia provided a much needed financial boost at a critical point in the writing process. I want to thank my excellent editor, Malcolm Sutton, for patiently nudging me to complete this project and for providing such insightful notes, suggestions, and queries throughout. And my gratitude also to head thugs Jay and Hazel for their ongoing efforts to bring unconventional work to light. This book, or any book of mine, would not have been possible without my parents, who surrounded me so completely with love, books, and the love of books that I experienced literature via total immersion. Lastly and above all, my endless, fathomless love and thanks to Sarah Faber, my first and last reader, without whom this book couldn't have been dreamed up, never mind written; and to Fianan and Neva, who daily leave me speechless with gratitude.